"Donohue does a fine job of weaving a clever web of suspense. . . . You know you're reading a well-told story when it leaves you hungry for more and that is precisely what the author has accomplished."—*USA Today*

"A fast-paced, exciting thriller—a fun read that pulls you into the intricacies, culture, and contradictions of the Japanese mind. . . . Clear-cut action, suspense, and tension . . . a well-executed book full of twists, subplots, and excitement."—Fighting Arts.com

"Strong story, good writing, colorful setting. Donohue, who has black belts in karate and kendo, has published extensively on the martial arts, but this is his fiction debut, and an impressive one it is."—*Kirkus Reviews*

"An exciting thriller [and] delightful tale. . . . Expect [the hero] to return in more top-rate novels like this one."—BookBrowser

continued . . .

SENSEI

John Donohue

AN ONYX BOOK

ONYX
Published by New American Library, a division of
Penguin Group (USA) Inc., 375 Hudson Street,
New York, New York 10014, U.S.A.
Penguin Books Ltd, 80 Strand,
London WC2R 0RL, England
Penguin Books Australia Ltd, 250 Camberwell Road,
Camberwell, Victoria 3124, Australia
Penguin Books Canada Ltd, 10 Alcorn Avenue,
Toronto, Ontario, Canada M4V 3B2
Penguin Books (N.Z.) Ltd, Cnr Rosedale and Airborne Roads,
Albany, Auckland 1310, New Zealand

Penguin Books Ltd, Registered Offices:
80 Strand, London WC2R 0RL, England

Published by Onyx, an imprint of New American Library, a division of Penguin
Group (USA) Inc. Published by arrangement with St. Martin's LLC. For information,
address St. Martin's Press, 175 Fifth Avenue, New York, NY 10010.

First Onyx Printing, February 2004
10 9 8 7 6 5 4 3 2 1

For Clare Donohue,
first teacher,
with love

Acknowledgments

A number of people have been instrumental in assisting in the writing of this book, and I would like to thank them.

Charles Fieramusca, former head of Homicide for the Buffalo Police Department and assistant professor in Medaille College's Criminal Justice Program, patiently answered my grisly questions and gave me the benefit of his expertise and insight regarding investigative procedure.

Kimura Hiroaki, one in a long line of excellent martial arts *sensei* I have studied under, taught me the types of lessons you don't get in school.

Deepest thanks go to my agent, Jacques de Spoelberch, for his invaluable support. My editor, Carolyn Chu, is a rare find. Her high level of expectation and unabashed enthusiasm for the project made writing the book a continuing revelation and a joy.

Most important, I would like to thank my wife, Kitty, who, as in all things, has encouraged and supported me in ways beyond measure. Her kind yet critical reading of the chapters and her willingness to enter with me into Burke's world have made the process of writing this book one of the best things we have done together, which is saying a lot.

Prologue

With what I know now, I can pretty much make sense of the whole thing. It's taken a while. Like making sense of the first file Micky showed me. The crime scene pictures, the coroner's report, the notes from the investigating officers initially seemed disconnected—a wealth of jumbled facts that didn't hang together. Random acts. A scene of senseless violence.

But the accretion of facts, the stories spun by witnesses, build on you. And then you can say here is where it begins. It's not that things are inevitable; they just look that way in retrospect. What you are left with is the sense of something that grows over time, the result of a thousand small and seemingly insignificant events. You can ask why. And to answer you can point to any one of the facts you uncover. But once isolated by clinical explanation, it's not very convincing. Or satisfying.

We're all looking for answers of some type. And we search for them in different ways and along different paths. We hope that knowledge brings control. But life reveals this notion to be a comforting fiction.

It's like explaining a storm. Waves are spawned by the dance of gravity and wind and tide. They gain strength and momentum until they hurl themselves at us, standing surprised and stupid on the shore. It's a hard lesson. Meteorology provides faint comfort to the survivors.

Ronin

He slipped into the empty building before anyone else. Fitness is big business in LA, so it must have still been dark, hours before the overachievers got there.

The killer knew his quarry well. The patterns would not have changed, even in America. The master—soon-to-be victim—would pad quietly into his training hall hours ahead of anyone else. He trained fighters, but a sound business was a diversified business, and he had branched out into general fitness and health. It meant a big jump for the bottom line. His school was clean and upscale, with a reception area and account reps who kept the budget fed, smoothly enticing the hesitant and recording it all on the PCs that sat like putty-colored fetishes in the office cubicles. For the master, even after fifteen years in America, it was, ultimately, a distraction. The noise, the coming and going, the lack of focus that was LA—all made it harder and harder for him to find time to pursue his art. And he was, despite all his success, still an artist at heart. Which was why, increasingly, he found himself before dawn, alone in the training hall, pushing himself further and further, in fierce pursuit of the moment when he and his art became inseparable.

*   *   *

His name was Ikagi, and he had been training in karate for over forty years. He had the tubular build of martial artists—all those movie fighters look like weight lifters because that's what they spend most of their time doing. Ikagi was a professional of the old school. In his time in LA he had led and harassed legions of aspiring black belts into his demanding vision of the martial arts. And he was no less strict with himself. Photos of him over the years showed a man who looked like a human howitzer shell. Even that morning, at fifty-eight years of age, his workout would be grueling. His fingers were thick and strong from countless sessions of *tameshiwari*—board breaking. His feet were tough and dry from hours of work on the hardwood floor of the training hall. You could see the calluses clearly in the stark contrasts of the crime scene shots taken later—they stood out as white patches, even with all that blood around.

Ikagi had come in off the street and changed into the white uniform of the karate student. His belt had become tattered and ragged over the years, but it still made a crisp black contrast to the pure white of the karate *gi*. He probably knelt and faced the small shrine at the head of the training hall. His students said that this was his usual pattern. Then the warm-ups and stretches would begin. Before dawn, Ikagi would be lost in a daily fine-tuning of his art: the punches moving faster and faster, a faint white blur in the predawn light; the kicks precise, balanced, and focused.

His attacker could have jumped in at any point, although the medical examiner's report suggests that the master wasn't dead for more than an hour before the building manager found him at five-thirty. Ikagi had probably just begun his routine when the challenger appeared.

The evidence suggests that Ikagi knew something of the threat by this time. Some faint rumbling was coming from Japan. And it quickly became clear to the *sensei* just what the intruder wanted. Ikagi was a little bull of a man, and he would have demanded to know why. Whether he was surprised to learn the reason, whether he was surprised to see his old student there in the flesh is anyone's guess, although they say some of the really good masters have a type of sixth sense about this sort of thing. Ikagi didn't mention anything to his family or friends beforehand, but that's no real clue. If you look at pictures of people like him, even when they're smiling, the eyes give you nothing.

Ikagi could have known that death was waiting that morning, but he said nothing to anyone.

The ritual of the challenge was almost certainly performed. The attacker enjoyed the symbolic trappings. The ritual was important. He was most probably dressed in street clothes—it's a bit hard making your getaway dressed like an Asian assassin, even in LA—but he most certainly would have followed all the Japanese etiquette: the bows, the ritual introductions and presentation of training pedigree, the request for a "lesson."

When the fight was actually underway, it was nothing like anything most of us have ever seen. In the first place, it was fast. Fighters at this level of proficiency, going for the kill, do not waste time. The more time you spend, the more fatigued you get. The more opportunities for error. For the killing blow.

These two opponents knew more about unarmed fighting than most people alive. It wasn't just that the blows uncoiled like a viper's strike. The reflexes at this level are so accelerated that feints and counterfeints occur with a subtle speed that means most people wouldn't even notice them taking place. There was some minor lividity on the victim's hands and feet, but they were so callused that it doesn't really tell us much. Ikagi was a *karateka,* though, and he probably unleashed the arsenal of kicks and punches that formed the heart of his art.

He got as good as he gave: his forearms and shins were bruised from parrying attacks. He had scuff marks on the shoulder from rolling on the hard floor, which means that they used everything they could think of, from strikes to throws. Ikagi must have tried a choke hold at one point.

You can tell, because he had the telltale bruise on the top of his hand between the thumb and first finger. He tried to slide in the choke and the opponent defended by lowering the jaw, using the bone to protect the potentially vulnerable artery in the neck.

The cops dusted the floor of the training hall to get a sense of how things went. The two fighters ranged all over the surface, lunging, tumbling, breathing hard in a feral type of ballet. Ultimately, they ended up near the weapons rack. I think the attacker panicked. Maybe it was doubt, rising like smoke in the heat of the contest. Maybe the jet lag. Ikagi was not just good, he was one of the best, and the whole thing was probably not turning out as planned. So when they tumbled into the corner, there were all those wooden staffs, stacked up like spears in a medieval castle. It must have seemed to the attacker like the answer to a prayer.

Ikagi probably smiled to himself when his opponent grabbed one of the staffs. Only the master would know that these were the beginner's weapons, made of inferior wood, which he could snap in two with little effort. And we know that, at some point, he did. Tiny wood fragments were found along the ridge of the palm—exactly where you would expect them if you broke something with a sword hand strike. The attacker, wielding what he thought was a potent weapon, must have been momentarily stunned when the power of Ikagi's attack snapped the staff in two.

But the recovery was equally sudden. The staff became a spike.

The first strike must have been almost instinctual—a straight thrust, hard and quick, into the midsection. The pain must have been intense for Ikagi, but the blood trail shows us he didn't collapse. After that first, electric jolt, the gasp as the point was driven home, Ikagi pressed the attacker for some time.

Did the jagged end of the staff stay buried in Ikagi's guts, or did the attacker yank it out right away? It's hard to tell.

Eventually, the loss of blood slowed the master down. The floor was growing slick. And then the attacker finished it.

He plunged that spike into the old man, perforating the abdomen repeatedly. There was massive trauma there. It went beyond functionality. Did the attacker enjoy it? The gasp each time as he drove the point home? The growing sense of domination? Did he smile even as Ikagi's lips were yanked back in a rictus of pain?

These are questions for the shrinks. That morning, it didn't matter. It was over. Ikagi lay there, agony dulled only by a lifetime of discipline. He attempted to reach the phone, slid in the fluids pouring out of him, and faded away. As he slipped out of this life, his athlete's heart pumped faithfully away, the pulse growing faster and threadier as shock set in and he died.

The killer paused long enough to leave a clue as to what he had become. And a warning. He dipped his finger in the blood and wrote in Japanese on the wall. The photo of it was mixed in with all the others, and even with the morbid fascination of Ikagi's death captured from all angles, the calligraphy was crude yet effective, demanding attention.

"*Ronin*," the characters read. "Wave Man."

A masterless *samurai*.

T W O

Heiho

You could usually hear a pin drop in that room. The slanting rays of the sun came in through the high windows. The angle was acute enough so that you never had to worry about being blinded (an important thing in a place where people hacked at each other with oak swords), but it showed the dust motes dancing around. Less wary students had been distracted by them. We had all been with Yamashita Sensei for a while, however, and that morning when he strode onto the floor, all eyes were riveted on him.

Yamashita was a small person: in street clothes he probably would have seemed surprisingly nondescript. In the martial arts *dojo*, his presence was palpable. It wasn't just the way he was dressed. Most of us had been banging around the martial arts world for years and so were pretty much used to the exotic uniforms. Yamashita was usually dressed like any other senior instructor in some of the more traditional arts: a heavy quilted top like the ones judo players wore and the pleated split skirt/pants known as *hakama*. The wide legs of his uniform swished quietly as he knelt in front of the class. Even in this small action, there was a decisive precision. He gazed at us, his round head swiveling slowly up and down the line.

Other than his head, nothing moved, but you could almost feel the energy pulsing off him and washing over you. He was the most demanding of taskmasters at the best of times, but today we were all tremendously apprehensive.

Yamashita was wearing white.

In Japan, white is the color of emptiness and humility. Many of us had started our training in arts like judo or karate, where the uniforms known as *gi* were traditionally white as a symbol of humility. Most mainline Japanese instructors I knew frowned on the American urge to branch out into personal color statements with their uniforms. The message was clear: a *gi* is not an expression of individuality. People wanting to make statements should probably rent billboards and avoid Japanese martial arts instructors. They are not focused on your needs. They are concerned only with the pursuit of the Way. You are free to come along. But your presence is not necessary.

You have to get used to that sort of attitude. In the martial arts, nobody owes you anything, least of all your teacher. The assumption is that you are pretty much worthless and lucky to be in the same room with your *sensei*. You do what he says. You don't talk back. You don't ask rude questions. You don't cop an attitude—that's the *sensei's* prerogative.

In the sword arts Yamashita teaches, only the high-ranking teachers are eligible to wear white. Yamashita could. He had done so in Japan for years. But he didn't do it much here. If he was wearing white today, it meant that he was symbolically adopting the attitude that he was the lowliest of students. Humility is nice, of course. The only drawback here was that, if Yamashita was being humble, it meant that, as his students, we were somewhere way down in the crud with other lower forms of life.

As we sat there eyeing him warily, I heard some very quiet sighs up and down the line: we were in for a rough workout.

You don't get in the door of this particular *dojo* without

having considerable experience and martial aptitude. In the first place, it's hidden in Brooklyn among the warehouses down by the East River. We occasionally have trouble with our cars being broken into and stuff like that, but then a few of us go out and spread the word that Mr. Yamashita is beginning to get annoyed. He's been in the same location for ten years and has had a number of "conversations" with the more felonious of his neighbors—there are people walking those streets whose joints will never work correctly again.

The neighborhood is dirty and smelly and loud. Once you get inside the *dojo*, however, the rest of the world disappears. The training hall is a cavernous space. The walls are unadorned grayish white and the floor is polished hardwood. There are no decorations on the walls, no posters of Bruce Lee or the Buddha. To one side there's a small office area with a battered green metal desk and two doors leading to the changing rooms. Other than the weapons racks, that's it. There is absolutely nothing to distract you from the task at hand. It also means, of course, that there is nowhere to hide, either.

We don't do a great deal of conditioning. What we do is basics.

Yamashita's idea of basics, of course, is bewildering. He thinks basics are essentially illustrated through application. This is where the bang and crunch comes in, but with a difference. Anybody can slam someone into submission—take a look at any tough-guy competition or kickboxing match. Yamashita is after something different. He thinks that the essence of any particular technique should be demonstrated by its effectiveness. He doesn't separate form from results. He doesn't even admit they are two separate things. He likes us to destroy with elegance.

There are technical terms for this in Japanese. They can isolate *ji*—the mechanics of technique—and *ri*—the quality of mastery that allows you to violate the appearance of form yet still remain true to its essence. It's hard to explain how they differ and how to separate them, since most of us have spent years in pursuit of *ji* and are pretty much conditioned to follow its dictates. Yamashita doesn't seem to have much of a problem, however. He prowls the floor like a predator correcting, encouraging, and demonstrating. And woe to the unlucky pupil whose focus slips during the exercise. Yamashita screams, "*Mu ri*,"—no *ri!*—and slams you to the floor. It's a unique pedagogical technique, but it works for him.

So, beyond the sighs of anticipation, once the lesson started, none of us spent much time worrying about how tough things were. In the *dojo* of Yamashita Sensei, the only way to be is fully present and engaged in the activity at hand. The unfocused are quickly weeded out and rarely return. The rest of us endure, in the suspicion that all this will lead to something approximating the fierce skill of our master.

We were working that day on some tricky techniques that involve pressure on selected nerve centers in the forearm. At about the time when most of us were slowing down—shaking our arms out in an effort to get the nerves to stop jangling—Yamashita called that part of the lesson quits and picked up a *bokken*. We scurried to the lower end of the floor and sat down as he began his instructions.

The *bokken* is a hardwood replica of the *katana*—the two-handed long sword used by the *samurai*. It has the curve and heft of a real sword and so is used to train students of the various sword arts that have evolved over the centuries in Japan. In the right hands, hardwood swords can be very dangerous. They have been known to shatter the shafts of *katana*, and people like the famous Miyamoto Musashi, armed with a *bokken*, used to regularly go up against swordsmen armed with real swords. The results were never pretty, but Musashi used to walk away intact, *bokken* in hand.

Bokken are also used in set series of training techniques

called *kata*, which is typically how Yamashita had us train with *bokken*.

Kata means "form": they are prearranged exercises. Don't be fooled, though. *Kata* practice in Yamashita's *dojo* is enough to make your hair stand on end. When we perform *kata*, we do them in pairs of attacker and defender, and the movements flow and the blade of the *bokken* moans through the air as it blurs its way to the target. There's nothing like the sight of an oak sword slashing at your head to focus your mind.

I was backpedaling furiously to dodge a slashing *kesagiri*—the cut that with a real sword would cleave you diagonally from your shoulder to the opposite hip—when movement on the edge of the practice floor caught my eye.

The visitors filed swiftly in, bobbing their heads briefly in that really poor American version of bowing. There were three of them in street clothes and the fourth was dressed in a *hakama* and top. The outfit caught my eye: the top was crimson red and looked like it was made out of some silky sort of material, the *hakama* was a crisp jet black. Quite the costume, really, especially when its wearer had a shaved brown head the shape of a large bullet. He had come to make a statement, I guess. They sat quietly with their backs against the wall, watching the class with that hard-eyed, clenched-jaw look that is supposed to intimidate you.

I suppose I should have been impressed, but my training partner would not let up. She was about as fierce and wiry as they come. And her sword work had a certain whip and quick snap to it, a slightly offbeat rapid rhythm that was hard to defend against, even though in *kata* you theoretically know what's happening. She wasn't at all impressed with the visitors. She was a relatively new student who was mostly intent on making one of Yamashita's senior pupils—me—look less than accomplished.

So even though I was pretty curious about these guys—

Yamashita did not, as a rule, tolerate visitors and one of them was dressed like he came to play—I quickly got more interested in not making a fool out of myself during *bokken* practice.

It's a pride thing. There's a lot of talk in the martial arts about letting go of your ego and all that, and we try, we really do, but the fact is that, at this level, you have invested a tremendous amount of time and effort into developing your skills and attaining a certain ranking in the *dojo*, and you really get just a bit ticked off when something happens to threaten that. All the bowing and titles, the uniforms and colored belts, are about status, your sense of worth. It's a closed little world with its own system for ranking you, but it's still a status system, and human beings respond to that.

This woman was good with her weapon. I could sense that and so could she. She was pressing me a bit—altering the tempo of the moves, delivering her cuts with something close to full force, shortening the time between parry and counter—delivering a type of challenge to see whether I could meet it.

I could, of course, but that wasn't the real point. For me, the challenge was how to respond to her force with something more refined. It meant that instead of parrying her cuts with a force that would make our *bokken* bark out with the shock of impact, I needed to finesse it a bit.

I changed the angles slightly, moving my body just out of the line of attack, which served to place me out of the radius of her strikes. I tried to keep my hands supple as I parried, accepting the force of her blows and redirecting them slightly, but things were getting a bit sweaty and I didn't want the sword flying out of my hands and shooting across the room. It happens occasionally, and if nobody gets hit we all laugh and the one who let go gets ribbed unmercifully, but this was not a situation where I was willing to get laughed at.

I knew this woman was a relative beginner at the *dojo*, and I counted on her weapon fixation. It was an unfair advantage in a way, but it's also an example of what Yamashita calls *heiho*—strategy.

Between shifting slightly and redirecting a bit more through the next series of movements in the *kata*, I built up enough frustration in my partner for her to overcommit in her next strike—a little too much shoulder in the technique, her head leading into it—and it was all over. I simply let go of my *bokken* with my left hand, entered into her blind side, led her around in a tight little circle and took the sword away. It wasn't a move that was in the *kata*, but Yamashita tells us any time you can do *tachidori* (sword taking), you should, just to keep your partner on his or her toes.

The pivot took her around on her toes, all right. She knew what was happening about a split second after the spin began, but it was too late to get out of it. I handed her back the *bokken*. She smiled a bit ruefully and we bowed just as Yamashita called the class to order in preparation to bow out.

He glided to the head of the room and waited for us to line up. He was studiously avoiding looking at the gang of four in the back of the room, but you could tell from his body language that he was annoyed.

You don't come dressed to play unless you've been invited. Only the *sensei* can give permission for a student to train in the *dojo*. If you show up uninvited and suited up, it means that either you don't know anything about Japanese martial arts teachers and are in real risk of being beaten up, or you are purposefully being insulting and wish to challenge the *sensei* to a match. In which case, it is anyone's guess who gets beaten up.

I've seen this happen before. Not often, but you don't tend to forget it once you've seen it. Especially if you're a student of the teacher being challenged. You get used as a type of cannon fodder for your teacher. He sends you or one of your pals out to fight the challenger, he watches the action, analyzes the skill level of the opponent. If the first student gets beaten, a more advanced pupil goes next, and so on up the line. By the time the challenger reaches the *sensei* (if he lasts that long), he has either revealed his strengths and weaknesses and so can be defeated, or become so tired that he's no longer much of a challenge to the *sensei*. It's not fair, of course. It's *heiho*.

We all knelt, a solid dark blue line stretching down the length of the *dojo*. Yamashita sat quietly for a minute, then turned to one of his senior pupils, a mild-mannered Japanese-American guy named Ken, who sat next to me at the end of the line reserved for higher ranks. He looked like he was dreading what was about to happen. Yamashita said to him, "I see we have visitors. Perhaps you would invite the colorful one to speak with me."

Ken bowed, got up, and scurried to the back of the room to deliver the invitation. The guy in the red top nodded, exchanged a series of ritual handshakes with his companions, and stepped onto the training floor. He struck a ready pose and let out a loud "UUS." A few of us rolled our eyes. Some of the karate schools out there think that kind of thing makes you seem like a real hard charger.

Yamashita nodded slightly and Red Top moved forward.

"I regret that I was unable to welcome you properly to my *dojo*. I am equally distressed to say that I do not know who you are or what you want, since we have not been properly introduced." The words came out quickly but were carefully pronounced. Sensei doesn't really have much of an accent, but when he is annoyed, his words are very precisely formed. I don't know if Red Top was picking it up or not, but there wasn't one of us who doubted that Yamashita Sensei was really ticked off.

"Mitchell Reilly, Sensei." He bowed, properly this time. Ken caught my eye. Mitch Reilly ran a notorious jujutsu school, pretty much specializing in combat arts of the one-hundred-ways-to-pluck-their-eyeballs-out variety. He was a mainstay of the nontraditional African-American martial arts community. He was built like a refrigerator and I could see his knuckles were enlarged from the damage too much board breaking creates. Mitch Reilly had the reputation of being a really savage competitor, a fair technician, and a guy staggering under the weight of a giant ego.

"So, Mr. Reilly. I must assume that there is a reason for your presence here. The school is hard to find and only a man in need of something would make a journey through such a dangerous neighborhood."

Reilly looked contemptuous. "No problem. I can take care of myself."

"And," Yamashita continued, "the obvious care with which you have selected your . . . charming costume tells me that you are, perhaps, interested in . . . ?" He let the question hang in the air.

I sat and watched the steam start to come out of Reilly's ears. I have to admit, he got it under control fairly well, which was a sign that he was probably a dangerous man. When the faint trembling stopped, Reilly finished Yamashita's sentence.

"A match," he said. "I'm challenging you."

You had to admire him. The guy pulled no punches. He was probably five years older than I was—in his early forties—and had been banging around the martial arts for at least two decades, and now felt he was ready to take on the closest thing the New York area had to a bona fide master. Most people don't even know Yamashita exists. He came to New York years ago from Japan for reasons none of us can fathom and hones our technique with a type of quiet brutality. The senior Japanese *sensei* send their most promising pupils to him, but he's never appeared in *Black Belt,* hasn't written a book divulging the ancient, secret techniques of the *samurai* elite, and doesn't have a listing in the Yellow Pages. Which was why Reilly's presence—and his challenge—was so odd.

You could see Yamashita's quandary. Reilly was fairly dangerous in a savage, commonplace kind of way. Yamashita was a harsh teacher, but he never needlessly put any of us in danger of serious injury. It was beneath Sensei's dignity to accept the challenge, but you could almost hear the clicks in his brain as he weighed various other options. Would this match serve any type of purpose in terms of teaching his students? Who would be the most appropriate opponent? Ken was a senior student and could be a logical choice. We all knew—and Sensei did too—that his wife had just had a baby and that a great deal of Ken's mental energy was not totally focused on training at this time. He was good (even on his bad days) but a match like this was bound to be one where both parties limped away. Ken didn't need that right now and Yamashita knew it.

Yamashita's head swiveled along the line of students, weighing each one for potential, for flaws, like a diamond cutter rooting carefully around a drawer of unfinished stones. The more experienced among us sat, trying to be totally numb about the situation, not really focusing on Reilly, listening to the hum of the fluorescents and the faint rumble of trucks. The newer students sat in various states: the smart ones were secretly appalled at the prospect; the really dense were excited.

When he called me, I tried to feel nothing. "Professor," Yamashita said. Ever since they found out I teach in college, the nickname has stuck. It could have been worse. Early on I had worked out at a kendo school where the Japanese kids simply called me "Big Head."

I bowed and scooted up to the front. In this situation, you sit formally, facing the *sensei*, which put me right next to Reilly.

"This is Dr. Burke," he told Reilly. "I am sure you will find him instructive."

Reilly jerked his head around to size me up. I looked back: flat eyes, sitting there like a blue lump with relaxed muscles, no energy given to the opponent.

"You think you want a piece of me, asshole?" Out of the side of his mouth, like he'd picked it up from old Bogart movies. I swung around—you could see a slight jerk before he realized what I was up to—and bowed, saying nothing. Silent. Passive. A shade. *Heiho* was keeping yourself in shadow.

Reilly looked back at Sensei. "You must be joking. I'm not fucking around with this piece of shit."

Yamashita is funny about foul language. He spends his days teaching people how to do serious harm to others, but he has this real thing about keeping conversation civil. Part of it's just that Japanese politeness, but I think the other part is that he is a man dedicated to an art that celebrates control of one sort or another, and foul language strikes him either as the result of a bad vocabulary and poor imagination or as a lack of mastery over one's temper. In either case, this kind of language is forbidden in his *dojo*. Reilly may not have known it, but he had just committed a gross breach of etiquette.

"I am sorry, Mr. Reilly. I regret that we cannot accommodate you in your request for a lesson. You are clearly not ready for any serious training." With that, Yamashita looked right through him and stood up like he was preparing to leave the floor.

"Wait a minute . . ." Reilly shot up and looked like he was going to reach for the old man. Which was how I got to wondering about whether I could poleax him. I was targeting him for a knuckle strike right below the ear (I figured with any luck I could dislocate his jaw), but there was really no need. Yamashita had about reached the limits of his patience.

As Reilly came at him, Yamashita shot in, a smooth blur. There was an elbow strike in there somewhere before he whipped Reilly around to break his balance. Then Yamashita was behind him, clinging like a limpet and bringing Reilly slowly down to the floor. The choke was (as always) precisely executed: the flow of blood to the brain was disrupted as he brought pressure to bear on the arteries and Reilly was out cold.

Yamashita stood up and beckoned to Reilly's pals. "Remove him. Do not come back." Not even breathing hard. They dragged Reilly off the practice floor and trundled him away.

"What a foolish man. An arrogant and violent man." He looked around at us all, then turned to me. "I am surprised at you, Burke. I would have tried for the jaw dislocation. Work on your reaction time, please."

He glided away and the lesson ended.

THREE

The Smell of Money

I live in Brooklyn because the rents are cheaper and Yamashita's *dojo* is there, but I work in Bloomington, a planned suburb on Long Island that, among its other unremarkable features, harbors the pedestrian university that employs me.

Of course, it's not that I really work there. Dorian, like many other colleges, pays a horde of part-time teachers to do the dirty work of modern education. As an adjunct instructor I labor in obscurity so that the full-time professors can think deeply in a measured, quiet, unpressured life that, in my more bitter moments, I think must be like the early onset of Alzheimer's.

A part-time college instructor typically makes about an eighth of the pay of a real professor, with no benefits, medical coverage, or job security. Everyone loves us because we're cheap, docile, and actually teach for a living. For our part, we labor on in the blind hope that we will somehow be plucked from anonymity and elevated to full-time status, where you work about nine months out of the year.

So I wandered in that day, my bag crammed with unmarked student tests and a collection of battered paperbacks, with the resignation of a gladiator who knew that his sword was made of lead. The letters for appointments for next semester were due out today, and I was not particularly optimistic.

The battered common room where I had staked out a claim to an ugly industrial gray metal desk and lopsided typing chair was fairly quiet as well. My mailbox, one in a series of slots labeled with neatly typed paper slips (easily replaced), was filled with the usual junk. There was an announcement about an upcoming faculty meeting—they insist on sending these things to adjuncts, even though we're not eligible to attend—a perky newsletter for résumé-writing workshops and other forlorn hopes; a flyer on blue paper advocating attendance at a continuing education seminar, "Selling Real Estate with Feng Shui," and a message that I was wanted in the dean's office.

Dorian is a small, obscure place, but even small ponds have big fish. I headed down the hallway toward the administrative offices. The university's brick buildings are old and heavy with the accumulated aroma of particulate matter: dust and plaster for certain, asbestos probably, and old paper. The halls smell old and used except when you approach the dean's suite. Here, the paint is brighter and everything smells like furniture polish and new carpets.

I once heard a full professor say that a dean had the education of a philosopher, the heart of an accountant, and the soul of a weasel. Joseph Ceppaglia was a slim, gray, academic weasel of the first order. He had a mop of salt-and-pepper hair, which he patted absently in moments of thought; a Douglas Fairbanks mustache; and every other month he tried to stop smoking through a variety of useless stratagems. He was slim and articulate, wily, and immensely pleased with himself.

He didn't get up from behind the desk, just swiveled around to see me better. "Hey, Burke. What have you been up to?" I didn't know it then, but it would be a question I'd hear asked more than once. The dean was chewing nicotine gum furiously and bending a paperclip back and forth.

And he had a plan. Which was how, the next day, I ended up in "officer country," waiting to meet the president.

This is not something mere mortals look forward to at the university. President Peter Domanova was an old-style autocrat. He was notorious for firing people on the spot, for denying tenure recommendations, and generally outraging the rank and file. He did have a few good points: sometimes he fired people who deserved it and, most important for the university, he was a relentless shmoozer who had managed to raise quite a few dollars for the institution.

Occasionally you caught glimpses of him churning across campus with any number of flunkies in his wake, but most contact with the troops took the form of various combative memos that ended up in everyone's mailboxes. The president thought of himself as something of an intellectual. He had graduated from Oxford, so maybe at one time this delusion actually held some water. He was on the far side of sixty now, however, and although he could be eloquent and charming, mostly Domanova came across as a cranky snob.

Ceppaglia had told me to "dress nice" for the meeting, which meant that I had to wear the one good blue suit I owned. The men in my family call them "wedding and funeral rigs." The dean had been a font of gratuitous advice about what to wear and what to say. But, true survivor that he was, Ceppaglia escorted me to the door of the presidential suite, wished me luck, and hightailed it out of there before I did something that got us both fired.

I sat in the muted air of the reception room while prim and efficient secretaries shuttled to and fro. Phones chirped discreetly. The furniture was cherry and polished and dust free. It was like being in a bubble.

Then the presidential portal opened. Polite laughter and the sound of gruff instructions spilled out into the hush and a cluster of harried suits tumbled out of the office, gazing back in there with the fixation of men who are still fascinated with their latest brush with death.

I was up. My basic plan for this interview was to say as little as possible, make the president feel I was competent, and escape with my life.

President Domanova beckoned magisterially from behind a desk the size of a pool table, inviting me in, and actually got up to shake my hand.

"Dr. Burke. Good. Good." He had an exaggerated Mediterranean accent of some sort, all rolling r's and carefully enunciated sentences. He talked as if he enjoyed the way words felt as they came out. "The dean tells me that you are an accomplished Orientalist. Sit down."

The president tended to talk at you, not with you. The sentences came out in tight little clusters, abruptly. They had more to do with some weird internal dialogue he was having in there than with anything occurring on the outside.

I shook hands, nodded at my Oriental expertise, and sat down.

Domanova picked up some papers and gave them a quick glance. "A decent university degree," he mused. "Some articles in minor scholarly journals, two books, with one forthcoming."

He looked up as if he was thinking. "You have been teaching for us for how long?"

He knew the answer as well as I did. It was right there in front of him. "Three years, sir."

"Three years." He smirked. "With our illustrious historians."

"Yes."

He got a bit more animated then, putting both hands flat on the slab in front of him and looking at me intently. "They are a total embarrassment, Burke. I wonder you can tolerate them."

What do you say to something like this? That adjuncts are on the bottom of the university food chain and that down there you get acclimated to a great deal of murk? I just sat there.

He shot back in his chair. If I did that in my office, I would go flying backward and end up on the floor. The president's chair was made of sterner stuff, however. Leather, with those tasteful little studs along the edges of the seams.

"So," he said finally, indicating the snappy repartee was about over, "I assume Dean Ceppaglia has described the nature of the assignment?"

"You need someone with expertise in the martial arts and Japanese culture to develop some descriptive material for an art exhibit being run by a potential donor. I don't see a problem, sir."

"Yes." Something shutterlike flickered in Domanova's eyes. "You understand that remuneration will be arranged with the client and not the university?" I nodded, but I don't think he was even watching for the prompt. The presidential close was coming. "Fine. My secretary will provide you with the name of the individual. Good day."

And just like that, it was over. He shot back into his seat and whirled away to gaze out the window. Like posing for a portrait: *Brooding Intellectual Surveys His Domain.* The afternoon sun lit up his craggy face and the shoulders of his expensive suit. For a university president, he had an awful lot of dandruff.

The name in the file I got from the president's office was Robert Akkadian. The martial arts universe is not that large, so I had heard of him. Akkadian, or Bobby Kay as he was known on the street, had been an early promoter on the New York karate tournament scene. He saw the business potential in the arts. Over twenty or so years he had gradually gotten his fingers into every piece of the martial arts pie he could. He was doing pretty well by now. I was surprised that he was rubbing elbows with Domanova, given his semisleazy origins.

Then again, as the Chinese say, money has no smell.

Akkadian had gone upscale, with an office in Manhattan that was part of his Samurai House art gallery. I strode through the glass doors off the street and entered the lobby. It featured an eight-foot waterfall splashing down a black rock face. The waterworks bifurcated the lobby into two halves—one devoted to the gallery and the other to offices. I wandered over to the right to the office suite area. It was sedate, with muted tans and greens, bleached wood wainscoting, and appropriately innocuous prints that Westerners would think of as vaguely Asian in character. The receptionist was blond, with that shiny, brittle look you get from spending too much time worrying about how well your cheekbones are showing. She gave me a smile, though, and ushered me into Akkadian's office.

Bobby had a horsey face and a mane of longish hair that looked like it was dyed to match the expensive camel-hair jacket he was wearing. His office was dominated by an expanse of U-shaped desk with the cyclops monolith of the desktop computer squatting in the corner—every modern executive's little electric shrine.

The desk surface was uncluttered. Some papers were fanned out in front of his chair the way a magician spreads out a deck of cards before beginning the act. I wouldn't have been surprised to find out they were glued together to make that display. The whole office didn't really feel like it was an actual work site. It had all the qualities of a replica showroom labeled "Important Executive."

The Important Executive came around to greet me. "Hello, Professor, thanks for coming by." He shook my hand and I noticed him taking a look at it. I was probably something of a disappointment. I'm not really big and I don't look particularly dangerous. Akkadian was checking to see whether I had the signs of hand conditioning you see in some karate students: enlarged knuckles, calluses, etc. My fingers are a bit thick. Weird muscles have also developed in my forearms, but the only sign of advanced training in my hands is the bulge in the web between my thumb and forefinger I've developed from all the sword work with Yamashita.

He motioned me to a small sitting area of low chairs and

we sat. Bobby and I chatted pleasantly, mostly about his experience training and deep love for the martial arts. He knew something of my background and I talked a bit about Yamashita.

"You know"—he smiled—"despite appearances, the Manhattan martial arts scene is a pretty small world."

I nodded. "Seems that way sometimes."

"But I don't hear much about Yamashita Sensei," he commented. Which was true. My teacher is almost as secretive as he is selective. "It would be fantastic to be able to visit the *dojo*. He really sounds impressive."

The subject of visitors was not one I cared to bring up with my teacher just now. I smiled noncommittally and nodded again. I noticed I was doing a lot of it lately. After a while I said, "I hope I can be of some help to you. You need some PR pieces done for a sword exhibit?"

That got him back on track. "Yeah. Let me show you what we've got planned." He gestured me toward the desk. It looked like it was made of marble.

We wandered over to the desk and he pushed the fan of papers to one side. To my surprise, they actually were unconnected. He ruined the display effect, but the creature outside would probably come in later and restore it. "I've managed to get some fantastic blades for this show. You would not believe what a pain the Japanese have been about letting this stuff out of the country. The security bond alone is killing me."

He opened a manila file and spread out some papers. "What I'm putting together, Professor Burke, is a display of rare Japanese weapons, all of which have a documented association with some of the most famous warriors in martial arts history."

I looked at one sheet of paper. It listed a series of weapons types, descriptions of individual pieces, and estimated value. There were *katana*—the long sword of the *samurai*—as well as short swords and knives, the spears known as *yari*, and *naginata*—long poles with wicked curved blades used to hack riders out of the saddle. They would interest any martial arts freak, but what was really fascinating were the names of the original owners of these items.

"Wow," I said, looking at the list.

Akkadian looked pleased. "You bet. Some of these pieces are being allowed out of Japan for the first time. Some of them, as a matter of fact, are already here. And every one of them linked to famous warriors."

He read aloud from the list: "Yagyu Munenori, Yamaoka Tesshu." He paused significantly, then continued, ". . . Miyamoto Musashi."

I could feel Bobby eyeing me for a reaction. He's famous, but Musashi had never been one of my favorites. He's known as the "sword saint," but it was a funny kind of sainthood. He was a minor seventeenth-century *samurai* whose single-minded pursuit of dominance in swordsmanship carried him through untold duels. Musashi pioneered the simultaneous use of two swords in Japanese swordsmanship but often faced his opponents armed with nothing but a wooden weapon. Once he used a carved-down boat oar. Whatever weapon he used, the results were always the same: a crumpled form in the dirt and Musashi stalking away, never satisfied, always hungry for another opponent. He always struck me as a man with something to prove.

He's known today for writing *A Book of Five Rings*, a treatise on strategy in swordsmanship. It's been touted as some sort of major work on strategy for today's businessmen, and deluded MBA students read it, thinking a tough merger negotiation is the twentieth-century equivalent of a sword duel. The dust jacket claims it's the secret guide to strategy for Japanese executives, but if you go to Japan, it's hard to come by and only antiquarians are familiar with it.

But I had to admit that it was a brilliant move. The weapons assembled were bound to draw a crowd.

Which was pretty much how he laid it out and where I came in. Bobby was a bit of an egotist, but he was also shrewd enough to know what he didn't know. A show like this would have martial artists as well as scholars coming out of the woodwork. Some in both groups would be lunatics, but a significant number would be fairly well informed. As a result, Bobby needed to make sure that his display hype was historically accurate. He could have tried to get some reputable name to do it, but Bobby was not really connected with those circles.

Domanova, like a shark smelling blood in the water, had sensed that Bobby was rapidly emerging as a successful—and wealthy—entrepreneur in search of some respectability. If I could do Bobby a favor on the cheap, the relationship with Domanova would grow and everyone would be happy. The president would give him a patina of respectability. Bobby would be slowly courted and stroked—you could imagine the dorsal fins circling—and eventually cajoled into making a sizable donation to the university.

It was a very finely choreographed dance where need, ego, money, and illusion swirled together. In higher education they call it "institutional development."

I don't pretend to understand all that, but my role in the process was pretty straightforward. Bobby called in his shiny receptionist to make copies of the documents in the folder and asked me to come up with some stuff on the different historical figures and their role in Japanese warrior culture. "Nothing too complicated, now, Professor," he reminded. "A little blood, a little guts, a little *budo* . . ." He grinned at me with that long horse face and I felt the urge to grin back. Bobby was not my kind of person, but it was hard not to respond to someone who was so obviously having so much fun.

"You ever been to Samurai House before, Dr. Burke?" I shook my head and he headed for the door, giving me a "come along" jerk of the head.

"I've been working on this place for years. Started as an Asian antique center. You know—vases, lacquer screens, that kind of stuff. I got a sense, though, that this martial arts thing was going to be big. So over time, I've been adding things—a mail-order house here, videos, a gallery for traveling displays . . ."

"Diversification," I commented.

He smiled. "It's a beautiful thing. My latest thing is the training and exhibition hall. Check it out."

The office suite was tucked away in a corner of the business part of the complex. From the other side of the lobby waterworks, you entered the public area through large wood doors that matched all the furniture in the office suite. On this side, instead of an office reception area, there was a rock garden. You walked around it and could then access the training and exhibition hall. "Some of the stuff's in there now," Bobby said as we walked past the garden. "Got a special security detail to watch it."

We went in through those sliding paper screen doors the Japanese call *shoji*. The *dojo* was bright and airy, with a good, hardwood floor and tasteful decorations. Of course, in a real *dojo* there are no decorations, but this was America. I had seen worse—a lot of people fill their schools with all kinds of Asian schlock and they end up looking like bad Chinese restaurants.

He watched me as I took a look around. "Pretty nice, huh?"

I had to admit that Bobby (or his interior designer) had done a good job. It was impressive. "Looks like you've got it all figured out," I commented.

He grinned again. "You bet. And, as a perk, I get to work out here."

"You still train?" I asked. What with all the diversification.

"I try to keep my hand in," he said with the false-modest smirky kind of reply people use in the martial arts when they want you to understand that they are good. "I'm training with this guy now; he's incredible."

Bobby glanced at his watch. Was that alligator for the band? "As a matter of fact, it's about time for my workout. Would you care to watch?"

And on cue, Mitch Reilly walked in to the *dojo*.

In street clothes he looked almost normal, although the tight polo shirt stretched across his torso gave the impres-

sion that this was a man who spent a great deal of time lift-
ing weights and looking at himself in the mirror. He probably got along pretty well with Bobby's receptionist. Reilly
came up short when he saw us and glared at me for a
minute.

"Mitch," I said, just to annoy him.

He looked at Akkadian. "What's going on here, Bobby?"

Bobby Kay did not get where he is by being dense. He
looked at me, then at Mitch, and realized that what he had
here were two unstable elements in very close proximity.
He moved in so he was at least partly between us. "Professor Burke is doing some consulting for the gallery. I didn't
realize you knew each other."

"It's a brief acquaintance," I noted.

Mitch muttered something under his breath. It sounded
like "asshole."

Bobby didn't pick that up. "I had just invited him to
watch our workout."

Reilly bristled. "I don't like outsiders watching me train,
Bobby." Akkadian looked a bit put out.

I jumped in. "It's OK, Mr. Akkadian. Maybe some other
time." I held up the file he gave me. "I'll get to work." For
a minute, I had the urge to tell him to get someone else for
his trainer. But, hey, he was hiring me to do some writing,
not to manage his business affairs.

As I walked out, Bobby Kay looked a bit disappointed.
But I figured he wasn't half as disappointed as he would
have been if I told him the last time I saw Mitch Reilly, Yamashita had knocked him out and Mitch had wet his pants.

F O U R

Trails

Owl's Head Park is in Bay Ridge, Brooklyn, and looks out over the Narrows leading into New York Harbor. It's one of the few parts of the borough left where you can still see how hilly it was before all that building effectively erased any of the land's texture. Every morning I run up the hill in Owl's Head, down the other side, and onto the pedestrian walk that borders the choppy gray water that churns between Brooklyn and Staten Island. It was almost summer, and I was praying for an offshore breeze. They built a sewage treatment plant right near the park in a fit of excellent urban planning and now it pretty much smells like you think it would. It helps when the breeze blows in from the ocean.

Yamashita's a big believer in running. He thinks it aids the cardiovascular fitness of his advanced students, and he's right. Once you get to a certain level in martial arts training, the physical effort sort of peaks out and technique takes over. What makes a novice collapse in a sweaty heap, gasping for breath, does not have the same effect on you. But Yamashita insists that we stay fit, which means some sort of cross-training.

One of his favorite stories is the one about the American who goes over to Okinawa to live out a lifelong dream of training with this karate master. The guy gets there for his first day of training and the master asks him, "What's the best self-defense technique?"

The American is pretty pleased with himself because he knows the answer. "Run away, Sensei," he says.

The old master nods sagely. "Good." Then, he adds, "Start running."

The American is absolutely perplexed.

The master repeats, "Start running. If I can catch you, I will beat you up."

And off they go, the student tearing down the street, running for his life, while this ancient karate teacher chugs relentlessly after him.

I'm not even sure whether the old guy catches the student, but Yamashita thinks it is tremendously entertaining. Like most things he tells us, the story has a point: a good martial artist needs to stay in shape.

So I run.

I hate running, even after all this time. I use it as an exercise in concentration and breath control. I tend to make up little chants to keep time with the flopping of my sneakers. I know the scientifically engineered, Day-Glo, rollbar-equipped and heel-cup-enhanced productions I wear are more properly referred to as running shoes, but I grew up calling them sneakers and I like to keep the memory alive. When I was a kid, you rooted around for these things in bins that smelled like inner tubes and contained hundreds of mismatched pairs. They cost seven bucks then, which is why I have a minor stroke every time I buy new ones today.

Mostly, I use the rhythm of exercise as an aid to thinking. It helps focus me, like the repetitive chants used in Shinto ceremonies that are believed to get the attention of the spirits. And, of course, when I think, I'm no longer dwelling on how much I hate running.

All the research I had been doing made me think about Yamashita, the closest I had ever come to a true master. I had presented myself to him years ago, with formal written recommendations from highly respected teachers. I knelt on the wood floor in the formal position, bowed, and offered him the neatly brushed testimonials with both hands, which is a sign of respect. I waited.

I knew that there was something missing from the training I had received up to that point. It was a quiet but insistent urging. My teachers could see it in me, revealed in my technique: it's hard to be focused when you're craning your neck to see around a bend. Whatever I was looking for, they knew they couldn't provide it. It must be a hard realization for any teacher to come to. So they passed me on to a higher level of intensity.

I knew a bit about Yamashita, even then. His prowess in swordsmanship, as a fighter with or without weapons, was grudgingly admitted by the more mainstream teachers. Stories about the rigor of his training were used to scare cocky black belts into a type of humility. So when I came before him that day, I looked at him carefully to see what part of my future was revealed in his form.

He was stocky and about average size for a Japanese man of his age. I'm not much bigger, but Yamashita radiated a type of power that you could feel. His hair was cut so short that from a distance he appeared totally bald. His eyes were hard and dark, and the expression on his face was one of total reserve. The fingers of his hands were thick and strong looking as they reached for the introductions I brought.

Yamashita glanced once at me, read the letters, and grimaced.

"So," he said. "Return tomorrow. We will see."

You couldn't tell whether he was pleased, annoyed, or optimistic. And in the early days of working with him, I despaired of ever finding out. But over the years, as I passed from one level to another, a subtle form of communication began to take place. I don't know whether it was just that I got more used to the nuances in him, or whether his training was making me more perceptive, but there it was. And, as I persevered on the hard course he charted for me, there were times when I swear I could see a glint of approval or satisfaction in his eyes. And just that hint was enough to keep me going. He was my *sensei*, after all.

In the last few days, there had been a subtle increase in the intensity of training. Not that things weren't normally pretty intense. But there was a pattern, a flow to the logic of what my teacher did. The years with him ingrain the pattern in you. And what we were doing lately seemed somehow out of synch. You could sense it in the nature of his comments to his students, in the stiff set of his back as he stalked the *dojo* floor. I wondered what Yamashita was up to.

Any *sensei* is a bit mercurial at times—they do it to keep you guessing. Part of the mystery of a really good martial arts teacher is the way in which you're perpetually surprised by things, kept just slightly off balance. I had a karate teacher years ago, and every time I thought, *OK, this guy has shown me just about everything he's got,* he would waltz in and do something I had never seen before. Then he would look at me like he could read my mind.

Yamashita was a master of this type, but even more so. You could glean clues of the inner workings of the man from the comments he would make after training. The students sit, row after row of sweaty swordsmen in dark blue, slowing their breathing and listening to the master. When he was pleased, Yamashita would offer parables that reinforced an important lesson. At that point in the training session, you're so used up that the mind is extremely open. As a result, the stories and advice are imprinted in your memory in a tremendously vivid way.

But there was none of that lately, just gruff admonitions to train harder. In response, each of us came back for more training even though its purpose was a mystery.

I slogged on in the rhythm of the run, mulling the situation over. There was nothing to be done. My teacher would reveal his purpose in time. Or not. It was his choice. He was the master. I thought about something else.

I had finished up Bobby Kay's project. It was not exactly

a brain teaser. I e-mailed the file and mailed a disk and a hard copy to him just in case. Now I was waiting for the check. The school semester was ending. It was the beginning of the lean season for all part-time college teachers like me, and Bobby's payment loomed large in my imagination. So I made up a little chant that kept my mind off the sheer boredom of running: Bobby Kay. You must pay.

I was on the hundredth repetition of my little mantra: Bob-by Kay. You Must Pay. It went well with the in and out of my breath. People were passing, going the other way, runners or people on mountain bikes, and I noticed after a while that I was getting some funny looks. Couldn't have been the sneakers; they were as high-tech as everyone else's. I was also pretty sure that I hadn't been actually chanting Bobby's name out loud. Then I started to pick up the crunch of car tires slowly approaching me.

The unmarked cop car came grinding up behind me with its light flashing and gave me a quick *bloop* on the siren just for kicks. I was glad for the breather.

There were two of them, and they had that cop look about them: faces that told you everyone is guilty of something, everyone lies. The driver was sandy haired with a clipped, military-style mustache. The other guy had a shock of dark reddish brown hair with a two-inch white streak to one side of his widow's peak. They were in shirts and ties, which told me they were detectives. You could eye their shoulder harnesses and hardware (gun belts being a pain in a car). I peeked in the back. Their sports jackets were neatly folded in the backseat, and the floors were cluttered with paper wrappers and empty coffee cups. I didn't look too hard, though. Cops get nervous when you appear too focused.

The driver's window geared down. I took one look and tried the time-honored civilian opener.

"What seems to be the problem, Officer?"

The driver eyed me silently, then looked at his partner. "How original."

"You don't get conversation like this just anywhere," the guy with the white streak commented.

Mustache continued. "Burke." It was a rhetorical question: they weren't nosing pedestrians to either side of the path just for fun. They were looking for someone in particular. I nodded.

"We're looking for some information. Could you come with us, please?"

I knew I hadn't done anything. But there's something about the Law. I got that feeling in my stomach. Like I had just gotten on an elevator that suddenly lurched down.

A black guy shot by on some in-line skates. "Hey man," he called, "don't let them roust you without ID. Could be anyone down here, know what I'm saying?" He had turned around to deliver this advice, skating backward. A few bicyclists swerved madly out of his way, and he spun forward and rolled on without giving us another look.

"I suppose I should ask for some ID." I'm not proud about some things: I took the skater's advice.

The driver made a show of patting himself absently and muttered, "Hmmm . . . badges . . . badges."

His partner chimed in with a really bad Mexican accent. "Badges? Badges? We don't need no stinking badges." I tried to place it. *Treasure of the Sierra Madre?* I always get those bandits mixed up with the ones from *The Magnificent Seven.*

They both chortled. Cop humor. The driver with the mustache flashed a detective's shield.

"You want me up front or in the back?" I asked. The sweat was beginning to pop out now that I had stopped running. I was hoping all the crud in the back of the car wouldn't stick to me.

"You sit next to me, Bruce Lee," the driver said.

His partner got out, eased the jackets over and settled into the backseat. It was an oddly fastidious motion. The jackets looked clean and pressed. They were the only tidy thing in the vehicle. I got in, bumping my knee on the radio console mounted on the dash, and we rolled slowly down the path until they could exit and we headed back onto the streets. No one said anything. The radio made soft gobbling noises. I asked if I could roll down my window. The driver eyed me and, deciding I wasn't about to make a break for it, rolled it down with the power console on his left. I turned to look over my shoulder at the cop with the white streak.

"So, Mick," I asked, "how's Mom?"

My brother, with the inevitability of salmon spawning and other inherited urges, was the latest product of the Brooklyn Irish diaspora who had flowed in childhood to Long Island and ebbed back home to the NYPD. He had been a rambunctious kid. He grew into a quiet adult who seemed to smother some deep, unanswerable anger and keep it under control only with a minute by minute exertion of willpower. He's like a lot of cops I know: a basically good guy who has seen too many bad things and is baffled, frustrated, and personally affronted by them and who, at a moment's notice, could go off like a rocket.

The family is mostly relieved he has found a constructive outlet for his energies. Micky is generous to his friends, an accomplished carpenter in his spare time, and a good husband and father. He also tends to wander off at family parties and stare vacantly into the distance while sucking on a Marlboro, seeing things the rest of us don't. Or don't want to.

It's a measure of his self-control that he's made detective. Since he essentially gets to wander the city with his partner, Art, tracking down criminals from the mobile trash bin they call a car, and doing it relatively free of supervision, Micky likes his job and is good at it.

Art Pedersen is a stockier version of Micky. He's also a little less gloomy. Art gets to play Good Cop most of the time, although I imagine that when the two of them begin to really work on an interrogation, it's probably hard for the perp to tell the difference between the Good Cop and the Bad Cop. Art is a movie buff, and after years of traveling together, the two of them have developed this annoying habit of recycling old lines of film dialogue into their conversation. They find it tremendously amusing. Many criminals, not as steeped in cinema, find it totally baffling.

Now I was treated to some of their patented charm. My older brother didn't rise to the bait of my question. He just eyed me and said flatly, "What have you been up to, you moron?"

Message

"Nothing much," I replied. "The teaching, working out."

We were driving on Fourth Avenue, heading north. This time of morning, it was a better bet than the Gowanus. Neither Art nor Micky said much. They had that smoldering cop silence about them, which was unusual. One of these guys was my brother, and Art had been his partner for eight years, so he was no stranger to me either. But I wasn't getting any information from either of them. They drove and watched out the window as the tired-looking brick of Brooklyn slid by. Somewhere down these streets, our parents had roller-skated as children.

"You're a little off the beaten path here, Mick," I said.

"Yeah," he admitted. Then he began to grope around for a Marlboro.

"Don't you light up one of those things in my car," Art warned him. He had quit about two years ago and was slowly, inexorably, forcing Micky into doing the same. "You light up in here, we're gonna end up like a bunch of hams cured in a smokehouse."

"Ah, gimme a break, Art."

"Give ME a break. Idiot," Art fumed.

"Asshole," Micky mumbled. It was like listening to a

crabby married couple. But I noticed that Micky didn't light up.

They also didn't say much about why we were heading over the Brooklyn Bridge into Manhattan.

Eventually, however, the stop and go of city traffic seemed to shake something out of them.

"Still doing that martial arts stuff?" Art asked.

I grinned. "Oh, yeah. A deadly weapon."

Micky snorted. "Some people never learn. Black belt, no black belt. No one can dodge a bullet."

"The trick," I said in my best Asian master voice, "is being where the bullet is not."

Art looked at me like I was insane.

"What's this I hear about you working for Bobby Kay?" Micky slipped the question in, but I sat up a little straighter.

"Yeah," I admitted. "How d'you find that out?"

Art slewed the car around a cab that shot across two lanes without warning to pluck up a fare, cursed under his breath, and asked, "You read the paper this morning, Connor?"

"No. Why?"

Micky was rooting around in the trash in the back and came up with a copy of the *Daily News*. He slapped it onto the seat back between us and said "Check it out, buddy boy."

The headline read "Kung Fu Killer" with the sort of creative alliteration I usually associate with the *Post*. The crux of the article was a homicide. Early this morning, Mr. Robert Akkadian, noted entrepreneur, had gone to his Samurai House gallery for a scheduled early appointment with his personal trainer. The trainer, identified as Mitchell Reilly, a martial arts expert, had been found in Samurai House's performance space, dead of an apparent broken neck. While NYPD was still investigating the cause of death, the *News* speculated it was caused by a "karate chop." Theft does not appear to have been a motive for the killing and the investigation was ongoing.

"Oooh," I said, "a karate chop. Hence the visit. Bobby Kay turn me in, fellas?"

I said it half-kidding, but the response I got was anything but. "Look, Connor," my brother said, "we just need to talk with you a bit on this." Micky wasn't exactly apologetic. If it bothered him at all to pick up his own brother for questioning, it didn't show. Just doing his job. The questions were really almost automatic for him by this time.

"C'mon, Mick. You don't seriously think I'm a suspect!" Micky held up a calming hand. Art, however, wasn't going to let it go. Today, he was Bad Cop.

"Akkadian likes you for it." There was silence. "Here's what we've got, Connor," Art continued. "The esteemed Mr. Akkadian, noted entrepreneur and tough guy wanna-be, gets a call from his janitorial staff early this A.M. to hightail it to his office. By the time he gets there, the uniforms are on the scene stretching yellow tape. Old Bob takes a good look around. Pokes about in his office. Then he goes over to the gallery. He takes one good look and that about does it."

"You mean he said I did it?" I asked skeptically.

"Well," Art continued, "first he had to stop barfing. Then he got cleaned up and started talking. And . . ."

"Presto," Micky concluded, "your name pops up."

I looked from one to the other and couldn't think of a thing to say.

"Here's where we are, Connor," Art went on. "You doing a job for Bobby Kay. Reilly in the mix. The two of you have some sort of confrontation. Some sort of mysterious martial arts stuff. Mitch tells Bobby about it. Day or so later, Mitch turns up dead. So . . ."

"So," Micky picked up the thread, "we got Bobby Kay babbling about some karate-grudge death match. I personally think it's a crock, but . . ."

"Motive." Art held up his hand, index finger pointing up like a DA making a telling point to a jury.

"Then we got all this 'death touch' hype. You should

read the *Post*'s version." Micky was digging around back there looking for it but gave up after a few seconds.

"So now, Mr. Martial Arts Expert," Art said, holding up finger number two, "we got the means."

"You do anything last night, Connor? Out with friends? A date?"

"No." I got a sinking feeling as Micky ran down the list of possibilities, trying to see whether I had an alibi. "I stayed in grading papers."

"Phone calls?" I shook my head.

"And," Art said with a flourish, raising finger three, "opportunity."

We came to a halt in front of Samurai House. There was a police cruiser on the scene and a cop by the door.

"Hey, come on. You guys can't be serious," I protested.

Art let out a long, fuming sigh. He put a cardboard sign with an NYPD sticker on the dash and shut the car down.

"Nah," Micky said. "We'll have to run it down in terms of an alibi . . ."

"And you'll have to make a statement . . . prints, that sort of thing," Art added.

"But what we really want is some advice on this one," Micky said as he climbed out of the backseat.

The three of us stood for a minute, looking at the front of Samurai House, the chrome and granite looking no worse for wear and the business of the city flowing past it as if nothing had happened there. But the cops were coming and going. Thirty minutes ago, I'd been running by the shore. Now I was in a very different world. Forensic guys in white coats were taking out little paper bags with stuff in them. Radios gabbled. My T-shirt had dried and my legs had that good, used feel they get from exertion. Though I stood there in my high-tech sneakers, feeling fit, it didn't do much for my confidence.

Micky tapped me lightly on the shoulder and took me by the arm. "Don't worry," he said quietly in a voice I recognized as my brother's. "It'll be OK."

"Besides," Art concluded, "we're afraid if we tried to

take you in, you'd kill us with your freakin' *ninja* death touch."

"Be afraid, Art. Be very afraid." I used my most menacing voice, but it was an effort.

Art appeared unimpressed. "Come on," he said as we walked toward the door. "You ever been on a crime scene, Connor?"

"No." I watched Micky dawdle on the pavement, fingering his pack of cigarettes and wondering whether he could get in a quick smoke.

"One cardinal rule," Art continued.

"OK." I looked over at him.

"Don't touch anything."

We went in past the uniformed cop, whose eyes briefly refocused as we approached, but glazed over once the boys flashed their shields. The waterfall burbled with a relentless lack of consideration for the solemnity of crime. The plastic yellow crime scene tape was strung across the scenic little entrance Bobby Kay had showed me with such pride the other day. Inside the gallery, the room was empty. I let out some air, realizing that I had been holding my breath in anticipation of having to see the body.

But it was long gone. There was the taped outline of Reilly's last earthly location on the floor, but that was about it. The room was an empty one to begin with, so there wasn't much to look at. There were some small pieces of paper and tape lying around—the detritus of the crime scene people—but not much else.

Then I saw the wall.

I could feel their eyes on me, but Micky and Art didn't say much. It's a thing cops develop. They're hunters of a sort. They learn by watching and waiting. They were both very still.

I did a double take and moved slowly toward the wall and what was written there. It must have been done with one of those thick magic markers. The black strokes had none of the esthetics of brushwork, but they were well formed and confident, nonetheless. It was calligraphy of a type. I had seen the characters before.

"Oh, man," I murmured.

"Can you read that, Connor?" Micky asked.

"Lookin' for a translation. We got a call in for a PD liaison from Chinatown, but no luck yet," Art added in explanation.

I turned to look at them. "You sure this wasn't here before? Not part of Kay's show?"

Art flipped through his notebook. "No such luck. This wall was set to have a display hung on it and was painted last week."

"We're assuming whoever got in here and nailed the victim did it," Micky added. "No trace of the magic marker, right?" He looked at Art, who shook his head. Micky ran a hand through his white streak and squinted at me. Our dad used the same expression: a squint created from a lifetime of looking at the world through the smoke from a Lucky Strike. "So, can you read it?"

"Oh, I can read it," I said.

"What's it say?" they asked in unison.

I looked from one to the other. A uniformed cop drifted closer to eavesdrop. "Fellas," I said, "let's get a cup of coffee."

We ended up in a diner, hunched over the table in a booth near the back. The waitress wandered over, a Pyrex in hand, and topped up our cups.

"Thanks, that's it," Art said to her. She looked disappointed that he didn't ask for donuts, but Art struggled manfully against stereotype.

Then they sat there and simply looked at me with the flat expectancy of their profession.

"What you've got here," I lectured, "is a message in Japanese. It says, 'I am here.' "

"Ooh. Ominous," my brother said.

"What's really interesting is that the note is signed." I dipped my finger in the coffee cup and drew the characters we had seen from the wall on a napkin. "The characters read *ro-nin*. Translates as 'wave man.'"

"Sailor?" Art suggested.

"Hmmm. Surfer?" Micky countered.

"Psycho surfer," Art grinned, happy with the sound of it.

"Guys," I said, trying to rein them in a bit, "in feudal Japan, a warrior without a master to serve was called a *ronin*, wave man. He was adrift, without moorings, without social place."

"Like Palladin," Micky said, eyeing Art.

"*Have Gun Will Travel.*" Art, more than equal to the task, barely missed a beat.

"Well, yeah," I admitted, "although it doesn't have quite the same attraction for the Japanese. A *ronin* was an essentially tragic figure. In Japan, your identity is bound up with the group. The individual outside group boundaries is an outcast. He has no status. In stories about a *ronin*, it usually doesn't end well for him."

Art snapped his fingers and pointed across the formica. "Like Shane."

"Well, yeah," I said, "but Americans tend to romanticize the gunslinger story. It pops up everywhere. Cowboy flicks. Private-eye flicks. Cop flicks. Same story, different costumes. The lone fighter is heroic for us, not really tragic."

"I think Shane pretty well captured the tragic aspect," Art began as a protest.

"So, what's that got to do with offing this Reilly guy?" Micky wanted to get to the point before Art digressed into the lesser known works of Jack Palance and Alan Ladd.

"Hey, you're the detectives," I countered. "Detect."

"What we have here . . ." Art began.

Micky picked up the thread. "Is a murder in the public space of an art gallery specializing in Asian objects related to all that martial arts stuff you do."

"Victim appears to have been done in without an apparent weapon," Art added.

"Then again, the perp could have used a pipe and taken it

with him." Micky nodded as he mulled over his own statement, looking at Art expectantly.

His partner nodded in agreement. "We'll check with the
ME's report. Pipe. Club. Cosh. It got done. We'll see if they
pick up anything from the autopsy that IDs a weapon."

"You mean like splinters or stuff?" I asked.

"Yeah." But he waved it away. "Now the graffiti. Here's
a new wrinkle. What's that all about?"

"People who sign their work, they want to be known,"
Micky pointed out. "Even with an alias."

"You don't think this was just a robbery gone bad?" I
said.

"Connor," my brother explained slowly, as if to a simple-
ton. "Someone breaks into an art gallery. They take . . ." he
raised his eyebrows, waiting for the answer.

"Well, art, I guess," I replied.

"You guess right. You don't thread an electronic alarm
system in midtown, go through all that planning, knock
someone off, and take . . . what?" He looked at Art for confirmation.

"Nothing of any real value. Nada. Zip." He consulted his
notes and quoted, "A personal inventory by Mr. Akkadian
confirms nothing missing except an old wooden sword that
formed a minor part of the display."

Micky nodded. "No thief is gonna act like that. Akkadian
had tons of valuable stuff in there." Micky seemed outraged
by the ineptness.

I sat, digesting this, and Art followed up. I think they
were both secretly enjoying lecturing to me. "And, if something goes wrong and you have to knock some heads, you
tend to boogie outta there quick. Your basic thief doesn't
whip out the old magic marker and do Chinese graffiti all
over the place instead of stuffing valuables into a sack."

"So what do you mean? What happened?" I asked.

Micky answered me. "This wasn't a smash and grab sort
of thing."

"Maybe just a smash," Art said. I guessed he had seen
the body before they came to fetch me.

"This is some weird, hokey murder," my brother said. "And that '*ronin*' shit is the clue."

"Guy like this," Art said, "is gonna leave a trail. And a trail . . ."

"Is just what two ace bloodhounds like us need," Micky said.

That seemed to do it for them. They drained their cups and headed out. Art paid the cashier, and Micky provided a running commentary as we headed out to the car, double-parked out front.

"We'll run a check. Connor, we'll need a statement. Compare your prints with any latents the lab people picked up. They won't match and you'll be cleared. Then, we see if there are reports with similar MOs. Shouldn't be hard to spot. The newspaper clippings alone should stick out a mile."

"Martial mayhem," Art offered.

"Samurai slaying."

"*Psycho* Samurai Slaying."

And off we went. This time, I had to sit in the back.

An Open and Shut Case

Progress has pretty much ruined everything. When Micky and Art invited me back to the squad room, I had all those B-movie images of where cops work lodged in my brain: dark and dingy rooms crammed with untidy desks, choked with cigarette smoke, and smelling of old coffee and stale sweat.

In reality, Micky and Art shared the wall of contiguous cubicles in a brightly lit, cavernous area made mazelike by the portable half-walls that divided up the space. Phones didn't ring; they chirped. There were even faxes in plain view, along with prominently displayed "No Smoking" symbols. Despite my disappointment, there were some comforting links with the past. The room was littered with coffee cups: anonymous Styrofoam ones, others with the very popular blue Greek motif, upscale types made of paper sporting various brand names, and even some ceramic mugs of the kind people get at conventions or as gifts from other people with no real clue about what to buy as presents.

The surface illusion of order and neatness was somewhat damaged when I got escorted to Micky's cubicle. Cartons awash in folders and dog-eared documents were shoved beneath the desk. Little slips of paper were tucked under blotters, half-empty coffee cups, and anything else remotely heavy. Art was on the phone, standing up and peering over the wall that divided him from us, murmuring "uh huh, uh huh" into the receiver and taking notes. His pen ran out of ink. He grimaced and snapped his fingers at Micky while throwing his dead pen in the trash. Micky opened a drawer that was crammed with paper and rummaged through a pile of ballpoints with mismatched caps, tossing one to Art.

"Excuse me," I said as I approached, "is this 221B Baker Street?"

Art sat down, rolled his chair out, and swiveled in it to eye me briefly. Micky pulled some paperwork off a chair and gestured for me to sit. Art hung up the phone.

I eyed him expectantly.

"Nah," he shook his head, "nothing. Other case."

He thumbed through some pages of notes in his little book. Art had thick, freckled hands and his fingers made the book look tiny. "OK," he said, "Connor's landlady confirms his statement that he was home the night of the murder. She heard him come in and various noises in the apartment for most of the evening. Seems to corroborate his statement."

Micky raised his eyebrows. "Noises? Way to go, bro."

"Don't get too excited, Mick, it's a two-family house. I live upstairs and the floors creak."

"Yeah, well. One less thing to worry about."

"Which is nice," Art said, " 'cause there's a shitload of other stuff to wade through here."

"What," I said, "you've got something?"

They swung their chairs to face me at almost exactly the same time. I felt left out because my chair had no wheels. Then they looked at each other.

"To the Batcave," they said together.

I followed them out of the cubicle and into a conference room, thinking that they really were seeing too much of each other.

* * *

It had only been a few days since Reilly's murder, but in that short time the investigation's paperwork had ballooned. Art and Micky both hauled various boxes, manila envelopes, files, and VCR tapes to the Batcave. It was pretty state of the art for cops, a carpeted conference room with a computer hooked up to a projector, a TV/VCR unit, and a large oval table. They dumped the stuff at one end and began sorting it, rooting around and grunting at each other like apes contentedly working a grub nest.

I sat and watched the process, waiting until they were ready. Finally, Micky popped a tape in the TV. The sound kicked in and it was some cop I didn't know narrating the examination of the crime scene. Date and time were automatically displayed, but he went through the motions anyway, identifying the location, the hour and day, and the fact that Art and Micky were the investigating officers.

The camera panned carefully around the room, noting entrances, windows (there were none), lighting and alarm controls, orienting the viewer. Then it carefully focused on the floor where Reilly lay.

The camera panned over the body. Reilly's form was like something discarded. It had the shape and dimension of a human being, but it was just flopped there on the floor, a heap, without any of the sense of connection you get from looking at a person at rest. The left shoulder looked droopy and it was obvious from the face that Reilly had taken a major blow to the head. What looked like an oak sword was pinned under the body.

Micky shoved some still photos across the table: Reilly from various angles. "OK," he began. "So much for cinema. Mitchell Reilly, aged forty-two. Casual employee of Samurai House. Ran a martial arts school in Queens. Some minor stuff as a juvenile, nothing on the record for the last twenty years or so."

"Saved for clean living by the martial arts?" I asked.

Art snorted. "Saved for the coroner's office."

"Doesn't matter," Micky said. "No apparent problems in

his life that would suggest he was anything but a guy who got in the way here."

"We put an end to that grudge match thing, by the way," Art said. "Once we squeezed Akkadian, we got to the bottom of it. Anyway," he continued, "we told Bobby Kay that you were clean."

"What was his reaction?" I asked.

"He seemed like his mind was on other things," Micky commented. "He did say that he never really thought it was you; you seemed OK."

"Yeah," I said, "I seemed so OK he couldn't wait to finger me for murder."

Art waved it away. "It happens." Then he picked up the thread, "Time of death is estimated somewhere between two-thirty and six-thirty A.M."

"Is that significant?"

Micky made a face. "There's a four-hour margin of error in this stuff. He was found at around seven-thirty in the morning, so it doesn't tell us much that we didn't already know."

"Deceased suffered a number of fractures, including a cranial blow that might have killed him," Art continued.

"Do you know what did it?" I was trying to remain as clinical as they were, but my eyes kept drifting to the frozen video and the stills on the table.

"Cellulose fragments from his shirt and scalp suggest the weapon was wood of some type; we haven't got it fixed yet."

"Let me ask," I said. "Reilly suffered a number of fractures. Collarbone?"

They nodded.

"The head wound is obvious. Any sign of damage to the right wrist or forearm?"

Micky consulted the ME's report. "No breaks that are noted. Did seem to have taken some bangs there, though."

It figured. I got up and shut the TV off so I could concentrate better.

"OK," I continued, "so Mitch Reilly is in the Samurai House guarding Bobby Kaye's exhibit. He got let in when?"

"Building shuts down about eleven. Lobby security logged the cleaners out and Reilly in at ten P.M. Reilly activated the Samurai House alarm and buttoned up for the night. There's no lobby security presence until five-thirty A.M."

"Custodial shift comes in at seven," Art said. "Secretary at seven-thirty. She takes a quick look in the gallery and all hell breaks loose."

"She screamed so loud, the guards spilled their coffee," Micky said. "They were very upset."

"So how'd the murderer get in?" I asked.

Micky snorted. "That's the easy part."

"Yeah," Art said. "Reilly let him in."

Reilly lay sprawled there in the photo with the bug-eyed look of head wounds and offered no clue to me as to why he let his killer in.

"What we need to know is whether you've got any insights into what happened," Micky prompted.

I nodded. "This thing wedged under the body, do you have it?"

"Sure." Art pulled another photo out of an envelope.

My first impression was right. It was a *bokken*.

"Murder weapon?" I asked.

"Nah. We're pretty certain it was Reilly's weapon," Micky said.

"What makes you so sure?"

"He carved his initials in the butt end."

"Then again," Art countered, "letters could stand for 'Master Robin.'"

"Murder Rampage," Micky suggested.

"Mister Roberts," Art offered.

I cut them off in mid-flow, "One of his students can probably identify it as Reilly's."

They seemed somewhat put out, and just stared at me.

Art shook his head and went on. "We're looking at fragments in his wounds. We can't type the wood yet."

"Wood of the murder weapon could be a lot of things," I said. "That thing looks like oak. You can also have the forensic guys check hickory. It's commonly used for *bokken*. If they really want to get exotic, they can try loquat."

Art looked at Micky and silently mouthed the question "Loquat?" Micky shrugged.

"The wounds seem fairly consistent with the kind of damage you might get if two people went at each other with wood swords," I said.

"How'd you figure the collarbone break?" Art asked me.

"You can see a little extra slump in the shoulder," I pointed out, spreading the different still shots out and pointing it out in each. "It's also a pretty easy bone to snap if you hit it right. In *kenjutsu*—swordsmanship—there's a pretty common strike that would do that. *Kesa giri*. Means 'scarf cut.'"

"Wouldn't that mean a cut to the throat?" Art was paging through the ME's report as I spoke, looking for details that would support or challenge my interpretation.

I shook my head. "Buddhist monks wore a large scarf draped from the left shoulder diagonally across their body. The cut was supposed to follow that line."

"Charming."

"Yeah, well. It's a basic technique, and if you do it with a blade, you can cut someone almost in half. With a wood sword, you would most probably break the clavicle.

"Now, if Reilly also had sustained some damage to his right wrist"—I looked inquiringly to Art, who nodded—"he would have a hard time using the sword. You need two hands to use it well. With his clavicle busted, Reilly would have been in big trouble. You could use a real blade one-handed, but a *bokken* would not be very effective."

"So what are you saying?" Micky asked.

"I think this guy had a duel with someone using a wooden weapon. The murderer could have been using a sword or a staff or a bunch of other weapons, but it seems like this was someone with some training."

"A duel?" Art was incredulous.

The light went on in Micky's head. He pointed at Art, snapping his fingers. "Sure, sure. Bobby Kay wasn't too far off the mark. Reilly sets it up ahead of time, lets the guy in for the big showdown. Otherwise, why carry around a stick?"

Art nodded. "Maybe." He looked at me. "This Reilly know what he was doing?" I nodded. "OK. So he's no virgin." He thought a bit and said, almost to himself, "Been around the block a few times. Knows the cardinal rule of weapons."

"What's that?" I was curious.

"Contrary to all that Asian less-is-more crap you've been listening to," Micky said, "with weapons, more is more."

"Or," Art said, "to phrase it with some more elegance, 'Never bring a knife to a gun fight.'"

"So, if Reilly's carrying a stick . . ." Art began.

"It's a *bokken*," I corrected.

"Yeah, whatever," Micky said.

". . . then it must have been on purpose. Reilly knew someone was coming and he knew he would need the sword."

"But, he got in over his head," Micky said. "A pop here, a pop there, the rest is history."

"What's the motive?" Art asked.

"Man, I'd be a lot happier if we had a theft here," Micky suggested.

"Yeah." Art nodded. "But if it was just a smash and grab with a little witness cleanup attached, the whole sword thing seems a bit elaborate, ya know?"

"I thought we agreed robbery wasn't the motive," I suggested. Micky and Art turned to look at me.

"What you tend to find, Connor," Art explained, "is that motives tend to be a mishmash of things."

I shrugged and went on. "Maybe here the duel itself was the murderer's real interest. This wasn't a robbery scheme that didn't come off. Maybe the killer got what he came for."

They chewed on that quietly for a minute. Then Art looked at Micky. "Burke, your people are weird."

"Look," I said, "whoever did this was trained. From what I hear, Reilly was pretty good."

Micky rolled his eyes toward the photos. "Not as good as he thought he was."

"No one's as good as they think they are," Art commented.

Art had never met Yamashita, but I let it go.

"Besides, if someone used Reilly to get into the Samurai House to rob it and then planned on killing him, don't you think they would have brought something fairly lethal along?" I asked.

"Looks like they did," Art said. He had a point. One way or the other, the man was dead.

I got back to my idea about the killing. "I mean that they would have brought a real weapon, Art, not a wooden replica of some sixteenth-century sword from half-way around the world. With these things, you're essentially bludgeoning someone to death. Look at him lying there."

They both eyed the photos.

"Reilly was an expert. If you had your choice, would you go three rounds with him?"

Micky shook his head. "Not even on a good day. In my prime."

Art laughed. "Like you ever had a prime."

"Seriously, guys."

"Nah, you're right." Art's eyes were narrowed as he sat and thought. "Typical MO would be to gain access in the middle of the night, get the stuff, and then point off to a corner and say, 'Hey Reilly check it out.' He turns to look, and *pow!* A nine-millimeter in the back of the head. Simple."

"A little hard on the carpet, though," Micky said.

The two men exchanged glances, suddenly aware of new possibilities.

"In each life," Art commented in rounded tones with a raised finger, "a little brain must fall."

"If theft were the primary motive, the methodology would be . . . what?" I had seen the glint in my brother's eyes and was trying to head off their usual routine.

"Get in and get out," Micky said.

Art jumped in. "But here, the perp chooses a time when someone's around. And there's this duel." He looked at me. "The ME's report says this guy took some beating. How long you think it took?"

"It's hard to say," I commented. "Theoretically it could have been over quickly. It depends on the skill levels involved."

"Was Reilly highly skilled?" he prompted.

"He was pretty good," I admitted.

"Lots of lividity on the arms and torso. Looks like the victim put up quite a fight," Art said. "So this did not go down quickly." He paused and looked down at some of the still photos. Then he fished out a sheet of paper. "Here's the report from the shrink liaison." He glanced at me and answered the look on my face. "We got a revolving group of forensic psychiatrists on call. You get a murder like this, we use 'em for profiling."

"Any good?" I asked them.

Art squinted and looked at the wall like he was focusing on something in the distance. "Depends on the case," he said noncommittally.

Micky snorted. "They're all a fucking pain in my ass."

Art just read the pieces of the report out loud.

" 'What we have here,' the good doctor concludes, 'is an elaborate killing. It took some time. It was carefully thought out and carefully executed.' "

"Nice pun," Micky said.

Art didn't rise to the bait. He just droned on: " 'The elaborate methodology, the apparent absence of other motives, the almost . . . ritual . . . staging. While the identity of the killer cannot be determined . . .' "

"There's a news flash," Micky commented.

Art didn't bat an eye. " 'The profile is a male, between the ages of twenty-one and forty.' " He looked up at me. "This is the profile of most murderers, Connor. So far, these guys are not impressing me." He scanned the next sheet. "Ooh, wait, there's more. 'The killer is intelligent, probably highly so . . .' "

"Unlike the writer of this report," my brother snickered.

"Doesn't stand out in a crowd. Quiet, polite . . . even affable." I looked from one to the other to get their reaction. They looked like they had heard it all before.

"Aha!" Art called. "Here it is . . . 'Somewhere in this man's past . . . in his childhood . . . behaviors of this type generated as a response to a life event . . . systematic abuse of some sort . . . often sexual.' "

"Thank God they got that in. I was beginning to worry," Micky said.

"There's more, Mick. Lemme see . . . 'Deep-seated feeling of insecurity . . . spawns a pathological need to exert control. The more intense the need, the greater the response.' " He looked up again. "These jokers wet their pants over serial killers," Art explained.

"I sort of get that impression," I said.

"Which is all well and good," Micky interrupted. "But every time I visit the morgue, I got shrinks spinning these theories about bed-wetting psychos. Know what? Most of the time, the person who put the stiff in the cooler is a friend or a family member, drunk or strung out. You know most murderers, Connor, they're not Hannibal Lecter. They're people who made bad choices, or got their buttons pushed one too many times, or just took it a little too far."

"You gotta admit the duel thing is a little kinky, Mick," Art said.

"Maybe so. But when it was all over, we're still zippin' someone into a rubber bag."

That seemed to sum up the situation nicely.

The door opened and another detective stuck his head in. "Oh. There you are. Art, a call for you from the coast . . ."

"Ooh, my big break."

". . . homicide guy named Schedel. Know him?" Art shook his head no. "Well, he says you'll want to talk to him."

"Can you transfer it in here?"

The cop looked offended. "Like I don't have anything to do but hunt you two morons down," he grumped as the door closed.

"Thanks, Kramer," Art called.

Eventually, the state-of-the-art phone purred, a light blinked, and Art's call got put through.

Which was how we heard about the Ikagi murder.

Detective Schedel, LAPD, gave a recital that was disengaged and clinical in that way cops have. Micky had him on speakerphone and the voice sounded like that of a bored guard coming from somewhere way in the back of a warehouse.

"Pedersen? I got the message you posted," he began.

Micky looked like he was going to ask something; Art shook his head silently.

"You asked for anything we might have in the files . . ."

"Martial arts related," Art finished.

"Buddy," the voice from the cave said, "this is LA. I got freaks in *ninja* suits falling out of trees."

"The West Coast is like another world," Art agreed.

"Maybe not," Schedel replied. "You also mentioned a crime scene with some sort of calligraphy left as a message."

Micky sat up a little straighter in his high-tech chair.

"What've you got?" Art prompted.

"Eight days ago, some Jap karate instructor gets the shit ripped out of him with a jagged stick. Also something written on the wall. In blood."

"You know what it said?" Art asked.

"Oh, yeah. One of the meat wagon guys is up on this kind of stuff. It was . . ." You could hear the papers shuffling around on the other coast, even with the echo. "OK, I got it. 'Ronin.' Is that what you're looking for?"

"Bingo," Art answered. "Where'd you go with the case?"

"The usual," Schedel replied. "Rousted the Asian gangs. Talked with the deceased's family, friends, business associates . . ."

"And?"

"And nada. Nothing. Zip. The guy was a straight arrow. No problems we could find, and we turned over all the rocks. Dead end so far."

"Tough," Art said without much conviction. They were both professionals and they had a pretty realistic feel for what was solvable and what wasn't. Cops knew you cracked a homicide within forty-eight hours. After that, the odds got slim.

"Yeah," Schedel continued. "Look, if you're interested in my notes and some crime scene shots, I can get 'em to you. Probably quicker if I sent it over the Net. I've got it on disk." Then his voice grew confidential. "Look. Pedersen?"

"Yeah."

"You turn up anything, let me know. This was my squeal, but it's on the way to the cold case file, ya know?"

Schedel hung up.

"What gives, Art?" Micky said.

"I've been fooling around with the Internet at home. I got on this secure listserve for homicide departments, and I sent out a description of what we had to see whether anyone had seen anything like it."

"So now," I said, "this detective Schedel tells us that we've got a similar type of murder taking place a few days ago on the other side of the country."

They both nodded.

Micky was standing and looking at the crime scene photos. "This thing," he said, "is getting interesting in a hurry."

"Just one thing, Connor," Art said.

"What?"

The two of them looked at each other and gave me their patented cop look.

"It's still an open case in California. Don't let Bobby Kay talk to the LAPD."

SEVEN

Things Not Said

Yamashita couldn't stand it anymore. "Cut him down," he called fiercely, as he churned across the floor toward us. "Cut him DOWN!"

The early morning training session is not heavily attended. Only the hard core tend to make it. As a result, Yamashita is usually a bit more approachable.

But this morning his mood had altered. It wasn't a lack of focus, exactly, but he seemed even more preoccupied. Yamashita's perception was normally ratcheted up way above that of normal people. On days like today, he would stare off into the distance and seem frozen with effort, straining to identify the hint of something that was beyond the threshold of his students to sense.

The nonverbal elements of communication and perception are highly valued by the Japanese; they prize their ability to grasp the essence of people and things using methods we can only guess at. They call this ability *haragei*. Yamashita has it. He can cross swords with a complete stranger and know the skill level of his opponent before they've begun. You can argue that it has to do with subtle physical clues people give off: a look in the eye, posture, breathing rates. The longer I train, the more I tend to agree. But there's also more to it than that.

On days when he's really cooking, it seems as if Yamashita can actually read your mind. What's scary is not that he knows what you're going to do before you do, but that he does it by getting inside you somehow.

I've experienced hints of it. The feeling is a weird, emotive certainty that washes up from the base of the neck and creeps over your scalp. It is often totally unexpected. And distracting.

I knew my teacher too well to think that his mood that day was fueled by anything but this sensation. I had seen it before. It was something he did not speak about. But, of course, it was possible to call him back to the reality of *heiho*.

I had been working with one of the more promising junior students. We had been going at it pretty hard and, although the late May morning wasn't actually hot yet, we were both sweating and constantly adjusting the grip on our weapons. He had a *bokken*. I was using a short staff known as a *jo*, which, at about fifty inches in length, gives you a bit of a reach over a sword. Sam was big and fast and good. He'd come to us from one of the better kendo schools in the area. As a result, he had amazing reflexes, so I needed all the help I could get. Which was why I was using the *jo*.

Far off, just on the edge of my attention, you could hear the sounds of another Brooklyn Saturday starting. The day was shaping up to be a busy one for me, and contemplating the details made my attention wander, which can be bad. Like trying to figure out the meaning of the distant whoop of a car alarm, it's not going to prevent you from getting cracked across the skull with an oak sword. I caught myself drifting and refocused on the task at hand. I worked with Sam and evaded a number of strikes that came a bit too close. It takes a certain amount of patience to wait for an opening in a situation like this and I had to force myself to do it. It finally came, though, and when the opening appeared I simply reached out and tapped his wrist lightly and backed away. Which was when Yamashita blew in like a small tornado.

"Burke," the *sensei* demanded, "what are you doing?"

"I had him, Sensei."

"You HAD him?" he asked incredulously.

"*Hai.*" Yes. "It was over."

Yamashita took a glance at Sam, who was wisely not getting anywhere near this conversation.

"Burke," my teacher said tightly, "look at Sam. Does he look like he has been, as you put it, had?" Sam looked like a large piece of granite in a martial arts uniform. When Yamashita turned to face me, Sam gave me a mocking grin behind the teacher's back.

"No, Sensei," I answered.

"You must take the opportunity when it comes. More focus, Burke. More spirit. Project. Like this."

Yamashita suddenly jerked his whole body toward Sam. He didn't really do anything—he wasn't carrying a weapon and didn't even raise his hands—but the force of Yamashita's presence made Sam step back in alarm.

"Hmm? So." He looked from me to Sam and back again, motioning us to continue.

We began again while Yamashita glided across the floor, his callused feet rasping along the wood. As he headed toward some other trainees he called out to the ceiling, not even looking at me, "And CUT HIM DOWN!"

It made the rest of that morning pretty interesting for both Sam and me.

Afterward, Yamashita brought me up to the living quarters he had in the loft portion of the *dojo*. He wanted to talk.

This is not a common thing with my teacher. The Japanese are suspicious of people who talk too much. But I had mentioned the fact that I was helping out Micky with the investigation of the Reilly murder. The martial arts community was buzzing about it. I imagined that the senior *sensei* would be deeply concerned, but Yamashita's reaction to my involvement was odd. It involved a hard narrowing of the eyes and a set of the mouth that told me I had displeased him in some way I couldn't fathom.

But when I followed him upstairs, he didn't say much right away. I sat down and waited while that little bullet of a man fussed in the kitchen making coffee. Oddly enough, Yamashita is a coffee fanatic. A while ago, someone signed him up for one of those gourmet mail services for what they insist on calling "kaffe" and it was all over for Sensei. Every time he tries to cancel, they offer him some free item to continue, and he does. His kitchen is cluttered with mugs with the company logo, a coffee maker with the brand name on it, and, his latest addition, a little white ceramic canister to hold his gourmet grounds.

Then, surrounded by the rich aroma of coffee harvested in one of those African countries whose name has changed about eight times since 1960, we sat and I filled him in on the Ronin case. He listened attentively, with the very intense focus he brings to things in general. But once again, I picked up a sense of agitation and displeasure from him. It was subtle and fleeting from a Western point of view, yet there nonetheless.

He nodded when I was done talking, blinked, and said, "Now, Burke. This morning showed something you need to pay attention to. The need for initiative and follow-through."

"Sensei," I protested, "Sam knew that I got him."

He sipped appreciatively at his mug, then grinned tightly. "No. YOU knew that you got him. Sam did not."

I started to reply and he held up an open hand in admonition. "Burke. I understand that you are at a point when you can anticipate what would happen and do not feel the need to follow through. Like a chess player, yes?"

I nodded.

"You must remember," he went on, "that, in fighting, TWO people are involved. Both are very sure that they are the best. Each thinks he will win.

"It is a delusion, of course," he went on merrily, "but a necessary one for a warrior."

His eyes locked on me, even as he sipped from his mug.

"But in a real contest, you must shatter the other's confidence. You must project your spirit in such a way as to let the other one know he is defeated. You cannot wait for him to act. You must take the initiative."

"I know that, Sensei, but in training . . ."

"You think you are being benevolent. Permitting the other person to develop skills. I understand. But you are really holding back, letting the other person exist in a type of delusion.

"Look." He walked to the table where his *katana* was nestled in a polished wooden holder. The long sword was elegantly simple, an arc of steel with minimal decoration that said something about the refinement and seriousness of purpose of its owner. "I know you have seen this." The sword came off the rack.

Yamashita pointed to the *tsuba*, or hand guard. On some swords, this is a highly ornamented spot. For a real swordsman, however, the *tsuba* is reduced to its functional essence. The only ornament on Yamashita's weapon was a character, etched in the surface of the hand guard that faced the owner when the sword was held in the ready posture. The character was *jin*, which means "benevolence."

"This is to remind me of my duty," Yamashita said, indicating the character. "The warrior's way includes an awareness of when to be merciful. But, Burke"—he turned the sword around—"look and see that my opponent cannot see the character when I hold the sword. Only the blade. That is as it should be."

"I understand, Sensei."

"Do you?" He paused as if considering just how far he wanted to push this. Candor and something almost like urgency won out. "You must commit to things, Burke. Otherwise you run the risk of not only deluding others, but deluding yourself too."

Yamashita believes that tact is an impediment to serious training.

* * *

I am sure he could have dwelt on my shortcomings indefinitely but the midmorning weekend class was beginning to arrive, and I had places to go.

Micky and Art were grinding away at the less glamorous side of detecting, but there was nothing yet. To make things worse I got a FedEx letter saying that President and Mrs. Domanova wanted the honor of my company for a cocktail reception to celebrate the end of the semester. Saturday at two at the presidential manse. I was happy to see that the money the university saved by exploiting adjuncts like me was wisely invested in really necessary things like the ornate copperplate invitation. I caught myself involuntarily admiring the fine bond of the card I held in my hand and felt flattered, manipulated, and gullible, all at the same time.

The president's receptions are the talk of the campus. They are lavish beyond the experience of the rank and file. The trajectory of a career at the institution can be measured at these events. People covertly watch one another, mentally ticking off a list of who is willing to be seen with whom. And who isn't. Domanova uses these things as public displays of his feelings about you. You can get invited so he can fawn all over you in that bogus Mediterranean way he has. Or you can get all dolled up only to arrive and learn that you've been summoned so he can pointedly snub you. In that case, the only consolation is that the hors d'oeuvres are great and the booze is free.

I took the car to the party. There is, of course, no real direct way to get from Brooklyn to Bloomington by car. The city planners designed it this way to keep the riffraff out. What they were thinking when they allowed a university to be established there is anyone's guess. In any event, the reception was already in full swing when I got there.

Domanova's residence borders the university but is shielded from the gaze of mere mortals by thick hedges. Inside the yard, a striped tent shielded the bar and food tables. The day was warm and sunny, with a light breeze rustling the higher leaves of the big oaks that bordered the property. Various clusters of people were spread around the grounds chatting merrily while a quartet of shanghaied music majors sawed away dutifully at their instruments.

I took a quick look around, getting the lay of the land. The Big Man was nowhere in evidence, which was a relief. I spotted Dean Ceppaglia in mid-scheme with a cluster of administrators. A few faculty members stared at me briefly, then turned back to the business at hand.

I went to the bar, swigged some beer, and looked out at the other guests. I rolled the liquid around my mouth. Just passing time communing with Sam Adams, brewer and patriot. I looked with appreciation at the picture on the label. They were giants in those days.

Out strode the president, projecting himself as if there were something tremendously fearless in his decision to brave the force of the sun. He was impeccably outfitted in a double-breasted blue blazer and gray slacks. He'd made the bold fashion statement of wearing a little paisley ascot instead of a tie. Domanova began working the crowd, stopping to have brief, authoritative conversations with small knots of administrators. He churned through them with the look of someone diligently pursuing an unpleasant duty.

Bobby Kay was in tow. He was dressed in much the same sporty style—a tan summer suit, blue shirt, and maroon patterned ascot—but seemed somehow out of his element. As he and Domanova made their way across the patio, the entrepreneur had the look of a small dinghy being sucked along the surface of a dangerous sea by the screw turbulence of an ocean liner.

Then Domanova's eyes met mine.

"Oh, no," I said. It was involuntary. The president changed course and headed right at me. Probably wanted to know why I hadn't worn a cravat. Then he turned the full force of that Mediterranean juggernaut on me.

Domanova doesn't really smile as most people know it. The best he can manage is a sort of long foxy grin—a baring of teeth that is more frightening than reassuring—and he gave me one of his best "I will eat your young" grimaces.

He took my hand. "Dr. Burke, Mr. Akkadian has been telling me what a marvelous job you did for him."

Bobby had been lurking in the background with that "sorry I had to finger you for murder, my mistake" look. On cue, he stepped forward to chime in.

"Fantastic, Burke. Thanks."

"Well," I said, stunned into courtesy, "my pleasure. Hello, Bobby." I eyed him for a moment to see whether he would squirm. Not a twitch. He and the president seemed in on a little secret that made them both happy.

But joy is fleeting at the top. The president's head jerked around. "Ah, there is my provost. I must have a word. Gentlemen, you will excuse me." We nodded and made room as the ship of state got underway.

As a parting shot, he added, "I was telling Mr. Akkadian how glad we were to be of service to him. We look forward to a long friendship. I am sure you will agree, Professor." He didn't even wait for a reply, but strode across the yard calling for the provost.

Bobby steered me to the end of the bar. He reached into his breast pocket and pulled out two envelopes. He looked at the identifying marks on them, put one back, and handed me what turned out to be the long-awaited check. It was for the amount we had agreed on. Was it rude to peek? My landlord wouldn't think so.

"Well," I said, "things are looking up." I was sure that the other envelope was for the president. It explained his manic good spirits.

"You bet." Bobby took a long, grateful pull from his glass. It told me he was finding a private session with Domanova to be somewhat stressful. He gestured to the bartender for another and seemed to brighten at the prospect.

"You would not believe the interest this thing is generating, Burke."

"So the brochure worked out for you? That was quick."

"Hmm? Oh, well, actually I went a step farther. I'm still

creating the glossy piece for the opening. But to get things moving I put it on the Samurai House Web page."

"How digital."

"You bet." The ice cubes clinked against his teeth as he drained the glass. "You've got to stay on top of this emerging technology, Burke. Otherwise the competition will eat you alive."

"And what is the competition doing these days, Bobby?"

He gave me that Bobby Kay smile, the one that told me he was feeling a bit more himself away from the president. "The competition is eating their hearts out, Burke. You know, I was worried. What with the killing, I was afraid that the whole show would fall apart. With the setup costs, it could have been a disaster."

Then his predatory optimism just ate right through that rare moment of doubt.

"But let me tell you, buddy"—he broke into a grin as his vodka was reloaded—"the news coverage has just revved up interest even more. Phone ringing off the hook. The Web page is getting, oh, I don't know, like ten thousand hits a day! All in all, things couldn't have worked out better."

"Except for Reilly," I mentioned. "What with the death thing and all."

He looked momentarily chastened again, but it was an emotion that struggled futilely with the selective conscience of the businessman. It took a lot to keep Bobby down for long.

"Want to see your stuff? C'mon, we'll use Peter's computer." He drained his third drink and we headed toward the house.

The transition from the sunny yard to the dim quiet of the Big Man's study was a bit hard on the eyes, and for a moment I stood there waiting for them to adjust. Domanova's home office was something of a disappointment. I knew some people who thought he slept there in a coffin, but it was really just a tastefully appointed study. Real wood paneling. Abstract artwork. The noise of our footsteps was swallowed up by a deep Persian rug.

Bobby booted up the computer. I noticed the machine had a university property tag stuck to the side of it. I wondered whether the art did, too. Bobby tapped merrily on the keys for a minute and wiggled the mouse.

The Web site loaded and we were off on a guided tour of his little cyber-kingdom.

"OK, here's the home page." It was a pretty nice graphic image of a waterfall, much like the one in the gallery. Vaguely Asian lettering identified various points of interest. He clicked on "Legacies of the Samurai" to show me the text and pictures of what would eventually be the exhibit catalogue. Sure enough, there was my stuff.

Something on the screen caught my eye: "Modern Masters."

"Hit that," I asked him, touching the screen.

A graphic appeared. It was a *shoji*—one of those sliding paper doors the Japanese use in traditional homes. Akkadian clicked on it and it slid to one side, revealing a shot of the *dojo* at the Samurai House. Superimposed over the picture were the characters for *meijin*, or master. He clicked again. A video clip of Mitch Reilly in action appeared.

The picture quality was not the greatest, but there was no mistaking the dense power of the man. It took about two seconds for the ghost to charge the screen with a slashing sword attack, then the image froze and a laudatory summary of Reilly's achievements and expertise appeared.

It didn't mention the fact that he was dead.

"What's this?" I asked.

Bobby tried to act surprised. "Oh. I guess we need to update that." He reached over for the mouse. Is it possible to click guiltily? We popped back to the home screen. A little message at the bottom informed us we were the 75,486th person to visit the site.

"See what I mean?" he asked. "You can't beat this thing for publicity. And cheap? Oh, man." He almost kissed the monitor. "I love these things."

"I don't suppose it hurts to have Reilly dancing around there so every reader of the *Daily News* can get a chance to

see him, huh, Bobby?" I never really knew Reilly, but flog-
ging his image to drive sales was a bit much.

The grin faded on him. "Hey, that was on for weeks before the . . . incident. Besides, I have it rigged so there's a
new master every month or so, and there are links to their
dojo and more free publicity than they ever imagined.
Don't get all cranky on me, Burke. Everyone makes out."

He gave me a hard look. "Including you." Bobby was
usually all smooth and glad-handy, but I had heard he
would cut a competitor's throat in a minute. Seeing that
look, I could believe it.

He was right, of course—the check I had in my pocket
was Samurai House money. But it didn't make me feel better. Bobby picked up on the sudden coolness in the room.
He looked at his watch.

"Ah, God! I better get back out to Peter. Got a little donation ceremony to do." He patted his breast meaningfully.
"See you, Burke." The tone told me that it would be quite
some time.

Links

The Burke clan springs from a very shallow gene pool: we all look pretty much the same. When I pulled up in front of Micky's house on the South Shore, a row of almost indistinguishable kid heads popped up from behind the palisade fence. "Hi, Uncle Connor!" they shrieked and collapsed back down out of sight, giggling.

"Hello, you monkeys," I called. Thomas, one of Micky's kids and the birthday boy of the moment, came charging out and grabbed me by the leg.

"Where's my toy? Where's my toy?" he demanded.

"Toy? What toy?" I said. Then, feigning surprise, "Who are you, little boy?" He stopped tugging at me long enough to look confused for a second.

"Uncle Connor!" He insisted, "You know who I am!" Thomas was almost sure of it, but kids are well aware that adults are strange and unpredictable. Almost anything was possible.

Micky's wife, Deirdre, had spotted the open gate and came scooting out to drive him back into the corral. "Thomas!" she said in that tone mothers everywhere use. "Behave."

I laughed. "OK, Mr. T. The loot's in the car." He seemed

briefly relieved that I hadn't lost my mind, then went scampering off to get his gift. "Hi, Dee," I said.

Dee has a broad, open face. She smiled, which made her eyes narrow into slits. "The riot is being held in the back," she said. As an in-law, Dee has a somewhat more objective view of the family than I do. She has also benefited from a decade of experience with us. Dee was nice but usually got right to the point. Life with Micky was not an adventure in subtlety.

Thomas lumbered by with a wrapped box almost as big as he was. Dee and I followed and closed the gate.

It was early in the season, but Micky had taken the bold step of opening the pool for the kids. Long Island is like the Mekong Delta in the summer: hot and humid but with more concrete. A succession of aboveground backyard pools had punctuated the vacation months of our childhood, and Micky had replicated that experience for his kids.

There were at least twelve bodies flailing around in the water. I knew there were redheads, brunettes, and even blondish Burke units in there, but soaking wet, they all looked alike. Occasionally, a skinny one would emerge for a toweling down, lips blue, trembling with cold, and then leap back in for a screaming, splashing dance with hypothermia. The fatter Burke kids only came out to eat.

Most of the guys were by the barbecue. My two other brothers, Tom and Jimmy, were there. So was Art. I spotted his wife, Marie, over by the sliding glass door that led to the kitchen and gave her a wave. My sister Peggy was doing lifeguard duty by the pool. My other sister, Irene, was probably in the kitchen, deep in recipes concocted with huge globs of mayonnaise.

My brothers-in-law were two pleasant guys who, as time went on, began to get looks on their faces that said life with my sisters was more than they had bargained for. Between the two of them, they had nine kids under the age of ten.

They enjoyed the barbecues: they got to talk to adults, tell off-color jokes they had been hoarding for weeks, and furtively drink more beer than permitted. Both men were starting to lose their hair.

There were music and stories, various minor accidents with the kids, and the normal type of socializing that goes on with a group of people who know each other very well, and generally get along well despite the fact. In short, the rest of the afternoon passed in the subdued riot that passes for get-togethers with my family.

After cake and presents, as evening came on, I sat on a molded plastic lawn chair, a little apart from the crush of the family. You could still smell the charcoal in the air. One of the neighbors had a baseball game on the TV and the faint roar of the stadium crowd washed in the background like the sound of the sea. A few of the smaller kids were rolling around in discarded wrapping paper from the presents.

This was pretty much the way it was for us growing up. When I think about it, I mostly remember crowds—kids and adults—Christmas, birthdays, and barbecues. I jerked my legs out of the way as one of Irene's kids shot by, trying to catch a lightning bug. I had memories of similar hunts, running with small tribes of children on broad expanses of freshly cut lawns. The breathless pursuit in the moist blue of a summer night.

My mother was in Maryland visiting her sister. Otherwise, we'd probably be at her house destroying her lawn. My dad, the king of barbecues, died five years ago of cancer. He gave it a good fight. But at the end, there wasn't much left. Just some fierce eyes. You'd think thoughts like that would get to you, but I smiled and looked around the backyard. At times like this, I recall him the way he was. I can almost hear him in the crowd. It's one of the reasons I keep coming to family parties, I suppose.

Micky had been shooting me looks all day, squinting significantly through the smoke of barbecue and birthday cake candles. With everyone fed and presents unwrapped, it was time to rendezvous in the family room. Art slipped in after me, pulling the sliding glass doors to the yard closed.

The family room looked like the place old overstuffed furniture went to die.

"What's up, Mick?"

"Art's been following up with that guy Schedel from LA. Getting details to see whether there's some sort of connection between the two murders."

I turned to Art. "And?"

"You, my man, are looking at the Dick Tracy of cyberspace," he commented with a big smile.

"Well, at the very least, we are looking at a dick," Micky commented under his breath.

Art shot him a look and went on. "It turns out that there have been at least two other homicides of this type in the last week."

"Come on!" I protested. "The papers would have a field day."

"Yeah," Art answered, "but they didn't take place in the same area. Homicide is local crime, and these things happened in different states. Unless you're looking, you wouldn't find 'em."

"Method is slightly different each time," Micky commented.

Art shrugged. "Basic underlying pattern is the same."

"What's that?" I could guess, but I wanted the details.

"The other two victims also were prominent martial arts instructors." Art ticked the points off on his fingers one by one as he talked. "They checked out OK. No problems with gangs or drugs. No disgruntled students."

"No disgruntled lovers," Micky added.

"Both were killed in somewhat exotic ways." I lifted my eyebrows and Art answered the unspoken question. "The first victim, the guy in LA, was stabbed to death with a broken stick. Coupla days later, a Japanese national in Phoenix named Kubata goes down."

"Sanjiro Kubata?" I interrupted.

"You know him?"

I nodded appreciatively. Kubata was the real thing. A champion in kendo who had capped a successful tournament career in Japan by relocating to the U.S. to promote kendo here. I'd never met him, but he was said to be charming and talented. He was, from all reports, a master technician, a skilled teacher, and had a real flair for self-promotion. The Japanese had loved him. They called him the "Jewel of the Budokan," and when he left that famous training hall in Kyoto, his fans wailed.

I couldn't believe that Yamashita hadn't mentioned it. I couldn't believe he was dead.

"Believe it," Art said. "He sustained a number of serious injuries from some sort of weapon, but the actual cause of death there was strangulation."

"No rope," Micky said. "Bruises are consistent with a fairly sophisticated choke technique."

"OK, pretty gruesome," I admitted, still trying to adjust to the surprise. "But how is it unusual?" I asked.

Micky fielded the question. Behind him on the wall, an old Republic Pictures poster for *Sands of Iwo Jima* was beginning to curl away from the Scotch tape that held it to the paneling.

"Most homicides are fairly routine in terms of MO. You got guns, knives, and blunt instruments."

"With beatings," Art said, "you usually get a victim who has been worked over. All over. Death is usually from internal bleeding and it takes a while."

"Now for stranglings," Micky jumped in, "you got your ropes, wires, and what have you. Ligature strangulation and manual. Crime of passion, lots of thumb marks on the front. They like their victims to see them." He and Art were really warming to their topic.

"But what we see here is different."

"How so?" I asked Art.

"Whoever did this was a pro," he said. "The victims in both LA and Phoenix were not subject to wild, unfocused beatings, which is what you usually get. Rage killings. In these cases, someone pounded the shit out of them, but boy oh boy, he knew where to pound. The choke job was the same type of thing. Focused."

"You know, it's hard work beating someone to death," Micky said reflectively, like he had considered the option. "Most times, it takes a while. Usually, some restraints are involved. But not here. These killings were almost surgical. The bruises tell us that a pro did it."

"Let me ask you a question," I said. "You're always talking about bruises on the victims. It seems to me that it takes a while for a bruise to form. I know you get some discoloration on a body after death . . ."

"Postmortem lividity," Art said.

"Right. But that has to do with blood settling. How do you get bruises like the ones you're talking about? If the victim is killed relatively quickly after the injury?"

Micky's eyebrows shot up. "Pretty smart, Connor," he said.

Art looked at him. "Are you sure you two are related?"

Micky grinned. He gestured for us to wait. The glass door slid back and let some of the party noise wash into the room. He came back in with some beers from the big orange cooler on the patio and shook the ice chips off as he handed them to us. Then he walled the family off again and continued.

"When you first look at the corpse, you don't see the bruises," my brother told me. "Then you have the ME stick him in the cooler overnight." He popped the tab on the can and took a drink. Micky had stopped being squeamish a long time ago.

"Then you see the bruises," Art commented. "Sort of like developing a picture."

"OK, I got it," I said.

"To get back to the issue here," Micky continued, "both the other victims appear to have been killed somewhere in the early part of the morning. And . . ."

"And," Art chimed in.

"Someone signed 'Ronin' at each scene."

I sat back in my chair. "Oh, no."

"Oh, yes," Art answered. "The messages are slightly different . . ."

"How so?"

"The LA murder just had the signature 'Ronin,'" Micky replied.

"In Phoenix, the killer added something: 'I am coming.' Then the same signature," Art said.

"So what does that tell you?" I asked.

"Details of the Ronin thing were not released to the press in the Ikagi murder. So a copycat is out." Micky trotted out the other details. "Killings are geographically dispersed, but they follow a pattern."

"We got a request in for a DNA sample from the LA killing," Art told me. "We'll compare it with samples from the Kubata and Reilly murders. It'll take a few days, but we'll see if they match up."

"You know they'll match up, Art," Micky said.

"OK," I asked, "and if they match up, what does that mean?"

"It means," Micky said, "that we have a nut job on the loose who gets off starring in his own Jackie Chan snuff film."

"Well, does it narrow things down for you in terms of suspects?" I persisted. "You know, give you a handle on what the killer might look like?"

"We know he's probably a male," Micky said. "But that's not a big help. Statistically, most killers are. He's about five feet nine or ten inches and probably right handed."

"Gee, Sherlock, did you figure all that out by yourself?" Art asked. Then he looked at me and smirked. "Don't be too impressed, Connor." He gazed at his partner. "I read the site analysis from the crime lab too, Mick."

My brother looked sheepish.

"They do an analysis of this kind of thing," Art explained. "You'd be amazed. From splatter marks, position of the body . . ."

"Star signs, phases of the moon, mood rings . . ." Micky added.

". . . they can come up with a profile of the killer. Probable sex, age, size. It's weird."

"Yeah," Micky agreed, "but I have to admit, it works. I know old-timers who claim the walls of a murder scene can talk to them." He looked at me. "But it's bullshit." Art nodded in agreement as Micky went on. "These forensic guys, on the other hand, seem pretty good."

"Yeah, but other than that, we don't have much. The DNA comparison is only gonna help us when we get a suspect in custody," Art pointed out.

Micky squinted off into the distant yard, thinking. "Right now, Connor, our assumption is that this guy is Asian. Japanese. Whoever it is has been pretty well trained. It's the same in both cases. He's into this martial arts shit as his method. You look at the victims; they're connected by the arts. And killed by them."

It didn't sound like much when you said it out loud. He continued anyway. "You don't learn this stuff at the neighborhood Y."

"So?" I asked.

"It narrows things down some more. Theoretically, at least."

"Does this help things?" I asked.

"Maybe," Art explained. He held up his empty beer can and looked at it as if he suspected evaporation as the culprit. Micky got us another round.

"On the one hand, we probably don't have any records like prints on this guy. Have to go through Interpol. Then again, if he's a Japanese national visiting the area, we should have INS records."

"Summer in the city," Micky commented. "I'll bet there are thousands of Japanese tourists in town."

"How're you gonna run him down?" I said.

Micky smiled evilly. "That, bro, is what newly minted detectives are for."

"Most Japanese tourists will be traveling in groups," I suggested. "This guy probably won't."

"Ya see? It gets better and better. We've got it narrowed down a bit more." He paused for a minute and looked significantly at Art. They didn't say anything, but I got the sense of messages flying back and forth through the air. Messages I was not meant to hear.

Art sat forward in his chair and began to speak very slowly and clearly to me. "So think about this, Connor. The link is through Japan. And the martial arts."

I said nothing, just sipped some beer and watched him work.

"So there are three prominent martial artists," he continued. "And this guy is . . . I dunno, tracking them down."

"You sure?" I asked him. He shrugged.

"Oh yeah," Art said. "The sequence is too tight." He ticked the points off one by one. "LA . . . Phoenix . . . now here. All within days of one another. The killer is traveling. Messages seem to pretty much bear that interpretation out: all that 'I am coming, I am here' shit."

"High drama," my brother agreed.

But something was bothering me. "Ya know, I don't see Reilly as being in the same class as Ikagi and Kubata. Not at all."

Art nodded. "There's a link between victims we don't see yet."

"Ya follow a trail, it's because it leads to something," Micky said quietly. "The trail leads here. The calligraphy confirms it. In LA, it was just the signature, a kind of general announcement. Then Phoenix and a type of warning. But here, the message is that he's arrived."

"Question is," Art commented, "who's supposed to be getting the message?"

"There's something we don't know about that's happening right under our noses," Micky groused. "Someone local is reading that message and knowing what it means."

"What!" I couldn't believe it.

The expression on their faces told me they were disappointed. So my brother filled me in.

"There's something your pal the *sensei* is not tellin' us."

"Come on," I said. "This is all speculation. We don't really know anything for sure."

"It feels right to me," my brother said flatly. He looked questioningly at Art.

"My gut says 'yeah' too," his partner replied. And they waited with that quiet cop intensity for me to say something.

"Maybe whoever is doing this is just a lunatic," I protested. "The victims might not be linked."

"Then why kill them?" my brother asked.

"I know something about Ikagi," I said. "He was a pretty prominent karate instructor. Real old school. Very well respected. Kubata was too. I can dig around and see what I can find out. But they're both celebrities of a type."

"Celebrities?" Micky sounded incredulous.

"Well"—I shrugged—"in the martial arts world."

"Connor," Art said, "are you saying that Ikagi and Kubata got whacked because Ronin thought they were famous?" He was dubious. "I dunno. We'll keep it in mind. . . . But what about Reilly?"

I shrugged.

"I still think there's a connection," Micky finished.

I shrugged again.

"But think of the fun we could have," Art said with glee. "A celebrity."

"Killed by a stalker." Micky had that look in his eye.

Art continued. "A celebrity stalker."

"Don't do this," I pleaded. But it was too late.

Micky went on. "A *samurai* celebrity stalker."

Art pointed triumphantly to the ceiling. "A psycho *samurai* celebrity stalker."

Which seemed to sum it all up nicely.

We sat for a while longer and swirled more beer around in fresh cans, like witches stirring a potion. As I went outside,

Micky was punching numbers into the phone. Working the angles.

"Connor," he called, and I turned back into the room.

"Yeah, Mick?"

"Something like this . . . we know what we're doin'. Trust me. Talk to Yamashita for us."

I nodded that I would, but I didn't feel too good about it.

NINE

Local Talent

At the heart of both sound and movement there is vibration. Yamashita wants us to be sensitive to sound; he says it has a message. Different types of activity, different places, have distinct aural signatures, he insists. They lay bare the essence of an activity, its spirit. Remaining open to the message that sound sends can help the warrior. Or so my *sensei* maintains.

The end of the semester at the university has the repressed, tense sound of papers shuffling, like the chitinous noise of frantic insects. I had sensed it all week, even as I grew increasingly distracted by the murder. When I closed my eyes to rest them from the strain of grading papers, I saw the stark finality of Reilly, collapsed and cold at the crime scene. And on the wall, the message that he was here. Ronin. The name spoke of a man adrift. Or free. But from what?

My brother was much more grounded. He was waiting for a DNA report, but it didn't slow him down. While I was still thinking about killers and exotic martial arts techniques, he got right down to the nitty gritty of police work. "It's not like the movies," he preached to me. "Whoever this guy is, he needs to eat. A place to sleep." Micky believed grunt work would eventually lead us to the killer.

But there was vibration here as well: the sense of the ticking of a clock, of time slipping away. Because Ronin was out there.

I had taken a quick look at things from my end, trying to get some information on the two victims. Anything that might give us a clue to Ronin's identity. And how he chose his victims.

The martial arts world is like that of a lot of other fringe interest groups. You'd think it would be a small place, but once you started looking, you found all sorts of organizations, causes, and publications. The mainstream popular martial arts world is pretty well covered by periodicals like *Black Belt* and *Karate/Kung Fu Illustrated*, but there are a host of others that spring up overnight and fade away almost as quickly. I found a library that kept back copies of the most well established and used them as a starting point.

Of course, the library collection was not complete—the martial arts reading public is poor but enthusiastic and tends to steal back issues with shocking regularity. I was able to plug some of the holes by consulting the back lists that get included with every month's issue. I used a contact at Dorian's library to request copies of missing back articles I felt might be useful. Like my brother, I would have to wait on some things, but I plowed ahead.

It was a fairly tedious process. I sat at a series of battered wooden tables, leafing through back issues that were limp and slightly aromatic with age. I clacked through innumerable computer search engines and Web sites, using up all my spare change printing relevant articles. It was a familiar sort of grind—not much different from academic research, really. By the end of the day, most of the information was coming together.

Ikagi was a fairly prominent karate *sensei*. The name was vaguely familiar to me even at the onset. There was coverage of him on and off over the years in the magazines I looked at. He had made a big splash when he first came to this country in the '80s. He had a tremendous pedigree: a gifted fighter and teacher who at one time had been honored by being asked to help train the emperor's guards. In short order he became a well-established instructor in LA. He was a big proponent of introducing weapons training— known as *kobudo*—into the more mainstream Japanese karate styles. We already knew that a jagged piece of a training staff had been used to kill him. In the weeks before the killing, Ikagi was in the news for helping out with choreography and technical advice for a new movie. It was the third or fourth installment of a shoot-'em-up where the wisecracking star is eventually stripped down to a sleeveless undershirt and takes a volume of punishment that would disable a platoon of Navy Seals. When it hit theaters, you would be able to glimpse Ikagi's ghost as an extra in one of the group fight scenes.

But there was more to him than this. For all his success, Ikagi was a *sensei* who never lost sight of the real purpose of training. He was quoted in one article as insisting that the true pursuit of karate was not in perfecting fighting technique but in the spiritual development Ikagi referred to as "mirror polishing." The phrase had strong links to Shinto and Zen Buddhism, and Ikagi had even adopted the name "mirror polisher" when he did calligraphy. From the various things I read, I got the sense that Ikagi was both tremendously skilled and unusually balanced in his approach to the martial arts.

Kubata, the Phoenix victim, was already known to me by reputation. He had been in this country for only a few months before he was killed. Welcome to the Valley of the Sun. He was part of a concerted effort to popularize kendo here and had launched a series of ambitious seminars that attracted a nationwide audience. Part of it was the result of the impressive charisma the man obviously possessed— they didn't call him the Jewel of the Budokan for nothing. But I also suspected, after a generation of training, that there were thousands of judo and karate students whose joints hurt too much to continue with their arts and were looking for something else. Not a week before his death, he had been prominently featured on the cover of one of the national martial arts rags with the caption: "Master Kubata Introduces the Art of the Sword." I knew of any number of teachers who had been laboring at this very goal for years, but modesty had not been one of Kubata's failings.

The two men were prominent and skilled martial artists. They were both Japanese. But other than that, I got no sense of how they were connected. And Reilly's connection was still unknown.

Which brought me to a dead end. So I considered Ronin. Micky looked at the basics. I followed that line of thinking from my own perspective. I thought that someone like Ronin needed not only a place to live, but also a place to train. You don't acquire those types of skills like you buy a suit of clothes. It's a high-maintenance commodity, which is why so many people begin studying the arts and so few persevere long enough to learn anything. In a consumer society, where everything is fast and easy, learning the martial arts is not. To make matters worse, martial skill requires practice. Constant practice and constant conditioning. And then more practice.

I explained to Micky and Art that training would probably eat up a big part of Ronin's day and be expensive. It narrowed things down somewhat: we had a much better chance of trying to find him by locating likely places where he could train.

At this skill level, some of your training takes place alone: you run, stretch, lift weights, whatever. But if you're serious about dealing with people, then you eventually have to confront a live adversary. You need bodies to work with, muscle and bone to leverage around.

For Ronin, however, the kind of place he would need would be special. It would need to be tough. And mean. This type of place the City had in abundance. But he seemed to gravitate to the Japanese arts. I'd look for him in a *dojo* but not some storefront school that was part day care and part yuppie commando fantasy center. The people in it would also have to be very skilled, which cut down the potential number of likely places considerably. I also thought, given the type of things that he would be training in, that there would have to be a high tolerance for injury. When this man practiced, there would be a good likelihood of collateral damage. It narrowed the list down even more.

I had some ideas, but this was a bit out of my league. It forced me to do the one thing that I wanted to avoid. I needed to talk with Yamashita.

I used the excuse that I needed to know about likely places to look for Ronin. The Japanese *sensei* like to pretend they ignore everyone except their equals. Believing they have no equals gives them license to appear totally disinterested in the great wash of humanity's inferior attempts at the fighting arts. Don't be fooled. The *sensei* watch everything from WWW wrestling to street fights. Their eyes don't blink as they bore into their subjects. They see and remember. And endure.

Yamashita didn't give me much. I spoke to him during a pause in a training session, so maybe he was focused on something else, but his whole manner seemed odd. I sidled in through the door and bowed, removing my shoes. I waited for the lesson to close and approached him.

Generally speaking, my teacher strides the practice floor in isolation. Even when he's not teaching, people watch him covertly. The way he moves, even the way he breathes can show you something. It was unusual that he should be approached and even more unusual that I did so in street clothes. But I bowed again, apologized for the intrusion, explained myself quietly to him and hoped he would have a suggestion that could help.

He didn't look at me when he answered the question. And he seemed pretty vague for the most part. Not particularly helpful. I've given up trying to anticipate his moods and chalked it up to some sort of Zen state, figuring that in his brain he was seated in an empty space, staring through nothing. But I was mildly surprised by the fact that, after I pushed him for a little more information, he began to appear almost visibly agitated by the whole thing. This was unusual in a man devoted to the idea that emotions be kept hidden from the world. It wasn't that Yamashita didn't have emotions. It was just that permitting others to see them gave potential opponents an advantage. As a result, his usual flat affect wasn't repression; it was *heiho*.

I mentioned Ikagi's name and saw no reaction in those dark eyes. He had heard something about the man's death, he admitted. It was only natural. But he was unaware of any connection between that incident and Kubata's murder. When I explained the theory Micky was working on, he dismissed it with a short chop of the hand.

"This country is a violent place, Professor. All those cowboy movies, no? Kubata Sensei's murder . . . I hope your brother does not waste his time chasing illusions. There is no mystery here. Only tragedy."

But I insisted that Reilly's death proved that Ronin was now in New York. And that he was a martial artist. If so, I wanted to help find him. And that's why Yamashita's insight would be helpful. In the end, I got little concrete information from him, despite my wheedling. Only a warning.

"This man you seek, Burke . . ." He stared off blankly at the wall for a moment, then finally turned those hard eyes on me and started again. "Human beings are conduits of power. Training focuses that power. Directs it. People like the one you seek . . . they are like . . ." Again the pause. "They are like electrical cable. Yes? Cable with cracked insulation. They leak anger. It is powerful. And dangerous. But it is the result of a flaw, not of real strength."

He held up his hand in the *tegatana,* arm extended in a loose arc designed to maximize the flow of energy, of *ki*. "They leak power, Burke, because of flaws in themselves. In their training. It appears impressive. Some people are seduced by it. But it is wrong. It is not the true Way."

And then he said, in the contradictory manner I have come to almost expect from him, "Such training is deeply flawed. But these people are very dangerous. I wish you would avoid them."

"I'm not looking for a fight, Sensei. We're just trying to track this killer down."

Yamashita shifted slightly on his feet and appeared to get more rooted to the ground. As if that were possible. "It does not matter what you wish. You place yourself in danger."

I was curious. "Are you saying, Sensei, that I would not be able to fight someone like this?"

His eyes narrowed. "Don't be an idiot, Burke. It is a child's question, who would win, who would lose! This man—whoever he is—is a killer." When he gets mad, my teacher grows quieter, more focused, more eloquent. "Evil has its own energy, Burke. Getting too close to it allows it to pull at your spirit. It is most unwise."

And he wouldn't say anything more than that.

Micky and Art planned to visit places where the types of body men they were familiar with would train. I could imagine it. They would slog through a number of dingy gyms, a universe filled with mats stained with skin grease and sweat and decades-old heavy bags patched with duct tape like victims of bad triage. You went downstairs or into an alley through a door and into a space where the bricks had been painted with diluted whitewash sometime during the Eisenhower administration. The clank of free weights hitting the ground would compete with the staccato rhythm of speed bags and the deeper thuds of bodies hitting the mat in a roped-in area farther back in the cavernous space.

The men training there would be mostly young and thickly built in the functional way you get when you leverage people's bodies around for a living. There was no Spandex worn here. There was lots of tape on hands and feet. Some of the denizens would take one look at Micky and Art and duck away, feigning a renewed interest in training. My brother would probably shoot his partner a look as well. Everyone recognized everyone else.

In those places the aural signature communicated effort and frustration, the quest for dominance. And anger. The air would be thick with the psychic radiation, spiky with sudden thuds and clanks, the visual field rendered gritty by bad light and human effort.

Micky and Art would ask whether anyone new had been training. They would be greeted with blank looks or faked attempts at thinking. They would go through the motions, leaving their cards and asking if anyone remembered anything or saw anything to give them a call.

They left the more exotic locations to me, figuring I'd have better luck. I knew some guys in some of the tougher *dojo* in New York. They weren't exactly friends, but you got to know people over the years, if only because when you bang on someone and they bang back, you tend to remember them.

I'd first come across Billy Watson when I was in college. He was a former wrestler who'd taken a shine to judo and was working out on the mats that got shared with the other martial arts clubs. He'd ended up hooked on judo and eventually began studying Yoshinkan aikido as well. It's an art form that adds joint locks to the throws and balance shifts of judo. Aikido in general is a beautiful and, in highly trained hands, somewhat effective art. Yoshinkan is a bit on the hard side, however. It uses more power than some other styles.

It suited Billy. There's a ritual pledge they use in Shotokan karate at the end of class. Among other things, trainees swear to "refrain from violent behavior." A more accurate translation of the Japanese is "to guard against impetuous courage." The Japanese *sensei* like to keep their students on a tight leash: they don't mind fighting; they just want to be able to control when and where it happens. Billy had enough impetuous courage to keep a room full of teachers worried. From what I knew of him and the type of people who gravitated to his Yoshinkan *dojo,* I thought he might be able to point me in a couple of good directions.

Like many other New York City *dojo*, Billy's had to offer classes practically around the clock to survive. There was an early morning workout for stressed Wall Street types (who got to the office still shaking out their wrists and trying to get the nerve endings to stop buzzing). There were typical evening classes and even an early lunchtime session on Sunday, which was where I found Billy putting his pupils through their paces.

He was an average-size guy but hard. Anyone who ever tangled with Billy learned that he was packed with muscle. He had a big, square head with bristly short, dark hair. It let you see the ropes of muscles that bound his head to the rest of him. There were nicks in his skull, white scars from old fights where the hair would never grow back. Billy took his training seriously. His eyes were a cool blue and he had that focused stare you see with really intense competitors. It was designed to frighten you. I knew. We had met more than a few times on the mats in my early days. His face was lean, and you could see that the straight ridge of his nose had been ruined when it was broken. I don't know whether he was still mad at me for doing it. I figured we were even: I can't sleep on my right side because of something he did to my shoulder.

The *dojo* was a pretty good size, carved out of an old downtown warehouse. The walls and pipes had been painted over and over again in that white color they use in the City to make you believe that things are new and clean. It mostly looks dingy and tired.

But the mats in Billy's *dojo* were in good shape. They were worn but repaired precisely. He had about twenty men, all at black belt level, working on some takedown techniques. In Yoshinkan *dojo*, they tend to just wear judo *gi* and not the fancier pleated *hakama*. It sends a certain message about the tough, no frills approach this style takes to fighting.

Billy was working with the class on what looked to me like *tenshi-nage*. It's a standard throw in the art: you deflect a lunging thrust and throw the attacker to his front corner by unbalancing him and moving in. Billy caught my entrance out of the corner of his eye. His eyes swept my way, but he made no sign of recognition.

Tenshi-nage in most styles is pretty elegant. Some

schools make it almost too stylized: trainees virtually launch themselves into the fall for their practice partners. Not here. Billy was obviously working on some variations that seemed predicated on the idea that your attacker would not go down. It was a good exercise: what happens when you give it your best shot and the guy will still not fold? It happens eventually to all of us.

There are a number of solutions to the problem. Billy demonstrated a few pretty convincingly: his opponents got propelled not only down but into the mat. Then the class got to try. He watched as they paired off and tried out his variations on each other.

I watched with him. And listened.

The aural signature here was a serious one, punctuated by the rhythmic slam of bodies hitting the mat. You could hear the deeper thud of body collision, the hiss of breath, the occasional grunt. I also picked up the higher-pitched sound of slapping.

Billy sidled up to me. "Burke. You come for a workout?" It wasn't a friendly comment. Billy and guys like him work hard at things, which is fine. But they also tend to believe that their way is the only way. I shook his hand—if we had been dogs, the hair on our necks would have been standing up.

"No. Just looking for some help with something." The slapping sound continued and drew my attention. Billy saw my glance and gestured with his chin.

"Check this guy out. The real deal."

The man wore a spotless white *gi* that looked soft with repeated washings. He was intent on working his partner relentlessly, moving in repeatedly to practice the move that Billy had shown them. The slapping noise was coming as he brought his cupped hand sharply into the jaw of his partner as a prelude to the throw. *Smack!* And in the brief moment of pain, the man would swirl into position and hinge down for the throw. His victim would be driven to the mat and then rise, red faced from the blow, to take more.

Billy's face didn't look a bit troubled as he watched. He didn't say anything. It was a tough place.

I told him about my problem. He looked at his class for a minute as if inspecting a lineup of suspects. "My people are rough, Burke, but I don't see any of them as a killer."

"Sure, Billy. But if anyone new comes by, anyone out of the ordinary, you let me know."

He gave me that hard look. "Hey, you know? I run a business here. People come in to train. I got transients coming by all the time. What's it gonna do for me if I start getting them involved with the cops? It'll kill me."

"Funny you should say that. The guy I'm looking for kills people."

He shook his head. It swiveled very precisely back and forth, yanked by muscle. "I teach people to fight. I don't get involved with their lives off the mat."

I could see he was annoyed. Billy always had a short fuse. I changed the subject and nodded in his student's direction. "He's going at it a bit hard, isn't he? Is he always this intense?" Part of me was thinking like a cop. Could this guy fit the profile of the man we were looking for?

Billy crossed his arms across his chest and watched the class. "Pretty much." Then he looked at me. "Don't get any ideas. He's been with me for a few years." I felt let down. I guess I wasn't going to crack the case. Billy watched as the man's partner took a particularly hard fall. I winced, but Billy was stoic. "Ya gotta keep him away from the beginners. They tend to break. He gives my advanced people a run for their money, though. Hang on a sec."

He glided over to the mat edge and called the group to order. It's always amazing to watch someone move like that: hard and crude though he was, he practically floated. He told everyone to take a short break and brought the man over to be introduced.

The Real Deal was cautiously polite in a way that's typical of a great many martial artists. They save most of their intensity for training. Some people feel we're repressed and only express ourselves in the *dojo*. They don't understand.

We're just resting between fights. "Sensei Watson tells us stories about your *dojo*," he said. "And your teacher. It would be something to meet him."

"Yeah," Billy said, "get in line. But don't get your hopes up. I've been trying to get in there for years." The topic seemed to revive his bad mood. "What he sees in you is anyone's guess, Burke."

I just shrugged. I sometimes wondered the same thing. But I knew that Billy wouldn't be getting to see my teacher soon. Yamashita had spoken to me about Billy in the past. Sensei wanted him to get a bit more experience. The impetuous courage thing.

Billy smirked at me. "OK, since you're here, how about a quick lesson for the class? Show us some of those exotic techniques you get to work on." Both men looked at me expectantly. If they weren't going to get to see Yamashita anytime soon, maybe some pointers from one of his students would do. But that wasn't the only reason. Way back in the eyes of the two men, I could see the predatory gleam of competitors. They wanted to see me work.

Billy ushered the class back into order and introduced me. I slipped my shoes off and bowed onto the mat.

I gestured for a partner. A student stepped forward. One-half of his face was still red from the slapping he had gotten. You had to give the guy credit for guts.

I looked around the group. "All technique should be guided by efficiency," I began. "Any of you who've studied judo know the principle of maximum efficiency for a minimum of effort." Some heads nodded around the circle that had formed around me. "In a situation like the one your *sensei* has given you—you try a technique and it doesn't quite work—the temptation is very strong to compensate by overpowering the opponent." I said to my partner, gesturing at him, "So. Half-speed, please."

He came at me with a lunge punch. It was a good, serious strike. "Someone centered," I continued as I moved, "someone strong and trained, like this guy here"—I grinned—"is hard to fight off." I let him barrel into me. I let his force push me back and down. I rolled backward and up onto my feet. "Too little force, or too slow a reaction time, will ruin your technique."

I nodded at him and we set up for him to repeat it. "I can do my *tenshi-nage* well. Like so." He came at me again, a little faster, a bit harder. "And now evade the strike, but he's still not going down." I slowly flowed into the technique and let him resist it.

"This is where the temptation to use too much power comes in. It's a natural reaction: crank up the volume." I pushed harder. He didn't budge. I could see the conviction growing in his eyes that I was a talker, not a doer. He wasn't alone. There were half-hidden smirks growing around the room.

"I could do this all day and a strong opponent wouldn't go down," I continued. "So now we get more focused, more efficient. Full speed, please."

I saw the light go on in my partner's eyes. This is what these guys lived for: full speed. We set up again and he came at me in a flash. I flowed into the technique and the sticking point where he refused to go over.

My left hand had parried his strike and now gripped his wrist, directing his momentum forward. Theoretically, my right hand should have pushed him, making him wheel a bit and lose his balance. But he wasn't going to cooperate. Which was the point.

Instead, I took my right hand and made an upright fist with my thumb sticking straight up. I slowly pressed the thumb into the soft area under the jaw, pressuring the base of the tongue. It's an uncomfortable feeling and the natural impulse is to draw the head back, which he did.

So I threw him.

"You need to make your opponent's head move if you want to break his balance," I said to the class. My partner looked surprised, but he stood up again. This time when he came at me, I pressed my forefinger into the point where the jaw hinges under the ear. It's a nice little pressure point.

Again, his head moved and down he went. He made a nice slapping noise as he hit the mat.

"The point," I concluded, "is to work smarter, not harder. Never use more force than is necessary." I bowed to my partner, who had taken enough abuse for one day, then to Billy, and to the class.

As I left, I felt the energy of someone staring at me. I turned to find Billy's hard-case student standing near the end of the mat. You could see the wheels turn in his head as he evaluated my performance. He probably thought he could take me. I bowed in his direction.

"Nice to meet you, buddy," I said. Then I got out of there before he got a chance to test his theory.

Court Warriors

It may be that all this training is paying off. I went home that night uneasy: I felt some sort of psychic barometric shift taking place. It was not a good thing. The Japanese describe *seme* as the type of pressure and intimidation a master swordsman can force on a lesser opponent, without seeming to do anything. It's unseen but nonetheless real. I had that sense of something pushing against me, probing my weaknesses.

If I had to explain it to someone, I don't know whether I could. There was a nagging thought just out of reach of conscious recognition, and I felt that if only I could drag it out things would be clearer. But I couldn't. It was like trying to gain a sighting of the moon through scudding clouds. All I was left with was a feeling. A storm was building.

And I wasn't alone. Yamashita was up to something.

He had an explanation, of course, but even as I listened respectfully I got the sense that there was something else going on as well.

Akkadian had gone on with his plans for a gala opening of the exhibit at Samurai House. Even if decency had made him reconsider it—and no one who really knew him entertained that thought for a second—the postmurder notoriety would have made the allure of publicity far too strong for Bobby's underdeveloped ethical muscles to withstand.

He had wanted to kick the night off with a demonstration of some of the best martial arts the New York area had to offer. In keeping with developments, he had gotten more than he bargained for. The old-time *sensei* wanted in.

The masters tended to keep people like Bobby at arm's length, but now honor was involved. Because with a little digging, I found out that the wooden sword that was taken the night of Reilly's murder was not a minor showpiece. It was a bit more obscure than Musashi's weapon—I could still remember the gleam in Akkadian's eye when he showed me that picture—but, in many ways, the stolen article was much more significant. It was a training weapon used by a man named Ittosai. The style he had founded, the *Itto Ryu*, had endured for four centuries and decisively shaped the technique and philosophy of Japanese swordsmanship. If the local *sensei* were relatively unmoved by Reilly's murder, they felt the theft of Ittosai's weapon to be a direct affront, my teacher above all. Ittosai had founded the school of swordsmanship that Yamashita had devoted his life to.

Yamashita had been to the meeting they held with Bobby. The senior *sensei* all vowed to help find the thief. In addition, the memories of both Ikagi and Kubata would be honored at the gala. The *sensei* felt that Bobby's stable of ersatz warriors, commando retreads, and closet *ninja* were not up to the task, but with the silent condescension of their culture they didn't tell him that. They insisted, instead, on their inclusion in the events surrounding the display.

Which is why I was there a day before the big event. Yamashita had sent me to make sure that the arrangements for the demonstration space were adequate. Bobby's staff had given assurances, but Yamashita refused to believe it. It wasn't just his contempt for Bobby Kay. It was that, in a matter of importance like a public display, you left nothing to chance. For the Japanese, the pressure of public performance is perhaps more intense than for anyone else. The possibility of technical flaws or accident is always present in a martial arts demonstration. For these men, the types of flaws they might reveal were so subtle that most people would not even notice them. People would, however, notice poor planning or inadequate facilities. Yamashita wanted these possibilities eliminated. It was exasperatingly painstaking, but it was the way you get at his level of competence.

So I went back to Samurai House and I spoke with the display curator. The wooden floor of the exhibition gallery was glossy with polish. You would never know that they had shoveled Reilly into a rubber bag in this very space just a week ago. The curator was a narrow-faced woman who sniffed constantly, as if catching a sudden whiff of something unpleasant. Maybe it was me. She seemed only too happy to let me wander off by myself.

The temporary dividers for the display had been removed, revealing a cavernous space. Behind a vacant performance area, you could glimpse the glass cases and muted lighting of the exhibit itself. Yamashita had given me pretty precise specifications to check. Even though part of me was consumed with a memory of this place as a crime scene, I complied with my teacher's wishes. I checked for obtruding pillars. I walked the floor surface checking for irregularities and splinters. I made sure the ceiling was high enough. The wall where Ronin had commemorated the murder with his message and signature had been re-painted. You would have a hard time identifying the area as the place where Reilly had looked, open-eyed with surprise, into eternity. I was alone in the space where Ronin had left his mark.

I paced the perimeter of the space like a monk in cloisters, focused on an interior reality, a search for something elusive. I tried to re-create Reilly's last fight. I could imagine the grunts, the hisses of air, the contained lunges. Were they barefoot? On this type of floor, I would have been. Did they speak? What do you say to someone when you realize they're trying to kill you? I would have saved my breath.

For something important like running away.

But I guess Reilly didn't use that option. When he finally looked into the eyes of his killer, what did he see? What does anyone see at that moment except the sudden realization that the idea of the ego's importance is a grand fraud?

In the martial arts, we train to diminish the ego. I've been chipping away at it for years, but I hope that someday the eventual blowing out of the candle of self occurs at my own pace and is not thrust on me like some violent, feral storm.

The next night, I stood uncomfortably at the reception with the Japanese *sensei*, outfitted like them in the layered robes of court warriors dead for three centuries, while a luminous crowd of well-dressed and underfed art afficionados waited for something to happen.

The *sensei*, of course, were seething. Standing there, elegant and self-contained, it seemed odd to think it, but it was true. You can't tell by their expressions, but there is an intense flatness the masters get in their eyes when they are truly angry. Looking around that room, I knew they were steamed. It added to the general sensory jumble of the event.

The emotional atmosphere in that room was cluttered. Yamashita wanted me to be more open to these unconscious signals, so I was trying hard to sense things. The vibes I was picking up were not very comforting. People tried to look smooth, but they bounced around like excited electrons. Only the Japanese masters were still. They regarded the crowds, dispassionate and removed, silent judges from another world. They stood there, mute and hard amid the smoothness of tuxedos and flash of jewelry, stark peaks in the sand sea of a rock garden. Waiting.

And I waited with them. Bobby had invited an eclectic mix to the opening. There were the inevitable media types lured in to ensure proper coverage. Given the exhibition, I assumed there were also art collectors here, although it's not a social circle I'm well acquainted with. Domanova was present, of course. He looked pleased at the prospect of being near so many potential donors, but also petulant that they weren't fawning all over him.

The lobby and exhibition room had been carefully prepped with discreet lighting and hors d'oeuvre tables. In the whirl, I caught a glimpse of Bobby glad-handing some celebrities. He looked flushed with pleasure at the way the evening seemed to be going, his long face nimbly registering sincerity, amusement, or respect as the character of his various audiences required. Music could be heard faintly at times, but it was drowned out by the ebb and flow of excited chatter coming from the well-heeled crowd. Waiters circulated with champagne in fluted glasses.

Amid the flat sameness of diamond sparkle, white teeth, and formal wear, the martial artists stood around, waiting.

"Bobby Kay looks pleased with himself," one of Yamashita's other students observed to me as she sipped her drink. She was one of the newer trainees, and had volunteered to help out. Actually, there wasn't much to do, so she was making the most of the situation.

"Bobby," I commented, "doesn't have the good sense to be worried. He smells money. It tends to cloud other issues."

"Like what?" she asked and sipped some more of Bobby's good champagne. She crinkled her nose fetchingly at the bubbles.

I had been watching things for a while and had a whole mental list of things I was worried about. I just smiled and shrugged, but deep down the thought intruded: money cloaks other things. Like the smell of blood.

Even before I arrived, I knew that the only thing the cops had to go on was the martial arts link between both victims. Micky and Art were still waiting for information about whether Ikagi and Kubata had connections back in

Japan. But if I was right about Ronin's attention being somehow attracted to victims who were prestigious *sensei*, then I thought the presence of some of the area's most prominent martial artists would be irresistible. Micky's response was much more succinct: "Oh boy," he had said, "fresh meat."

It brought me back to the state of heightened anxiety I was experiencing. I thought about why the *sensei* were here: they thought that Ronin was going to strike again. And soon. They weren't alone. What little I had been able to find out from my brother suggested that the NYPD thought so too. We all knew that Ronin's last message meant that he wasn't done yet.

This was the source of another complication. There was a fair amount of public pressure to solve the case. The potential for media hype was irresistible, and Micky's lieutenant had made it clear in no uncertain terms that things were not moving fast enough to satisfy the mayor, the commissioner, and *The Daily News*. As a result, a whole team of detectives had been put on the job. Micky looked on it as less than a ringing endorsement of his investigative skill.

To make things worse, the newspapers told me that the Japanese community had posted a $25,000 reward for the return of the sword. Micky and Art thought the reward would draw every lunatic in the five boroughs and make their job that much harder. My brother was almost speechless with rage.

You couldn't get a good sense of Micky's lack of contentment from looking at him. The Japanese are not the only people to have perfected the poker face. He and Art were here tonight, circulating discreetly around the fringes of the reception. Their suits were appropriately dark, but the wider jacket cut you needed for a shoulder holster tended to make that elegant cocktail-reception look somewhat hard to achieve. Micky's blue eyes swept over the crowd, a searchlight groping for a subject. Art looked tense. Neither was really sure that Ronin would show. Yet both men suspected, in a visceral cop way, that the mix of Bobby's odd guest list and the pattern of Ronin's crimes made it a good bet that something was going to go down. Besides, Micky had reminded me tightly, there was all that reward money.

But for my brother, like the *sensei*, it wasn't about money. It was about pride. Something had been taken. It needed to be returned.

As one of the players in tonight's demonstration, I wasn't really free to roam the party. I caught Art's eye and jerked my head to one side to signal them to come over.

"Technically," Art informed me, "we're not even supposed to be here. Violation of Lieutenant Colletti's orders. He wants us to rework the paper trail."

"Oooh, Art," Micky spat, "a violation. We'll get in trouble. Maybe a note home to our fucking mothers." His partner looked around. No one had noticed or overheard: the wash of noise from the crowd had drowned Micky out. But Art had seen Micky like this before and wanted to head off the explosion.

"Hey, Mr. Furious. Relax."

"Relax yourself," Micky shot back. "Pussy."

"Asshole."

"C'mon, guys. Let's keep it down."

You could see the muscles in Micky's neck and jaw work a little with the effort involved in rage suppression. He finally let out a thin stream of air, like a pressure valve gradually bleeding the needle down off the red zone. "OK. OK."

"Look, I'm here, all right?" Art offered to him. You could tell he didn't want to be, but the alchemy between cops, particularly partners, is strong.

"So what's the deal?" I asked them, hoping that conversation would further calm Micky down.

"Three things," Art answered. The thick, freckled forefinger came up. "One, if Ronin is stalking martial arts celebrities, he'll be here. Tonight's an opportunity for him to scope them out in the flesh. Probably too good to pass up. And if he's here, we want to see whether we can spot him."

"Probably a long shot," Micky grumbled. "I gotta believe there's something else we don't see here. But what's the harm?"

"Other than to our careers," Art reminded him.

Micky started to respond and the "F" sound had already escaped him before he realized it. "F . . . orget about it," he said flatly. "Just two private citizens out for a night on the town, watching my brother prance around like an extra in *Shogun*." He eyed my outfit. For a formal demonstration of this type, the normal practice uniform is replaced by much more formal wear. I had on a gray *hakama* and black silk top that bore the small *mon*, or crests, of Yamashita's family on both sides of the chest and the back. My feet were covered in white *tabi*, split-toed socks, and I wore *zori*, the straw sandals of old Japan. My brother concluded his assessment. "Nice dress, Connor."

"Thanks, Mick. Always so supportive." I turned to his partner to pick up the thread of their analysis. "And what's the second reason you're here, Art?"

He looked at me with a deadpan expression. "Two is that if there's some connection between the victims, some of your martial arts masters know the reason, and they're just not telling us. We wanna scope them out."

"Come on," I protested. "You really think these guys are holding out on you?"

Art sighed. "First rule of being a cop: everyone lies."

My brother nodded. "And the third reason," Micky jumped in, "is that nobody throws me my gun and tells me to run. Nobody." He grinned as he said it, but it wasn't a pleasant look.

I looked at Art with raised eyebrows. He was grinning too. It was nicer to look at.

"James Coburn," Art answered. "*The Magnificent Seven.*"

I paused to digest the return to cinema. These guys could shift gears so quickly that it was hard to keep up with them.

But I tried. "It didn't end well for his character as I remember," I reminded them.

"Shut up, Connor," my brother ordered.

The crowd ebbed and flowed around tables of food and waiters bearing trays. I stood near the performance area, trying not to let the party atmosphere distract me. It was almost show time.

Bobby's demonstration had been effectively hijacked by the *sensei*. Masters of their arts and of the etiquette that cloaked them, they had put together an impressive plan for the display. Armed and unarmed systems would be featured. Reflecting etiquette, the senior ranking master in the senior art form—*kendo,* the way of the sword—headed the list.

Asa Hiroaki Sensei was compact and dignified, possessed of a gravity created by the accretion of experience. Iron-gray hair was swept back from a wide brow. His eyes glittered black, peering at you over high cheekbones like a rifleman taking aim over a parapet. His lips were thin, as if pressed flat by the effort of forty years of training.

Even Yamashita respected him. Kendo is an art form inspired by the fencing techniques of the *samurai*. It includes free sparring using split bamboo foils known as *shinai*, and trainees wear elaborate armor for protection. Kendo is fast, elegant, and furious, but it's a highly stylized fury. Asa was a master of the art and combined dignity and elegance with lightning reflexes.

Kendo students are supposed to study sword *kata*, but most people have been seduced by the more sportive element of competition in free fighting. It's not unusual to see middle-level black belts, impressively ferocious in their sparring skills, fumble through a *kata* sequence. Yamashita thinks simulated fighting with armor is delusional; Asa thinks kendo *kata* are neglected. The two men practice very different arts but found common ground in the study of sword *kata*.

Asa and Yamashita were originally scheduled to open up

the demo with the kendo *kata*. Kendo's free fighting is fast and subtle; the *kata* are elegant and more appropriate for a formal gathering. But to everyone's surprise, Yamashita begged off and put me in his place. He'd damaged the ulnar nerve in his left arm, he explained, and wouldn't be able to wield the sword correctly. It was a valid excuse, I suppose. Even though the *katana* is normally wielded with two hands, only the right guides. The left does most of the real work. In a demonstration of this magnitude, it would be a serious handicap.

The only problem with the excuse was that I had never seen Yamashita with an injury as debilitating as that. And just this morning he had been going at it with some novices, all of whom would have sworn there was nothing wrong—and with good reason.

The *sensei* were annoyed. They never come out and say it to your face, but deep down the Japanese feel that no Round Eye can really know the martial arts. Each *sensei* knew exceptions to the rule, but as a category non-Japanese are thought of as decidedly second string. Yamashita might have vouched for me, but for a public display of this importance, my role was a cause for concern for the other masters.

So here was another thing that worried me. Asa, all dressed up, was now being forced to work with what he considered an inferior product—me. Only his respect for Yamashita and his need to maintain a dignified public appearance kept him from storming out of the room.

To make things more complicated, we were going to be using real swords. Most times, you use wooden weapons for these *kata*. At formal occasions, steel swords are used, but usually they are unsharpened replica swords known as *iaito*. They have the balance and look of a *katana* but they can't cut. Tonight's performance, however, would be with *shinken*—real swords.

So. A big crowd. The possible presence of a killer. My brother about to explode. A deeply annoyed performance partner. And live swords. The Burke luck was holding true to form.

Yamashita fussed around me, making sure the line of my garments was right. The paired swords, long and short, that we each would use rested in finely wrought wooden holders in a place of honor. Yamashita checked the sword fittings. The blades are held in by only a small bamboo pin, called a *mekugi*, that is inserted through the handle. If it breaks, the blades have an alarming habit of flying out when you do a cut. The rumor mill says a hapless spectator was impaled some years ago in Tokyo when a pin snapped and a blade went rocketing across the room. There were probably people who would pay to see Bobby Kay skewered that way, but Yamashita wanted this thing to go off tonight without a hitch.

Some people saw my teacher pick up the swords for inspection. When Yamashita knelt to remove them from the lacquered wooden racks they rested on, a buzz started as people thought the demonstration was about to begin. Yamashita ignored it and went on with his work. Satisfied, he rose and crossed over to the other side of the area to speak briefly with Asa. I tried to stay calm and watched the crowd, looking for anything unusual. What does a killer look like, anyway? It was pretty much a swirl of party heads. You caught a sense of personalities in motion, brief glimpses. But any insight was lost in the crowd's motion, like a view into another room blocked by a closing door.

My *sensei* returned to me. "We begin in ten minutes, Burke."

I noticed that a small envelope had been left by Asa's sword stand while I was distracted. Asa Sensei moved smoothly to the sword rack and picked up the note. He glanced at it and placed it inside his top. Then he picked up his swords. With a final tug on my *hakama*, I followed suit.

The demonstration finally began. I was relieved, because I couldn't deal with any more psychic clutter. There was a fanfare and some words of welcome. The mayor, who was up for reelection, had gotten wind of the press coverage, and he was there. It meant that there was some extra verbiage tossed around while Asa Sensei and I edged over to the side of the performance area and worked on our breathing. The crowd clustered around and I scanned the faces. I saw Art, who winked at me. Akkadian, looking pleased. There were lots of strangers. Some looked distracted. Some looked bored. Some looked rich and quite a few looked drunk. But no one looked like a murderer.

The words bubbled away eventually. There was applause and then silence. We were on.

The *kata* series Asa and I were to perform is highly choreographed and dense with significance. Each of the ten sets is a paired exercise in attack and response; each is an illustration of a vital lesson in the Way of the Sword. Entrance, initiative, attack, and even response are all known ahead of time. But the tension generated throughout the performance is considerable. You expend a great deal of energy looking confident in *kata*. There can be no hesitation in your actions, no flaw in your technique. Add to this the vagaries of dealing with a partner, and the *kata* performance becomes a nice test in how you balance the tension created by almost infinite minute variations in human activity with the need to maintain fidelity to the form and spirit of the *kata*.

When you are done with an exercise like this, perspiration trickles down the small of your back, under the stiff *koshita* that forms the back of the *hakama* you wear. Your hands are slick with sweat from handling the sword. Mine were wet even before we started.

Just for kicks, Yamashita had arranged for a *tameshigiri* exercise to precede the *kata*. This is a test cutting that you perform to show the audience that the swords are real. Asa and I faced each other about twenty feet apart. Behind each of us and slightly to one side, three bamboo shoots, each as thick as a man's wrist, stood upright.

At Yamashita's command, we strode forward, closing the gap between us and crossing to the opposite side. I drew my sword and cut at the bamboo. You have to hit it just right with the sword. Although lethally sharp, you need to draw the blade in so you cut at the target a bit. If you don't, the *katana* will actually bounce off.

I got it right and sliced though the green stalks, one after the other. As I spun to face Asa, the bamboo stumps quivered and swayed slightly with the force of the attack. Then the *kata* began.

It only takes about six and a half minutes to perform the entire kendo *kata* set. But when you do it, time feels different. We slid toward each other, the balls of our feet rasping across the floor, the tips of our swords pointed high over our heads in the position known as *jodan*. Our hips drove us forward.

Asa exploded into an attack. In the first *kata*, the attacker tries to cleave you in two by cutting through the top of your head. I dodged the blow by stepping back just far enough for the cut to miss. When you're using wooden swords in this *kata*, it's a bit dicey because you can get clonked pretty good if you misjudge the distance. With live blades, it's infinitely more interesting.

Asa's intent was to cleave me in half down to the waist, and he followed through with his blow. It presented the critical opening needed. I dodged back, then slid forward and countered with a decisive cut to the head, my shout of attack coming a split second after his and punctuating the decisive moment in the exercise.

We concluded this *kata*. We met and our swords crossed. They say a good swordsman can make your sword "stick" to his at this juncture. Asa's blade and mine felt held together by a magnetic force. We broke and backed up to our initial starting points, eyeing each other warily, feet dragging along the ground as if we were wading through thick mud.

Each of the next nine exercises contained different techniques, but the same tension. After number seven, I switched to using the short sword, which reduced the margin for error even more. When I put the long sword down in the pause between the seventh and eighth series, the cloth wrapping on the handle was dark with perspiration.

When it was finally over and we bowed out, I had no real idea how the audience thought we had done. In many ways, the reality of the crowd had faded for me during the performance and it seemed as if the universe were filled only by the blades, their points and edges, and the threatening darkness of Asa's eyes. I had some vague memory of crowd noise washing over the sibilant whisper of my partner's blade as it whipped by my head a few times, but that was it. Asa, it seemed to me, had not been as precise as I would have expected, but it was only an impression of a microsecond's hesitation. Not something a casual viewer would have noticed.

The crowd applauded. We stepped out of the performance area, sat in the formal posture, and, bowing, thanked each other. I'm sure his error bothered him, but even when they're annoyed, the Japanese are usually polite. Asa got up and went to Yamashita. He bowed to my *sensei* and they spoke for a moment. Then Asa left. It was a surprise, but maybe he felt the need to get out of the area after what I'm sure he thought of as an embarrassing performance.

I turned to watch the next demonstration. I spotted Art and Micky, but they were looking at the faces focused on the performance area.

A noted karate master strode to the center of the crowd's attention. Thick and confident, he bowed to the makeshift *dojo* shrine and to the assembled masters. He stood silently for a moment, the breath coming and going with a tidal rhythm. His hands rose up in front of him higher than his head. The thumbs and forefingers of the open hands touched, making a triangle shape through which he looked for a moment. It was *Kanku Dai*, one of my favorite black belt routines. The name was suggested by the hand posture: Gazing at the Sky.

I felt a presence behind me. "Burke," Yamashita hissed in my ear, "something is amiss. Get your brother."

We gathered behind the audience, off in a corner. There were small clusters of people more interested in the free champagne than what was going on in the stage area. Back here, you could hear people talking and the occasional discreet laugh.

Micky and Art listened quietly, still watching the crowd, as the *sensei* explained.

"Something is wrong. Asa Sensei." He looked at me. "You noticed?"

"He wasn't as focused as I thought he would be."

Yamashita nodded. "So. He took two tries at one of his cuts. There were moments where his awareness seemed clouded."

"He looked pretty scary to me," Art said.

Yamashita smiled tightly. "Yes. You would not know."

"Is that all," Micky asked with some exasperation. "The guy was off his game?"

"No, Detective. That is not all." Yamashita's tone was not something they were used to hearing from people, and Micky and Art turned on him with the full power of their cop stare. My *sensei* didn't flinch. "As he left, Asa Sensei apologized to me for his faltering performance." He turned to face me. "He asked me to offer congratulations to you on the level of your skill, Professor."

"Yeah," Micky said, "I give it a nine and it's got a good dance beat. Can we get to the point?" My brother was still a bit cranky.

Yamashita was not used to being addressed like that, either. I saw it in his eyes, but he went on. "Asa Sensei apologized and told me that he had received a note. And that he hoped to be able to redeem our honor tonight."

The only reason we were able to catch up with Asa at all was that he took a while to fold his formal uniform. Even with all that was on his mind, Asa Sensei was a methodical man. His *hakama* would be neatly folded, his other items carefully packed. He had spent a lifetime learning not to cut corners and that night was no exception.

We spotted him as he left the dressing room. He was less conspicuous in his street clothes, as if they were designed to shield the world from seeing his true nature. He threaded through the crowd and headed out the door. I ducked into the dressing room, grabbed my clothes bag, and headed out with all the speed that I could. Running in sandals is tough work. Besides, I had watched men like Asa move for years and knew how deceptive he would be when he got going.

ELEVEN

Gazing at the Sky

The car, with its NYPD card on the dash, was pulled up in a No Parking zone close to the Samurai House entrance. Micky and I piled in and we shot down the street.

"He just entered the parking garage," Art reported as he ran back from the corner and then thudded into the seat beside my brother. Micky had the car in gear before Art's door was even closed.

"Where's the exit?"

"Around the block." Art picked up the radio handset and asked for a record check for auto registration.

"Right or left?"

"Left."

"Thank God." The streets here were one way, and Micky was afraid we'd lose Asa if we had to circle around the block.

Micky raced the car across the traffic. His high-speed turn made tires squeal; some of them were ours. The maneuver drew a few cranky horn blasts from a cruising cab and threw me up against the car door. Art worked the radio like nothing was happening. He seemed to be glued to the seat. "How do you spell his name?" he asked me.

"What's he drive?" Micky demanded.

"A Toyota."

My brother grunted. "Figures."

The radio came to life. "Camry four-door," Art told Micky. He gave him the tag number and they scanned the road ahead. The garage was one of those multilevel affairs buried in the wall of buildings that lined the street. Cars sprung out of the gated exit directly into traffic, like rabbits from a hole. The night road ahead was flecked with red taillights. From the backseat, I couldn't see their expression, but you could almost feel the eye strain as the two men peered into the distance to try to spot Asa. The tension evaporated and they both settled back into the seat with relief as the Toyota exited the garage.

"OK," Micky breathed, "here we go."

We trailed Asa through Manhattan's night traffic.

Micky was cursing softly under his breath, trying to stay close but not too close to Asa's car and avoid the vehicles that passed by. Art quietly narrated their progress across town. I noticed that they didn't bicker at all.

We were headed down the East Side.

"He live down here?" Art asked me. I shook my head no. "OK," he said quietly. "Is he heading for the bridge or the tunnel?"

"Please God," Micky said, swerving around and then ahead of a bus that lumbered into our path like a whale breaching, "let it be the bridge."

Roebling's bridge is an architectural wonder, even after all these years. It was built in an age when aesthetics and technology hadn't been split apart. At night, the Brooklyn Bridge is lit up, a brick-and-cable causeway spun across the oily churning of the East River. It could be seen as the initiate's path to the mysteries of Manhattan or as an escape hatch from the menace of the urban beast. It's hard to tell. Traffic goes both ways.

"So what's in Brooklyn?" Micky mused. "Asa have a school there?"

"No," I replied.

"And he doesn't live there?" Art reconfirmed. All I could do was shake my head no. "OK. No problem; I got the address," he said.

My brother shot me a quick look of pure fury. "Fuck, fuck, fuck," he breathed. "I told ya these guys were holdin' out on us, Art."

"Maybe he's headed for Little Tokyo," I suggested lamely. There was a growing Japanese and Korean community in Queens.

"Seems a roundabout way of getting there," Micky commented with acid in his voice.

He edged a little closer to the Camry, muscling his way through the close-packed lanes. The exit ramp from the bridge was a bit dicey and he didn't want to lose Asa. The traffic squeezed in as we reached the Brooklyn side, the drivers getting ready to head north to the Long Island Expressway or south to the Gowanus.

The blacktop was uneven, with seams and holes that made the car grumble. Micky was jockeying around in the middle lane, swinging his head quickly over his right shoulder to check the blind spot in case we had to go in that direction. The exit ramp from the bridge was coming up. "So whattaya think, Art?" my brother asked quietly.

"I think if he was heading to Queens he would have taken the Fifty-ninth Street Bridge. I don't think he's going home. I think he's got a meet set up."

"Me too," my brother said.

"Why?" I asked. I swallowed when I said it and the word came out with an odd, strangled sound to it.

Micky let out a breath. Then his shoulders shrugged. "Think about it. If you were gonna try to catch this guy, where would you look, Connor?"

"I guess I'd stake out a *dojo*."

"Correct," Art jumped in. "And why is that?"

"Well, because . . . I guess because the other murders took place in *dojo*. Or places like them."

"Right." Micky jerked the car over and followed Asa

through the exit toward the Gowanus Expressway. We passed the silent group of warehouses and refurbished office buildings that cluster around the foot of the bridge, and drove along the waterfront for a time. A navy destroyer hulked, a gray form in the grayer expanse of urban night. Then we drove up past the plaza where cars clustered before entering the Brooklyn Tunnel to Manhattan and we moved onto the expressway proper, which led through the Red Hook section toward Bay Ridge. "And the one thing that trips most murderers up, Art?" Micky continued, as if the intervening silence had not existed.

"Pattern. Predictability," his partner responded.

"So, buddy boy," Micky continued, "we got your teacher's pal shootin' out of the reception like his tail's on fire. A mysterious message that obviously got to him. And now he's headin' somewhere. Not home. My guess is something's goin' down."

"Maybe," I said grudgingly. I was still trying to digest the swirl of action that hadn't seemed to let up since Asa and I crossed swords for the *kata* demonstration. It felt like it happened a month ago.

The expressway was a bland, brightly lit stretch of elevated concrete. You got occasional glimpses of the upper stories of brick row houses that piled up in clusters right in the shadow of the roadway. Church spires stuck up out of the sea of tar roofs—Brooklyn is the borough of churches. Billboards advertised for car dealerships. Up ahead, the sky looked dark, but the stars were washed out from the ambient light. Soon the road would arc left to lead to the bridge to Staten Island. The traffic had eased up here and everyone was more or less in their own lanes. It reduced the tension and the two men were more willing to talk.

"Ronin has got to know someone's looking for him," Art commented.

"And our basic assumption is that there's something he's after we don't know about. So he may be crazy," Micky said.

"But he's not dumb," Art finished.

"So, after all the publicity in the papers, he's got to find another spot to get at his victim. Now that ya think about it, maybe the whole Samurai House reception looked to him like a great way to get us lookin' in the wrong place."

"Sure." Art nodded sagely. "And while we're all tied up there, he sets up another location."

"But he's got to have a way to lure someone to the meet. I wonder what he's got?" My brother had been giving this some thought.

"Gotta be some powerful mojo," Art commented. "He's already used it on two others."

I grunted in affirmation. Part of me was wondering whether my brother hadn't been right all along: the *sensei* knew something they weren't telling. I had the sickening feeling that maybe my *sensei* knew something. But at that moment, I was trying to figure out some way of getting out of the ceremonial outfit I was still wearing: I had anticipated changing into a suit after the performance. But not in a car.

The *hakama* and other clothes are not easily disposed of. I finally gave up and just pulled on the shoes I had in the bottom of the bag. The *zori* would be useless if we had to go anywhere on foot.

As I looked up, the Camry exited onto Fourth Avenue and we kept pace.

"Mr. Man, Mr. Man," Micky murmured under his breath, "where are you heading?"

He was heading south. But we couldn't figure out where. Down Fourth Avenue, Asa took a left. It led along a strip of park that served as a buffer between the neighborhoods of Sunset Park and Bay Ridge. It was lined with trees whose bark was mottled like camouflage. The chain-link fencing around the playground was ten feet high and iron swing sets and monkey bars made odd shapes in the darkness. A squat brick Parks Department building hulked in the middle of the grass strip. Passing headlights picked out the fluid wash of graffiti.

A left again, and we were heading north onto Sixth Avenue. We passed under the expressway, and the Camry's brake lights flashed as Asa turned right onto Sixty-second Street.

At this spot in Brooklyn, the subway comes up for air. The R and N lines run out here from Manhattan. The R continues south to the tip of Brooklyn, which is capped by Fort Hamilton. At Fifty-ninth Street, the N line turns east and emerges from its tunnel into a trench that rises slowly until the subway becomes elevated and you get to Coney Island. A growing Chinese population was moving into the area around the point where the trains come out of the tunnels. New immigrants got simple directions to the first stop the N makes after it bursts from darkness: get off at Blue Sky. For the local Chinese, the Eighth Avenue stop on the N is known as the Blue Sky station.

Asa slowly rolled down Sixty-second Street, which goes one way, east, and parallels the N train's trench. Small factories and warehouses dotted the street, shuttered tight and washed in the odd light of sodium lamps. There were narrow garages here as well, former stables from the 1920s that had been converted for cars. The block ended ahead, where it met Seventh Avenue.

The subway lines themselves were dug out here early in the last century. The token booths and entrances get an occasional facelift, but if you walk far enough down any subway platform in New York, you come face to face with the thick riveted girders and arched struts that generations of New Yorkers have stood near, glancing impatiently down the track for the light of an oncoming train. On the block where we were trailing Asa, the old stables were a reminder that, a short sixty or seventy years ago, horses were still lugging ice through Brooklyn's streets.

"What's the deal here, Connor?" We weren't too far from where I lived and Micky was relying on me for some information.

"Seventh Avenue's coming up," I said. "The street dead-ends. Not much there. A few shops around the corner. More people closer to Eighth Avenue."

Asa pulled over and we nosed into the curb, farther back on the block. Micky dowsed the headlights and we watched.

The Camry's lights went out. Asa got out of the car. He took a quick glance around, sweeping the shadows. His eyes were dark slashes in the sodium wash of the street-light. I felt myself shrink back into the seat almost invol-untarily. With anyone else, it would have been foolish. But I knew this man and what he was capable of. I felt as if he had sensed our presence. But it didn't seem to bother him. He popped the trunk and removed something long and narrow from the car, and began walking toward the corner.

Micky gestured. "What?" he asked me quietly.

I let out a tense breath. "It's a sword bag."

"OK." Micky's voice was sharp with excitement. "It's happening. What's there?" He pointed as Asa turned right at the corner.

"Nothing," I said. "The overpass is blocked off for con-struction."

"C'mon, ladies," Art urged, "time's wastin'. Something's there."

"Nothing," I insisted. Then it came to me. "Wait." I sat forward to peer through the windshield into the murk. "There's an old entrance to the Eighth Avenue subway stop."

"In use?" Micky had already started to roll the car for-ward.

"No. It's closed down."

They looked quickly at each other. "Perfect," Art said. He reached under his coat and checked his pistol. Micky handed him a two-way radio and Art squelched it for a test. "There's an exit further ahead on Eighth?" he confirmed.

"Next block." Things were beginning to speed up and the conversation, the movements, everything had the feeling of getting tight.

"OK." Art was doing three things at once. Checking his gun. Handling the radio. Undoing the seat belt. His brain had to be racing. "I go in here. You block the other exit?" He looked at Micky for confirmation.

Micky nodded in agreement and we rolled ahead to the corner where Asa had turned right. Art launched himself out the door. Asa was nowhere to be seen. On the east side of Seventh Avenue, the closed subway entrance was dark. An old sign, dirty with time and neglect, hinted faintly at the old platform's presence. One of those old metal turnstiles marked the entrance. It was essentially a cylindrical cage that was about seven feet high. Part of it rotated to permit access. In the dark it looked like a torture machine from a medieval castle. At one point, it had been chained shut. Art shined a flashlight on the entry. He held it like a club, with the shorter, light end projecting from the bottom of his fist. The chain hung, swaying slightly. The light picked up the fresh cut where the links had been severed. Art gave us a last look, nodded, and followed Asa into the shadows that led down to the trench.

"Shit, Art," Micky said to the night where his partner had been, "shoot first, will ya?"

Micky started to wheel the car into a left turn to get to Sixty-first Street and head to the other end of the station, but never made it. The sequence that followed is jumbled in my mind, even now.

Art's voice crackled over the two-way radio. "Mick," he hissed cautiously. Then louder, more urgently, "MICK!"

My brother jerked the car to a stop and sprung out, the door hanging open. My window was closed but the sound of the gunshot was clear as it punched its way up from down on the old platform. It cut through everything and snapped my head in its direction.

My brother sprinted around the front of the car and headed for the subway turnstile at a run. His gun was out and he was calling into his radio: "Art? Art?" As if contact would put things right again. But he was wrong.

I sat for a moment, watching things unfold with a bewildering rapidity. I popped open the car door, unsure of what to do next. The engine was still running and the keys glinted in the darkness, dancing with vibration. The radio mounted on the dash chattered. I got out of the car and headed toward my brother. Micky hit the entranceway and, from down in the trench, a muffled string of concussions thudded into the night.

Things were bad. They were about to get worse.

The turnstile entrance was dark and the metal moaned as I moved through it. The brief corridor smelled of damp concrete and urine, and I hurried onto the stairs leading down to the old station.

A hundred yards to my left toward Eighth Avenue the platform was brightly lit. But here, it was dim. I took the stairs as fast as I could, but it was awkward in the Japanese clothes. The steps were slick with dead leaves and old newspapers and the thick wet stuff that subway floors secrete like mucus.

I don't know what I expected. Movement, I suppose. Some kind of action. But it was still down there, and it scared me. There was just enough light to ruin whatever night vision I had, but I could sense faint forms huddled at the bottom of the landing.

I could also smell the residual scent of gunfire in the air. And the damp. And something else that I couldn't identify yet. You could hear the faint hum of the traffic in the distance, the pulse that never really stops in Brooklyn. The high whine of tires on the expressway floated above. Then I picked up the odd *zzzing* noise carrying through the metal rails on the subway tracks that told you a train was approaching. But there was something else as well, another noise I couldn't immediately identify.

As I got closer, cutting through the background noise, small, liquid gasps floated up into the night air from below me on the landing.

A Manhattan-bound train pulled in at the Eighth Avenue stop, three hundred feet to the east. Its light washed the scene. Asa crouched in a corner, gripping the handle of his sword like a talisman. His face was an angry mask, rigid with the intensity of emotion. He tried to say something as I slid down the stairs, but the noise of the approaching train swallowed it.

The light intensified as the subway train got closer. The roar of its approach grew in volume as I reached the last step. The train shot by, a fierce explosion of light and speed and noise. Then I knew what I smelled.

In the strobelike flutter of the light from the train cars, Micky knelt in a black pool of blood that washed across the platform. In his arms, Art lay stretched out. It was dark, but I could see the stump of a wrist where blood pulsed out onto the concrete. His shirt was dark and slick from the gash across his torso. He was sliding deep down into shock and gazing up frantically as if trying to pierce the night sky for a last glimpse of the world. His face was straining in the effort, a response to some inner prompting we could only guess at. Art gulped spasmodically at the air, his lips working in frantic haste.

The noise of the train passed and I could hear Micky screaming at me "Put some pressure on it, Godammit!" and jerking his chin at the gushing arm. Then into his radio: "Officer down! Officer down!" In the rapid pattern of dark and light thrown by the train, he looked wild, caught up in a mix of rage and frustration and despair.

Ronin was nowhere to be seen. In the distance, a siren whooped, its frantic call a faint offer of hope.

I knelt across from my brother and pressed down hard on Art's arm as if sheer diligence could set things right. "Hang on, buddy," Micky was telling him. "Hang on." Micky was rocking back and forth, cradling Art's head in one hand, working the radio with the other. The force in his utterance was like something palpable: a rope to bind Art to us, a light in the dim, wet valley we huddled in. A prayer against the night.

The sirens got closer. I could hear shouts. People were

moving cautiously down toward us from the lighted platform.

Art seemed to seize up; his back arched and he made a
glottal, choking sound. Micky dropped the radio and held
him tight. Art's face calmed a bit as if reassured. It was
hard to tell at that point if he was even aware of us. I felt
like something essential had just been wrenched from me,
deep down in my guts. I looked about in that dark place,
searching for help. It seemed to take a long time to come. I
turned back to face my brother.

Even in the washed-out light of that place, the tears in
Micky's eyes glittered like the last sparks of a dying star.

Night Noise

When Art married Marie, he converted to Catholicism, so amid the tubes and beeping machines of the ICU, there were the whispered implications of the Last Rites. The priest was youngish, with that well-fed and sincere look priests get before the hard life they choose drives them to furtive sins and quiet resignation. For now, he sat uncomfortably with us in the waiting room, pink-faced and round, ready to speak, eager to comfort. But he took a look at Micky and the other cops who had come to be with the family. They were hard-faced men. The priest wisely squashed his impulse to tell us all the Good News. No one was in the mood for it.

Marie sniffed once or twice but held it together. Dee sat with her. Art's daughter, red-eyed and washed out, stared at a world that had been blown apart and revealed as the uncertain place it really was. It was a hard thing to learn. At any age.

They couldn't say whether Art would make it. We waited around the hospital, not saying much. It was a busy place, and each group keeping vigil thought they were somehow special, but we were all the same. For every red-eyed cluster, the universe had contracted into a tight knot of people hesitant to come to grips with the grim possibilities before them. It had been a long night, but it seemed like there were better things to do than just wait. The cops arranged shifts: some stayed; some went back out on the streets. After a while, I emerged into the bright sunlight, blinking with the suddenness of the glare and the harsh, relentless way of the world.

The ride home was a leaden progression through different mental landscapes. The growing summer heat beat in through the windshield, fighting with the air conditioner for dominance. It added to the general feeling of impending disaster. For distraction, I watched the scenery rush by, but it didn't work. My eyes were open, but I was really just seeing the aftermath of that night.

There is nothing so frantic as the scene where a policeman has been taken down. A transit cop at the Eighth Avenue station had heard the shots and called for backup—the radios Micky and Art were using were encrypted stakeout sets that couldn't reach the police communication network. A cruiser from the local precinct was the first on the scene, both cops nervously waving guns and lights around until they were sure who all the players were. By that time, Asa had joined us by Art's side, which was a good thing; if he'd still been crouched in the corner with a sword, the cops would have drilled him for sure.

The ambulance got there at about the same time. Two beefy guys in tightly tailored uniform shirts snapped on latex gloves and got to work. They surveyed the scene and knelt down across from Micky.

"Shit," one breathed. He was looking at the mess of Art's chest and his stump, trying to figure out what to do first. You could see the judgment register in his eyes like a shutter flickering, but his hands never stopped moving. "Shock suit," he told his partner.

Micky's voice was flat and far away. "He's already bled out."

The EMT nodded in acknowledgment. "Maybe. Maybe not. We gotta try, man," he said gently. "Hey," he shouted to one of the cops, "put that piece away and find the hand.

Then bag it in ice." The cops holstered their guns sheepishly and did what he said. "Make yoself useful fo' a change," the EMT mumbled under his breath.

Then he began with the arsenal at his disposal. Tubes. Shock suit. Blood expanders. They trundled Art out of that trench and away with grim, firm moves, a ritual of succor performed in equal parts for victim and witnesses. The ambulance whooped away into the night.

Then Asa and I got hustled off the platform and back up to street level. The area was thick with cars. Red bubble lights were strobing around the site. Radios crackled and sputtered and cops rushed back and forth, frantic to impose some sense and order on the jumble of witnesses and blood and darkness.

We went to the Sixty-eighth Precinct. No one there was happy to see us. A cop walked us into the main foyer, they buzzed us through a door, and the patrolman silently put Asa's sword on a desk. It was wrapped in brown paper and tagged. Then Asa and I were split up and the desk sergeant told someone to put us in interrogation rooms. They let me change into regular clothes. There were dark smudges on the *hakama*. I'd been kneeling in blood and was glad to get the smell of it away from me. I'd seen enough of the stuff.

Micky arrived in a separate car. He was covered in dried blood too, and the desk staff fussed about him, repeating all the blood-borne pathogen stuff that the age of AIDS has made a daily reality for cops. I heard his voice in the hall asking where Asa was. The door to my room opened and he stuck his head in. His face was closed and hard. His only comment to me was "What a cluster fuck." Then he was gone. He must have ID'd us to the people at the precinct; things got a little less tense. But a cop was down, and the fluorescent lights did little to dispel the dinginess of the station or the somber tone of the interrogation.

Asa was still gray faced and silent when they led him away. After I had my statement taken, a series of different detectives came in and asked me the same series of questions all over again. They had a real knack for making you feel like you were lying, even when you were telling the truth. You know why they do it, of course, but it doesn't make things any easier.

It was after two A.M. before I saw Asa again. He looked old and remote. His face was a wall; only the eyes moved behind it. The *sensei* sat in a chair with his hands cupped in his lap, palms up. It's the *mudra* hand gesture used for meditation in swordsmanship. But his mind was still on the platform, not in the *dojo*.

I sat next to him and watched the ebb and flow of a station house at night. I didn't look at Asa—among the Japanese, you don't look directly at higher ranks in tense situations—although when he spoke his voice was so low that I had to resist the urge to look at him so I could read his lips.

"He was waiting there," the *sensei* murmured, as if picking up the thread of a conversation already underway. "In the dark. The note I received said he would be." He took a long breath in. "I was not sure it would be so.

"It was a narrow space." His right hand stirred faintly in his lap, as if coming alive with the retelling. "Dark. Dirty. I said it was not a place . . . of honor."

What did he say, I wanted to ask. But I was afraid the sound of my voice would shatter the spell. Asa's eyes weren't focused on the room, but looked back into the trench.

"He told me it was regrettable but could not be avoided." A pause while the wheel of memory turned for Asa.

"I told him I was there to accept his challenge. He seemed surprised. But he understood courtesy, that one. We bowed. It was a narrow place . . ." he said again, as if stuck on that detail.

"I circled away from the stairs toward the wall. It was dark, but I could feel him watching me. By the wall, I could look out and the light around him made him a better target." He smiled tightly. "*Heiho.* We drew our swords. His *nukitsuke* was strong, Professor." It was the only indication

I had that Asa was even aware of my presence. For him to classify Ronin's sword drawing as strong told me volumes.

"Then the policeman came. The big one. I do not believe he even saw me in the shadows. He came down the stairs so fast, he had little time. Just some words in the radio." He took a breath to continue, then paused as if editing his thoughts. "The stairs were slippery. The platform too. I called out a warning to the policeman . . .

"The . . . man . . . he turned on the policeman. The gun went off." Asa paused as if the memory of the shot punctuated his narrative. "I saw the rage in his eyes by the light from the gun's flash. It was like the heat of a furnace, his anger." He paused. "The old warriors must have known this feeling: 'relentless as fire.'" It was a reference to an ancient *samurai* battle slogan.

Asa sat forward with the tension, then subsided. "He struck *kote*," the old man said simply. The wrist cut is one of the most common used in kendo. "He cut at the right hand. In the dark, it looked as if the policeman had a gun in it." But Art was left handed.

Asa continued. "The first shot came as the blade sliced down." I could imagine the flash of gunfire and the glitter of the blade's arc. "It froze the *ronin* for a moment." And that fractional pause was probably why Art was clinging to life.

"But he recovered. He was quick, that one." He stopped again, caught in the vividness of his memory. "I began to move, but he had already crossed to the other side. I could not get a clear strike . . . It was *irimi*," he said flatly. An entering technique that brings you to your attacker's side for a counter. "He moved in," Asa spat.

"I am not sure what technique he used then," he said apologetically, as if identifying the simple mechanics could change the ultimate outcome of that night.

"But he took the pistol away from the big one. Close in." Asa seemed to bring himself back into the room with an effort. "The rest you know."

We sat in the white noise of the station, in the time before dawn when the unconscious mind works hardest, and listened again to the memory sound of the shots, a string of muffled blasts that Ronin squeezed off, the pistol muzzle searching for Art's side like an open mouth.

I nodded. The rest I knew.

Later that day, after the vigil at the ICU, I drove out to Micky's. I had spoken to my brother in private only briefly since the night Art was wounded. He was monosyllabic and distant, on administrative leave until Internal Affairs had investigated the incident.

Even as night approached, the sun hammered down on the Island, not letting up. Micky's kids were in the pool, paddling around and playing with face masks and little plastic boats. They were subdued, but the cooling effect of the water had begun to revive them a bit. Dee was out there, a faint sheen of perspiration on her flushed face, trying to keep them quiet.

I came through the fence and around the house to the pool side.

"Hey, Dee," I said. She smiled wanly at me and the kids waved. We watched them splash around for a bit. "Mick around?"

She looked at me. Dee looked beat too, but sunburn made her high cheekbones stand out with a type of false vitality. "Sort of," she said. "He's in the family room." She picked up a glass and sucked at a straw and watched me walk up to the sliding doors.

The room was dark. I put my face up to the screen and peered in. I glimpsed a suggestion of motion and heard the faint clink of ice cubes. The thunk of a glass being set down on a wooden table.

"What?" His voice was raspy.

I slid the screen over and stepped inside. Micky was holed up in the gloom like an animal in a cave. I pulled a chair over and sat down without saying anything. He got up and fumbled in the dark, set a glass down on the table in front of me, palmed some ice cubes in, and poured me a drink. In the dark it was hard to tell, but as I lifted the glass up I could smell the Irish whiskey.

He settled back in the chair like an old man and tipped his glass at me in a toast.

I swirled the glass around, making the cubes clink. I took a sip and watched him. "You been in here long?" I asked.

"A while." I listened to him carefully. You can only drink so much of this stuff before it hits you. But Micky was doing a good job getting his tongue around the words. He was stone-cold sober.

"Got a plan?" I asked.

He reached over and turned on a light. My brother's eyes are a bluish gray and they seem to lighten or darken depending on the mood and his surroundings. At that moment, they were dark, like pieces of rock.

"Course I do," Micky said. "I'm gonna squeeze your man Yamashita until he pops."

"What!"

Micky took a hit of his drink. You could hear him inhale as he brought the glass to his lips. He squinted at me as the whiskey went down. "I told you there was something goin' on with those Japs."

He says things like that just to get a rise out of me.

"You got anything that proves it?" I demanded. "I mean, other than some hunch?"

"My hunches pay off, buddy boy."

"Hey, Mick. Just because you're comin' up empty doesn't mean that Yamashita or any of the other *sensei* are involved."

"Oh no?"

"No," I said.

"Well you tell me how this fits together." He sloshed, some more whiskey into the glass. The lamp glowed through the green of the Jameson's bottle, like luminescence from the bed of the ocean. "You got a major homicide here. One in LA and another in Phoenix. Same martial arts MO. Cryptic messages on the walls at the crime scenes. In Japanese. Also martial arts related. Then, last night, who gets a meet set up with the guy? Your teacher." He glared at me.

"Whattaya mean? It was Asa who got the note."

Micky gave me a hostile smirk. "You dope. Your teacher was scheduled to do the demo. The note was for him. Asa picked it up by mistake."

I thought for a minute. "OK, when you string things together like that, it sounds plausible," I admitted. "But, look, we know that whoever's doing this has some sort of martial arts fixation. I mean, the whole 'Ronin' thing . . . the theft of the *bokken*. Don't you think it's possible that Yamashita got singled out just because he's a prominent martial arts *sensei*?"

"You still working that celebrity stalker angle, Connor? It's thin."

"No thinner than you trying to pin Yamashita for something he's not involved in."

Micky looked hard at me. "You sure of that, Connor?"

I thought of Yamashita. His silences and the sense you had of trying to pierce through a shield any time you looked at him. His unpredictable nature. The ways in which he made you feel both awe and fear, often simultaneously. I nodded.

"I'd know, Mick. He wouldn't hide something like this from me. It's too important."

"Everyone lies, Connor. Even your teacher."

"You don't know him."

"Buddy boy," my brother said, taking another drink, "don't be fooled. You think he's so special . . ." The contempt in his voice was palpable.

"Fuck you, Mick."

"Fuck you, Connor." The height of brotherly debate.

I waited. All I got was sullen silence. The cubes rattled as he drank. "Ahh, I don't see how this is gonna help with anything," I finally prompted. "You got anything else?"

"Not yet."

"Any new leads?"

"Hey! I'm working on it," he snapped.

"You're not working on anything but a hangover."

Micky made no response.

"You gonna let this guy walk? After what he did to Art?" I demanded.

"No one's gettin' away," my brother said. He sounded like doom.

"Then what?" I persisted.

He waved his glass vaguely. "I got some things to work on." Then Micky seemed to deflate a bit in the chair and he mumbled something at me.

"What!" I demanded.

Micky leaned forward and said something, but it was low and to himself.

"No," I insisted. "What'd you say?"

"Nothing," my brother protested.

I don't know what I was madder at, the whole situation, Micky's accusation of Yamashita, the fact I had to defend him, or the nagging doubt I felt. Something gave inside me. I stood up, reached down, and grabbed him by his lapels.

"Tell me what you said, you dumb fuck!"

I must have touched something raw and hurtful way down inside him. He jerked to his feet. I heard the bottle go over. I wasn't expecting the sudden move and fell backward, tripping over a piece of furniture in the dim room. I sat sprawled on the floor as he stood swaying over me, furious.

"Don't push it, Connor! You and all that martial arts bullshit. I shoulda had myself more together, but I was too busy payin' attention to you."

"Whadaya mean?"

"You asshole! I never shoulda let you come along last night."

"Wha . . ."

"Don't you get it?" he yelled. "We had vests in the trunk! We had vests in the trunk and I forget to make Art put his on!"

I thought for a minute that he was going to attack me. Then he retreated back into himself, collapsing into the chair. I looked at him in the silence and slowly got to my feet.

Micky had the hard-edged fatalism of a cop. He knew, more often than not, that the worst thing that can happen usually does. You hear about the guilt of survivors. Old soldiers and anyone who works on the sharp end of things know about it. The feeling that you could have, should have done more, or something else, to stave off the disaster. It doesn't matter whether someone is just wounded or blown away. Whatever the event, you still get the intimate revelation of your own mortality, the electric brush with death's close passage. The secret joy that it wasn't you whose number was up. All those feelings get mixed into an acid stew that can eat away at you, drop by drop, over days, or years, or a lifetime.

In a sense, it's not rational. In another sense, it's totally understandable. At least that's what I told myself. People crave certainty. And control. We spend our lives erecting coping mechanisms, little games we play to preserve the illusion of safety. The plain fact of the matter is that bad things happen. And when they do, all our efforts at staving them off are revealed as inadequate, delusional. The innocent finger-crossing of a child in the face of the killer's bludgeon.

I took a deep breath and tried again. "That's crap and you know it. It's not my fault. And it's not your fault either, Mick." He didn't respond. "We didn't do anything wrong. Ronin did."

My brother just grunted.

I tried another tack. "You know Art doesn't blame you."

Micky just sat there and I went on. "Do you think if your positions were reversed that Art would do what you're doing? Blaming yourself? Feeling sorry for yourself? A guy like that?"

Micky leaned toward me, his face ghosting into the shadow thrown by the lamp. "Don't you tell me what kind of guy he is. I know."

"Yeah. Even last night . . ." In my mind's eye I saw Art gasping in the dark as the EMTs worked on him. "He was trying to tell us something."

My brother took a deep breath and looked at me like he was both surprised and disappointed. "Connor, Art just had some fuckin' nut job try to empty the whole clip of a 9-mm into him. You think he was together enough to send a message home?" Micky gave a harsh snort. "He was making noises, but they were just sound. Art's brain was already shutting down, Connor. His body just hadn't caught on."

I didn't believe it, mostly because I couldn't face it. I still held out hope. So did the surgeons; every day Art hung on was a good sign. Micky and I sat for a while longer, looking out into the yard where the night grew stronger with each passing minute. The kids' voices drifted in, muted sounds from another world. It was probably what Lazarus heard. My brother sat there like a stone, deaf to the call.

I finished the whiskey and set the glass down next to him. As I got to the screen, I turned.

"It doesn't matter, Mick," I said. I got nothing from him in response. "It doesn't," I prodded. Through the screen, I could see Dee toweling the kids off as they came out of the pool. The image was softened by the filtering of the screen door and the arrival of full darkness. The sheer normalcy of the scene pulled at me, but I looked back into the room one last time.

"We're going to have to get him, Mick. It's personal now." I said it softly hoping for a reply. Ice cubes tinkled softly. I went outside, closed the sliding screen door, and walked away.

I went home and sat alone in my apartment.

It was hot. The windows at both ends of the railroad-flat-style houses that lined the block were wide open, worshipers praying for a breeze, waiting for a blessing. I sat down on the floor in the position known as *seiza*, which is used for meditation in the *dojo*. I waited as well.

The masters advocate letting all conscious thoughts bubble off in trying to attain what they call "no-mind" as a way to deal with the challenge of life. My thoughts churned, but they didn't bubble off. I waited for calm. For insight. For a plan.

What I got were mental images of the platform. Of Art. Of Asa. Of my brother drinking in the dark.

The apartment is the place where I sleep and write. I looked about it in a harsh, introspective state of mind. I had a corner where I do work on the computer. It was lined with books and papers. They were like bricks in a wall. It seemed to me that I used them for a variety of reasons.

I studied history. Did I do it because the past was safe? A place you could observe without responsibility? You could argue about its interpretation, sure. But you never had to really act to shape the outcome.

And what about Yamashita and his art? It was archaic, a step removed from things. I trained day after day in the choreography of a lost age, the urgent moves of battles lost or won a long time ago. I was a fighter who never fought, the disciple of a teacher who hid as much as he revealed.

And now I was confronted, it seemed simultaneously, with all the things I had worked so hard to elude. Questions of trust. Of responsibility. Of life and death.

And I could sit there, pretending to meditate. But deep down I knew one thing with a subtle, yet sickening, certainty: I was afraid.

From off the sea, a breeze stirred and moved the curtains. Out in the Narrows a ship's horn sounded like the distant moan of a lost soul.

I went to bed. The only insight I was left with was the one I had given Micky earlier: it was personal now.

THIRTEEN

Oracle Bones

Shamans chant in the dark to summon the dead. People have peered into the depths of caves for thousands of years, hoping the voice that sounded from the blackness could tell the future. It usually ends badly: what we want to hear most is almost always something we will regret learning.

It had rained in the night. When I went for my jog by the Narrows that ran between Staten Island and Brooklyn, the morning sun made the blacktop of the pathway steam. The air was warm and thick with a rich mixture of dust and exhaust, saltwater, grass. The day was heating up and the moist air was thickening with particulate matter. It made the distant hulk of Staten Island look dreamy and indistinct. I pounded my way along, trying to think of nothing. Instead I thought of everything.

I was none the wiser for the experience.

There was a knock on the door. Dee stood there with her husband.

"Is he sober, Dee?" I asked. She laughed and gestured at him.

My brother looked miserable. He squinted at me. "What kind of fucking question is that?" Micky said.

"A good one. Are you?"

"Well," he admitted, "I'm a little under the weather."

"Under the weather? That's one way of putting it. Dad always used to say he had 'the malaria.'"

"I may have that too," my brother admitted.

"Ignore him," Dee said. "He's just being a baby."

After considerable back and forth, they trundled a box up the stairs into the apartment. It contained Micky's copies of the Ronin case files. Technically, he wasn't supposed to have them. It was against departmental regulations. But like most cops Micky figured that the ends justified the means.

Finally, Micky sat huffing in a chair. Dee put a six-pack of Coke directly in front of him. Micky pulled a can off and held the cold aluminum to his forehead for a minute. Then he popped the tab. "We need to look at all this stuff, Connor. Think about some things." He said it like there was some significance there for me, but I didn't get it.

Dee helped me uncrate the files. Micky sat in a chair, sipping the Coke. He was green.

"OK," he began, taking a deep, exploratory breath, "here's what we've got. Asa's statement confirms that this guy is middle-aged and Asian."

"D'you talk with him again?"

"Not yet. I'm on leave, remember?" He seemed like he wanted to say more about it, but went off on a different tangent. "We don't know what would have happened the other night, but the MO seems the same. I gotta assume this guy is our killer."

"OK." I nodded.

"DNA samples from the other crimes match up."

"You never got any fingerprints that you could check from Samurai House, did you?" I asked.

He sat back again with his eyes closed. "No." It seemed like the word took a lot of effort.

"What about . . ." I hesitated, ". . . the gun." I meant Art's gun, but I couldn't bring myself to say it.

Micky opened his eyes and looked at me. "We got partials. They're still running 'em down. Right now, we got zip. And if we gotta go through Interpol, I wouldn't hold my breath."

Remembering Art made me think of his advice: when you hit a wall, you go in a different direction.

I sat down across from my brother. "What was it Art said trips most killers up, Mick? Pattern?"

He nodded. "Yeah. And predictability."

"So what do we have here?" I said it gently, because he was wincing at the sound of my voice. "What's the pattern?"

He made a concerted effort to pull himself together. The copies of the file were spread out on the coffee table like the scattered bones of a carcass. Micky started to gingerly push the papers around. Dee silently offered him a fresh Coke. Out of his vision, she put a hand to her lips and warned me into silence.

My brother moved slowly at first. He began pulling things out and making groupings, pausing to sip at his drink frequently. Gradually, the tempo built up. Papers got arranged, spun around, compared. His watery, bloodshot eyes moved from spot to spot. He sat back and covered his face with his hands, moving it around like the skin was made of rubber.

Micky gestured at the reports. "It's always the same. He's into this martial arts shit. You look at the list, and all the victims are connected by the arts. And killed by them."

"The pattern holds with Asa," I commented. "The other victims were somehow ambushed or lured into some sort of duel. And," I said significantly, "as far as we can tell, the victims had no connection to the killer."

"That we know," my brother objected.

"And neither does Yamashita," I finished pointedly.

My brother made a face. "Bullshit. You gotta start thinking clearly about this, buddy . . ."

"OK, OK," Dee said to calm us. "At least we agree that the link is Japan." We both looked at her. "I mean, it's obvious. Most of the guys he killed or tried to kill were Japanese."

"Reilly's the exception," I said.

"Reilly's also unusual in that there was a theft associated with that homicide," Micky added grudgingly. I could tell that he wasn't letting go of the whole topic of Yamashita.

"Well, they're all into the Japanese martial arts," Dee continued. "And this guy is . . . I dunno, tracking them down. Looking for something."

"And the trail leads here," Micky said quietly. "The messages at the crime scenes tell us that. There's gotta be a connection between the victims. And Ronin's lookin' for his next one here. So there's something we don't see. Something right under our noses."

"Come on," I said, knowing where he was headed, "not that angle again."

"The shoe fits, wear it," he said with rising conviction. "You may not want to hear it, but there's something your pals the *sensei* are not tellin' us."

I took a deep breath and tried to stay calm. I remembered last night's debate: we hadn't gotten very far. "OK, lay it out for me again, Mick."

He shrugged. "Seems obvious. Ronin's after somebody in New York. Someone linked to the victims in LA and Phoenix. So let's think about it." His voice was getting stronger and harder as the words began to match the quickening cadence of his thoughts.

"All the victims are martial artists," Dee offered. She was looking at a *National Geographic*.

"Good chance whomever he's hunting now will be one too." My brother eyed me.

"OK." I nodded. "What other links do we have?"

"Both Ikagi and Kubata were at the top of their game," he answered. "They were so good they were involved with the emperor."

"They were pretty well known. In the public eye," I commented. "You could see how they'd be chosen."

"True," he admitted ruefully. "But look at it from a

slightly different angle. Let's assume we got a Japanese national, traveling alone, looking for somebody. He's stopping off at various cities. With the first two victims, we don't see much time wasted in terms of the homicides. Ronin kills Ikagi in LA and within a few days he shows up in Phoenix and snuffs Kubata. Then he breaks into the Samurai House, grabs some junky sword, and whacks Reilly. But he hangs around. Why?"

I thought it through. "Because Reilly was not who he was after."

"Maybe Reilly was part of the message," Dee said quietly. "Or maybe he just got in the way. I mean, why steal the sword?"

"It pissed off the local *sensei* pretty well," Micky said. "Maybe that was the whole point." He sat back again and sipped at his Coke, his eyes far away. "Think about it like a hunter. You know, like in India when they hunt tigers. They're not sure where the tiger is, so they send those guys out into the bush to make a racket . . ." He looked at me for help.

"Beaters," I said.

"Right. They do something to flush the tiger outta the grass."

"Are you telling me that the whole thing with Reilly was done just to get a reaction out of somebody? Come on," I said.

"Yeah, I do," he said with grim conviction. "The theft wouldn't have made any kind of splash—some junky old wooden sword. But you link it with a killing and the papers are all over it." The expression on Micky's face was dead certain.

"I don't think Reilly's murder was an accident," he continued. "It was designed for effect. Just like with the first two. These killings weren't accidents. And the next time, the attempt in the subway, that was no fluke either . . ." He looked up at me. "Except his message got crossed and he ended up with the wrong *sensei*."

"There are alternative explanations," I offered. "There have to be."

"Bullshit," Micky growled.

"I can't believe Yamashita has anything to do with this," I protested.

"Bull. Shit." I could see my brother starting to fume. Only his hangover was delaying the explosion.

Dee snorted in amusement at the two of us. "Look, how long will you two go around and around like this?" We shrugged.

"Connor, I know you don't like to hear it, but think it through," Dee said. I opened my mouth to speak, but she smiled and went right on. "No, no, no. It's my turn. Let's go with your idea that your teacher isn't involved."

I nodded in eager agreement.

"OK," she said, "but we agree that the murderer is looking for someone, right? At the first murder scene in LA, were there signs of a search? Same in Phoenix?"

Micky looked through the reports. "Yeah," he grumbled.

"OK." Dee nodded. "The killer's looking for someone. He doesn't know where he is. The first two victims weren't random. They somehow gave Ronin clues. They lead him to New York. But he doesn't know where, exactly. And so maybe he comes here to find out. And tries to do it through this guy . . ."

"Reilly," I answered.

"Sure," she said. "He was a pretty big martial arts name?" I nodded. "You'd expect him to know things? Know people?" I nodded again. "So there you are: this guy that the killer is looking for is like the other victims. A martial artist. He's really good but really hard to find. The killer wanted Reilly to tell him."

I started to get an uncomfortable feeling, a vague tingling. Dee seemed unaware of the effect of her words on me. She flashed the *National Geographic* at me. "There's an article here about the Imperial Palace in Tokyo. There's some link between the two Japanese men who were killed and the Japanese emperor, right?" I nodded.

Dee was still looking at the magazine. "Did you see this picture?"

It was a shot of the Imperial Guards training in kendo. They're pretty distinctive because they train in uniforms that are snow white. I said so.

"So," she concluded. "Work this angle. I mean, come on"—she looked at me, eyes and mouth wide open in mock stupidity—"who do you know among the Japanese martial artists in New York who's good? And hard to find." She waved the picture at me. "And dresses like these guys?"

I stayed quiet because I didn't want to have to supply the name.

My brother rubbed his temples with his fingers and watched me. He poked at the paper on the table in front of him. Schedel's notes were there. "First, the Mirror Man in LA," he murmured.

"Huh?" Dee asked.

"The first victim, Ikagi. His pen name for calligraphy was 'Mirror Polisher,'" I said wearily.

"Then the Jewel Guy in Phoenix," Micky added, with a bit more energy.

"His nickname was the Jewel of the Budokan," I told Dee without prompting.

"So who's next?" Micky asked. "Mirror, Jewel . . ." He let the question hang in the air.

And, after a time, the answer struck me. Hard. "Sword," I said.

He looked up at me with a hard light growing in his bleary eyes. "That mean something, Connor?"

"It's the imperial connection," I admitted slowly, with growing dismay. I was still fighting it hard. "The imperial regalia were three items given to the first emperor by the gods: a mirror, a jewel, and a sword."

"There's the pattern," Micky breathed. "Both victims outside New York were connected to the Japanese emperor. So . . . first the mirror, then the jewel, then the sword."

"Reilly's got no connection like that," I pointed out.

"Forget Reilly," Micky said. "He's window dressing."

Dee made a face. She pointed at me. "No. Think about him. Why's he important? What's he guarding? What gets stolen? What gets all the local Japanese all hot and bothered?"

"The sword," I sighed. But I brightened a bit. "Asa's a pretty well-known kendo master." I looked at Dee. "It's the way of the sword. Maybe Ronin was after him."

"Let it go, buddy boy." Micky shook his head slowly from side to side. "We know that Ronin was not expecting Asa to show up down in the subway. He was looking for someone else."

"Who was he expecting? Who fits?" Dee asked simply.

"The intended victim should have some connection with the pattern," I said. I was on my feet and walking restlessly around. Dee and Micky remained quiet and simply watched me as I added up the pieces of the puzzle. I tried not to, but there was no avoiding it.

"Yamashita," I breathed finally, as I slumped into a chair. "He signs his calligraphy *kenjin*. Sword Man."

I felt like I had been struck. But part of me still struggled against the realization. I looked from Micky to Dee and back again. "There's got to be some other explanation," I began.

Micky began to intone the word "bullshit," but Dee shushed him.

"He wouldn't keep something like this from me. . . . He knew I was working with the police. . . ." I started out gamely but quickly ran out of things to say.

"Maybe, Connor." My brother sounded sad, as if he were giving someone bad news. Which, in a way, he was. "But maybe not."

Micky looked down and shuffled some papers around in a rare moment of delicacy. A photocopy of a handwritten note in Japanese caught my eye. An English translation was penciled in between the lines.

"What's that?" I said quickly.

"The note that Ronin left for Yamashita at Samurai

House. It says, 'Please meet me' and gives directions." My brother handed it to me.

I took a deep breath and asked, "Where'd the translation come from, Mick?" I didn't want to hear the answer.

"Yamashita. Why?" Micky asked very gently. His manner had the soft quietness of a hunter.

"The translation is . . . wrong," I sputtered. "It says, 'I look forward to meeting you again.' And it's signed with a name. Tomita."

Micky silently mouthed the name and wrote it down. I stood there with the paper clutched in my hand and felt the heat rise in my face. "I can't believe it," I finally said. "He knew . . . all along . . ."

My brother and his wife sat and said nothing. After that, I didn't either. We all knew where this was heading.

Yamashita's *dojo* was quiet, its entrance as flat and unwelcoming as a hostile face. Micky was right next to me. He still wasn't firing on all cylinders, but you could almost feel the anticipation boiling up in him. I pushed the buzzer but got no answer. There had been no activities planned at the school since the attack on Art. But as a senior student I have a key, so I let us in. It's not unusual. Yamashita encourages us to train relentlessly. Class doesn't need to be in session.

Anger clouds perception. I wasn't focusing on the dim, empty space of the training floor as I entered. I never even sensed the presence behind the door until the snout of a pistol was shoved in my face. The guy holding it took a good look at us and relaxed. I wish I could say the same.

My brother had gone very still. Micky's eyes were narrowed down into slits and he looked at the man with the gun like he was imprinting him on his memory for later. Because I could tell that there would be a later.

The man was a street thug, a gang member of some sort. He had the look written all over him. A young, Asian face, with flat brown eyes. His hair was cut short on the side and spiked on top, with blond highlights. His gun was nicely chromed, completing the with-it, happening look.

He had relaxed slightly, but he never took his eyes off us. And the gun didn't waver.

"Visitor!" he called upstairs.

Two men appeared at the landing above the training space.

"Please, Mori-san," I heard Yamashita say, then his voice dropped to a whisper and I lost it.

Another voice called out an order. The gun came down. We went up.

I had generated a real head of steam on my way down to the *dojo*. But the experience of having a gun shoved in my face knocked me off balance mentally. At any other time, I knew if I mentioned this to my teacher, he would nod and reply that emotion does this sort of thing. But I wasn't in the mood for any of his mystical advice. I wanted answers to something much more pressing.

Even someone not as skilled as my teacher would have sensed the tension roiling off the Burke brothers. But part of me was surprised at Micky's emotional control. At least one of us was calm.

Yamashita could see it all in my face: the anger, the hurt. I had labored long with him to perfect the stolid projection of *heiho*, but I felt all that skill slipping away, melted down by emotion. He saw that reality in my face, but Yamashita said nothing. His face was flat and closed in on itself.

"My apologies, Mr. Burke," the Japanese man called Mori said, "my assistant meant no disrespect."

He was an older man, probably in his early sixties, but he had the thick, solid look of someone who was still formidable. He was impeccably dressed: dark blue suit, white shirt, and gleaming black shoes. His crimson tie was a slash of deep red. It reminded me of the color of blood.

Micky pulled out his shield. "I don't know who you are, but you just made a big mistake." Then he bent down and pulled a small revolver out of an ankle holster. He gestured at Mori. "You call down and have him drop the piece. Then we'll talk."

Mori grimaced. "Please, Officer, I think there has been a misunderstanding."

My brother was watching everyone carefully, turned partially so the gun was shielded from sight from the man downstairs. "Oh, I think there's been a misunderstanding, all right . . ." Micky continued.

"Burke, please!" Yamashita hissed.

I ignored him for a second. Then I said, "That guy is a street thug," pointing downstairs. "He doesn't belong here."

"Indeed," my teacher said, in a tone that told me to take it no further. Mori had presented Micky with credentials that managed to pacify him. But barely. Yamashita watched my brother put his gun away. He saw me prepare to speak, and continued, "Please come in, Professor. Since you are both here . . ." He gestured back into the sitting area and glided in without a backward glance.

Old habits die hard. I obeyed and followed him in, pulled into the wake of sheer power that radiated from him. It has a subduing effect. But I fought it. Micky's presence helped. Once in the sitting room, Yamashita began the process of formally introducing me to his guest. Micky drifted to a wall and leaned against it, keeping an eye on everyone. And the stairwell.

I gave a half-bow to the man with the tie like blood, but I had no time for introductions. "Excuse me," I said to Mori, "I have business with Yamashita Sensei." Then I faced my teacher and could feel my lips tightening, curving down with emotion as I prepared to speak. He stood there, unblinking.

"Who is Tomita?" I demanded.

"The matter does not concern you," Yamashita said, his eyes narrowed.

I heard Micky snort. "The DA will have a different idea."

"Doesn't concern me!" I blurted out. I took a step toward him. Out of the corner of my eye, I saw Mori's body shift as if he were preparing to move. I got the sense of a matching shift from my brother. "Art was almost killed. My brother was down there too." I felt my stomach muscles clench with tension.

My teacher was unmoved. Mori spoke: "Mr. Burke, please . . ."

I ignored him and glared at Yamashita. Mori hissed in Japanese to Yamashita. It was half statement, half warning: "This is not for *gaijin*."

Mori probably didn't think I understood Japanese. The look I gave him told him otherwise.

Gaijin. The translation is innocuous enough: "foreigner." But it has ugly connotations in Japanese. Foreigners are barbarians. Inferior. Incapable of the subtlety of a true *nihonjin*, a Japanese. In that brief statement, Mori had crystallized the situation. However long I had labored with my teacher, I was still not accepted as a true disciple. Whatever the secret he harbored, I was still unworthy of learning it. *Gaijin* literally refers to an outsider, someone beyond the bounds of friends, family, and nation. I felt the bitter realization that all I had attempted to achieve with Yamashita was an illusion. The community I had believed I was forging in his *dojo* was an exercise in wishful thinking.

That night I performed at Samurai House, I had felt the undercurrent of these sentiments from the other masters there. But I had believed my *sensei* to be above that kind of narrow thinking. As the true situation hit me, I had a sensation of vertigo: a jet of alarm deep within the body's core, a swirl of disorientation.

Yamashita stood there, rooted to the ground. And said nothing. He was like a piece of granite on a rocky headland: waves pounded against him but with no visible effect. His students admired this in him. A day ago, I had, too. Now, I wanted to wring his neck. But even after all this, I couldn't.

I brought my face close to his. "You knew," I hissed. "You knew and you said nothing . . ." It was as close as I could come to an actual physical attack. The closeness, the emotion made my words like nothing I had ever done to him. It's odd, in a place devoted to combat, that there is normally so little emotional contact. Everything is sacrificed in the pursuit of *heiho*.

"Yamashita," Micky said quietly. He had stopped leaning against the wall. "I think you've got information related to these murders." His words came out clipped with anger. "You held out on us, and my partner's in a world of hurt. I'm gonna get a warrant. And I'm gonna bring you in. And when I do, you're gonna be in a world of hurt too."

"Sensei, please!" I said. "Whatever you know, you've got to tell us. I was down there. I saw what the killer did." But the novelty of the exchange didn't move him. Yamashita didn't even flinch. "My brother was down there!" I protested again. My teacher said nothing.

"You owe it to me," I finally said, and loaded the words with all the bitterness I felt. Even now, I still hoped for something, some reaction. An acknowledgment of his complicity. But my teacher stayed mute and I turned away. "My brother was down there," I repeated quietly, as much to myself as to my *sensei*.

I stormed down the stairs and through the *dojo*, heading toward the street. Micky slipped in behind me, but he gave the two men in the upper room a look that said he would be back. The thug looked up as we came down the stairs and our eyes met. His were like the oily surface of a murky well, briefly lit with the effort of target acquisition. My eyes were hot and scratchy and I felt a lump in my throat. But emotion had no place here. Yamashita had taught me that much. When the anger burned through, all that was left was a type of pride.

I set my eyes like flint and we left that place.

F
O
U
R
T
E
E
N

Connections

There's a spot on the Belt Parkway heading east toward Bay Eighth Street where the road curves and you get an expanse of grass right along the Verrazano Narrows. On any given weekend, hordes of kite flyers are there. The kites, ranging from simple to elaborate, are brightly colored, and they whip and twist in the ocean breeze like living things. Even on a weekday morning, there were a few retired guys, in baseball hats and clothes slowly growing baggy on them, clutching lines and watching the kites intensely. They looked as if they expected a revelation of some sort to buzz down the wire.

There were young mothers with strollers who paused, pointing out the spectacle to their children. The colors and motion, the bright blue of the day spoke of good times, leisure, and joy uncomplicated by anything but the vagary of the breeze.

In Tibet, kites were used as instruments of war. The thought came unbidden to me as I watched the scene. The realization made me suddenly aware of just what a mess everything was. It was a sudden jet of resentment. In the beginning of all this, I started to think that working with cops changes the way you see things. Now I wondered whether anything was ever as it appeared to be.

*   *   *

I had run flat out that morning, as hard as possible. As far as I could. It didn't help. In some ways, it showed just how confused I was: I ran in pursuit of the Way that Yamashita had opened to me. Now, even though I was turning my back on it, the discipline would not release its hold. The tether had been forged over years and years. No matter how I lunged and tried to break free, these connections still had mastery over me.

I stood, sweaty in the breeze, and watched the kites swoop in vain attempts at liberation, buffeted by winds not of their choosing.

The day was bright. I turned away from watching and sat on a park bench. I closed my eyes against the deep, warm push of sunlight. After running, even on a bad day, there is a type of calm. I know it's just endorphins at work, but it was welcome anyway.

It is, of course, at times when we are most relaxed that the more subtle powers come into play. The Japanese think that *ki* is the invisible energy that fills the world. The ability to connect with *ki* is latent in all of us. And it flowers when the accretion of our mental tensions dissipates. You can learn how to do it consciously—*ki* is what martial artists are supposed to harness. But sometimes, the ability springs to life in disturbing and unexpected ways. Like the insights we are left with on waking after a bad dream.

The breeze played against me on the bench. I could hear the distant rush of cars as they shot by on the parkway and odd fragments of voices from the kite flyers. I drowsed on the bench with my eyes closed and gradually felt a type of awareness wash over me.

I felt him there.

I know it sounds far-fetched, but I did.

It wasn't a mental thing. It had a far more visceral feel, almost like a low-level electric current was passing through the body. And, as it came, I acknowledged a certainty so deep that it failed to surprise me. My master was near.

I remained perfectly still in the sunshine, eyes closed,

and explored the experience. When I was ready, I opened my eyes.

He stood with his back to the water, against the metal railing that lined the pathway. The wind pushed at his clothes, but the fabric danced around his body like smoke against an immovable pillar. We looked at each other in silence. When he started to move toward me, I stood up.

"The awareness has come for you," Yamashita said. He had felt it, too. At any other time, I would have been pleased at the comment. But I was still too hurt.

"Not bad for a Round Eye," I said.

His face tightened with displeasure, but he gestured to the bench. "Please."

I eased myself back down. Yamashita sat stiffly, facing the choppy blue water of the Narrows as if bracing himself against an unseen force.

"I'm surprised they let you go," I told him.

He looked off at the water. "I made a statement. Mori-san enjoys . . . certain privileges . . . The district attorney seemed content. You must understand, Professor," he began. But I jumped in.

"Oh, I understand, all right. Micky was right. You've been holding out on us."

"It is not as simple as that."

"Oh, no," I agreed. "Probably complicated by having to deal with all these *gaijin*."

"Stop!" he grunted and made a short chopping motion with his hand. "You are guessing at things you know nothing about."

I stared right at him, sitting there and gazing off into the distance. He felt the look and his head swiveled slowly around to face me.

"I don't know about things because you haven't trusted me enough to tell me," I hissed. "Me! After all this time."

He blinked once and seemed on the verge of saying something, but movement came easier to him. Yamashita rose slowly and walked across the path to the railing by the water's edge. I followed, like a fighter pressing an advantage, exploiting a weakness. There was some sort of subtle projection going on here. Maybe it was *ki*. Maybe I was just fed up. But we both felt it, like a barometer shift.

Yamashita leaned his forearms on the railing and grasped his hands. "It is not your place to question my motives, Burke. Have I ever held back in teaching you?" He knew the answer and continued. "No. I have not. I have worked with you for years . . ."

"And I deserve your trust," I insisted. I wasn't going to let him wiggle out of this.

Yamashita straightened up and regarded me with those deep eyes. "I have trusted you with the most precious thing I have. The Way."

"Don't give me that," I said, waving my hand in dismissal. I watched his eyes briefly track the movement. "When I needed you the most, you held back. And I want to know why."

Yamashita got an odd expression on his face, as if he were seeing me for the first time. "This has changed you, Professor, *neh*?"

I shrugged. This was a favorite tactic of his, changing angles of attack. I wasn't going to be suckered in.

"There are some things we regret learning," he cautioned.

"I need to know," I said simply.

Yamashita began to walk slowly along the path, speaking softly. I had to come along to hear what he had to say.

"I remember when you first came to the *dojo*," he said. "You were so hungry for knowledge . . ." His mouth tightened in a small, wry smile.

We walked along, an old man and a younger one. Sharing memories in the sun.

I could think back to the years I had spent searching with him: searching for release from the pressures of graduate school, for solace when my dad died. For a sense of place. And belonging.

"Sometimes, our desire for something can work against us . . ." he said. I took a breath to answer and Yamashita held up a hand. "I am thinking of your early days, Professor. There is an occupational hazard of people who work with their minds too much. It creates an imbalance. It is revealed in motion, of course."

I remembered that he used to yell at me to stop moving my head, but I refused to say so.

"Yes," Yamashita replied as if reading my mind. "When everything you do involves your brain, you tend to involve your head in everything that you do. You would telegraph your movements through odd little jerks of the head. . . ."

"I stopped," I said, leery of a warm walk down memory lane. My tone conveyed the sentiment.

"Yes. You have approached a place where thought and emotion are more equally at balance. It is revealed in your technique."

I said nothing.

"Part of what you sought with me was that balance," the old man said. "It was what drew you to the art of the sword."

"I thought I was pursuing an honorable Way," I said. The words felt bitter in my mouth.

Yamashita stopped and peered at me. "And now you will reject the Way? And all your hard work? For what reason?"

I stood there with my fists balled on my hips. I leaned close to him. "You know the reason."

"I know what you think the reason is, Burke," he said calmly.

"Don't play with me!"

Now he really smiled and it made me even angrier. "Burke, it is interesting that a man so involved with the life of the mind should now let his emotions run so strongly." He cocked his head to look at me as he began to walk again. "But that too is part of what you sought, *neh*?"

It's a hard thing to explain to an outsider. Studying an art with a teacher like Yamashita was many things: a physical challenge, an act of will. And it was a process of creating links between yourself and others, of making connections between human beings that were so strong because they were forged in heat and discipline and hope and vulnerability.

As I stood there in the sunlight, I squinted to see Yamashita. The glare was intense, and he was hard to see with the sun at his back. I could still feel him with *haragei*, however. And the sense of connection I felt was only partially eclipsed by anger. And fear that we were being driven apart.

I swallowed. "I need to know why you held back."

Yamashita reached out and touched my arm. It was an unusual gesture. "The reasons are . . . not simple."

I snorted. "Things never are, with you."

"So . . ." he mused. "That does not mean that they are not true." He seemed to straighten a bit, as if shrugging off a weight with a sudden decision. "You are right, Burke. I will explain. But not here. You should come to the *dojo*," he concluded.

"Why?"

Yamashita began to walk away. "Because you are my student," he said.

My resentment was strong, but ultimately the connection between us proved stronger. I followed him back.

The training hall was once again empty of activity. The man with the gun was there. And so was his boss, Mori Masataka.

Our first meeting had been a brief and awkward one, so we went through the niceties the Japanese cling to in moments of discomfort. Mori bowed and proffered a *meishi*, a business card, to me. I bowed back to Mori and gave the card a quick glance. It was simple and elegant. The card stock was a fine cream and the lettering was gold. It contained his name and contact numbers, one side in English, the other in Japanese. And that was it.

Except for the chrysanthemum pattern of the Japanese Imperial House.

*   *   *

You show something like this to an old-time Japanese *sensei*, he would probably pass out from excitement. The Japanese have the oldest ruling dynasty in the world. MacArthur made the old emperor admit he wasn't a god after World War II. Hirohito said it and the people listened respectfully. But they didn't buy it. The Japanese are a polite people and routinely say things they don't really mean. Especially when dealing with foreigners.

The two men watched me carefully for my reaction. But I had learned well. I said nothing and waited.

"Mori-san is a member of the Kunaicho," Yamashita prompted.

I must have been a disappointment to them both, since I didn't swoon. I had more pressing issues on my mind. I wished they would get to the point. But the Japanese are elliptical and you have to accept the idea that explanations emerge at a somewhat slower pace than you might want.

"What do you know about Kunaicho, Mr. Burke?" Mori asked. His voice had a forceful, precise tone.

"You're a branch of the prime minister's office," I replied as we sat down. The arcane structuring of the modern Japanese bureaucracy is not my area of specialization.

"Yes. The Imperial Household Agency has been placed within that branch of government," he said. "Do you have any idea what our responsibility entails?" he continued. It was a rhetorical question, and he went right on without waiting for my response. "The Yamato House is an ancient lineage that extends back to the very beginning of the Japanese nation. The imperial family is the symbol, the living embodiment of my country."

"*Kokutai*," I commented.

Mori looked quickly at me. The phrase *kokutai*, national essence, has some unsavory connotations for many people since it was widely used during the war years by the Japanese government. You don't hear it bandied about much anymore. But the old *sensei* still refer to it, and I had heard it used with reverence before this.

"The status of the royal family has been diminished in

some ways since 1945," he said woodenly, as if referring to an unpleasant event best left unexplored. "And, in a political sense, that is, perhaps, appropriate. But the reverence for the emperor continues to be an important part of Japanese culture. And, as such, his person and his family members must be protected."

"Which is where you come in?"

"*Hai*. The Kunaicho is the agency responsible for seeing to the needs of the emperor. This includes the maintenance and supervision of the imperial Palace in Tokyo, secretarial duties related to the imperial schedule, travel arrangements for public relations activities, and so on."

"Mori-san," I said quietly, and he turned his head slightly to look right at me. "I don't believe you're a travel agent or a social secretary. People like that don't travel with gunmen."

"Ah," he said. "So. You refer, of course, to the young man below us." Something like an ironic smile appeared on his face. "He is not Kunaicho. Oh, no . . . I am here"—a pause while he licked his thin lips—"unofficially. In light of events, I thought his presence expedient."

"A hired gun?" I prompted. "What was there to be afraid of?"

"In addition to more . . . mundane needs," he eventually said as he studiously ignored my comment, "the Kunaicho has more specialized duties. We must remain alert to threats to the royal person. In the contemporary world, Mr. Burke, being in the public eye brings with it certain potential hazards."

I let him duck my question for the moment. "Fame," I noted sagely, "has its price."

Mori seemed unimpressed with my insight.

"I am sure that, to Western eyes, the emperor seems an obscure, remote figure. A vestige of another time. But the fact that the institution has endured for over three thousand years makes him a target for disgruntled elements in society."

It was a very bland statement, but the reality was probably sobering enough. Japan has extremely low crime rates, but the human propensity for odd behavior is a global phenomenon. Japan is a refined nation where elaborate paper folding and perfume smelling are arts. It's also the world's largest producer of pornographic comics. Cradle of the Red Army faction. And a religious cult that released Sarin nerve gas into the Tokyo subway.

"So in addition to supporting the emperor's public and ceremonial activities, we are charged with security. This includes things like providing bodyguards as well as more sophisticated activities."

He stopped talking and looked off into the distance. All he could see was a wall. Somewhere, beyond the brick of the buildings, was the sea. Mori came from an island nation. He probably smelled the salt in the air and thought of home.

"I don't think you realize just how complex a mission it is, to protect the emperor, Mr. Burke. The unit I head in the Kunaicho is known as the Konoe-tai." The pace of his words was hesitant, as if he were mentally reviewing what could be divulged before speaking. Now the tempo picked up, as if he had made a decision. "We use special tactics in containment and neutralization of threats to imperial security." He sounded like he had that part memorized. Probably came from the mission statement, or whatever they called it in Japan.

"Konoe-tai trainees receive extremely intensive training in unarmed fighting systems. An individual must hold a *dan* ranking of at least the fifth degree. And that is just the beginning. We are able to call on the most skilled of our martial arts masters to assist us. And the training never really ends."

Questions flickered through my mind in a steady stream. We were somehow treading on very sensitive ground here. You could sense it from the body language of the two men. I didn't want to spook them with my *gaijin* directness, but little bells were going off in my head. Highly trained martial artists. Links to the Imperial House. And a trail of bodies that stretched across the country. I looked at those two closed faces in front of me and knew I had to ask.

"Sensei," I began tentatively, like a man edging out onto thin ice, or probing a wound that had only recently started to heal, "is there a connection between this Tomita and the Kunaicho?"

I looked from one face to the other. In the quiet of the room, you could hear traffic from far away. A car door slammed. Down below us, a man with a gun waited with the mute intensity of a raptor.

Mori regarded me silently. The air quivered with tension like a vibrating crystal. The two men exchanged looks. Mori seemed angry at having to disclose things. Yamashita seemed resigned.

"What does this have to do with the murders?" I demanded. "Why is he here?"

"The answer is simple," Yamashita finally said. "Tomita is seeking me."

Which is all he said for a time.

The story Yamashita eventually told unfolded with a hypnotic cadence that brought the images he evoked vividly to mind. The tale spun out in starts and stops, a line of events anchored in his past and pulled painfully into his present.

When we think of Tokyo's Imperial Palace, it's a place of calm and control. It is set off from the bustle of modern Tokyo by moats and walls, the precise lines of traditional Japanese architecture at the gates set as if they were mystical boundaries leading to another realm. Like the minutely tended gardens that dot its acreage, however, this placid environment is the result of an almost savage discipline.

So it is with the men of the Konoe-tai who serve the emperor. The tradition of an Imperial Guard stretches back to the very beginnings of the Yamato House. And, despite their youth, the modern members of the Konoe-tai hearken back to another time in Japan. They take the issue of duty and obligation seriously. More seriously than even most Japanese, which is saying a great deal. And in their pursuit of sincere efficacy, they forge themselves in the crucible of martial arts training.

Yamashita came from a family with a long-standing relationship to the Kunaicho. A prodigy of martial skill, he was recruited very early in his life to train the specialized corps of bodyguards within the Konoe-tai that Mori directed. Which is where, eventually, they met Tomita.

They spoke of him elliptically, as if he were a family member who had shamed himself and, by extension, them. It was as if neither Yamashita nor Mori could bring himself to actually name the man. But it was clear they had thought a great deal about him and about what had happened.

Yamashita described this in a very matter-of-fact way. He merely related the details of Tomita's life in the same way you would read off points on a map: significant only as reference points that lead somewhere.

My teacher recruited Tomita himself. He frequented the major college, regional, and national contests, searching for likely recruits for Mori. Yamashita was a noted swordsman in his own right and had both a personal and professional interest in the young champions he watched in tournaments. His dark eyes watched countless young people slam each other into judo mats and clash together in kendo armor with all the ferocity of pit bulls. At the level of play he observed, they were all impressive. But he was searching for something else, something more elusive and harder to identify.

Yamashita saw that the young Tomita had within him the potential for greatness. It was unusual that someone so high up in the ranks like Yamashita would personally extend an invitation of this type. But he did. Among the Japanese, superiors get involved only in the late stages of any negotiations to avoid the possibility of an affront. But, although not really coming out and saying so, Yamashita gave the impression that he got carried away.

Even as he described the events of twenty years ago, he was at a loss to coherently explain what he was looking for among the *bugeisha,* the martial artists, he watched.

"The training process for Konoe-tai is a unique one, Burke," he related.

I could imagine. Most special groups of this type consciously create training ordeals. Some make it; some don't. It's like military elites anywhere: you take your best and brightest and essentially grind them up in the interest of serving the cause. The Japanese put a nicer spin on it, but they do the same thing.

"In ancient times, you heated bones until they cracked under the heat. The patterns created by weaknesses can foretell the future. We do the same with men. Following a true martial discipline is a process of"—Yamashita paused to do the mental translation—"spiritual forging."

The Japanese phrase *seishin tanren* was something I had heard for years. For Yamashita, it wasn't a theory or a philosophical abstraction; it was his training blueprint. "I have attempted to expose you to this as well," he said. I nodded in acknowledgment.

Mori commented, "The Konoe-tai must be impeccable, Mr. Burke. Smooth and flowing as water. Hard as rock. The challenge and the responsibility are such that only the very finest can be selected."

"And Tomita had what you were looking for?" I asked incredulously.

They looked at each other for a moment as if sharing a guilty thought. "I take responsibility for the selection." Yamashita sipped at the air as he spoke, as if the admission hurt him, even now. He looked down, half bowing in my direction.

I thought about the toll this statement imposed on such a proud man. Even after all that had happened, it made me uncomfortable to see my teacher like this. I looked searchingly at Mori.

"Yamashita Sensei has nothing to apologize for, Mr.

Burke," the other man said. "His assessment of Tomita's potential was quite accurate."

"He was flawless," my *sensei* continued. "The *waza*, his techniques, were"—he seemed at a loss to express himself, even now—"beautiful."

"He was a fine candidate," Mori commented, as if comforting him.

I imagine that for a young, gifted martial artist in Japan, the opportunity to be exposed to the level of training the Konoe-tai could provide, as well as the prestige involved in being a member of the Imperial Household Agency, must have been irresistible. And, of course, it was meant to be.

But for Tomita, I believed that there were other, more subtle attractions as well. Yamashita didn't speculate on them, but Tomita must have basked in the attention of a senior man like Yamashita. As I sat there and listened, I could imagine how Tomita must have felt.

He felt like he was coming home.

The two men seemed lost in memory for a moment. So I asked the question. It emerged into the still air of the room and hovered there.

"What happened?"

It was Mori's turn to look vaguely guilty.

"The training proceeded well," he said.

But I got the sense that there was more.

"So he got into the Konoe-tai? At the palace?"

Yamashita smiled and nodded. "No. Potential members are trained in a separate location . . ."

"The emperor might find the activities disruptive to the harmony of the palace," Mori said. How he kept a straight face is anyone's guess. He was a very serious man.

"The training period is a long one," Yamashita continued. "It is done at a different location in the North." He looked at me significantly.

To the Japanese, the North is the equivalent of our Wild West. It's where you go for the wide-open spaces. And the rough life.

"A little more rustic," I commented.

Mori nodded. "The training facility is quite isolated. It permits more focus on the part of the students. There are fewer distractions."

"Much of the training is done outdoors, Burke," Yamashita said. "In the field."

"So what happened?" I was through being patient.

The furtive looks passed between the two men again. Mori cleared his throat. "In our enthusiasm and haste over Tomita, certain things were overlooked." I said nothing and he continued.

"There are a variety of requirements for membership in the Konoe-tai," Mori explained. "The young man was more than qualified in terms of training and ability. Education. It was almost a year before . . . irregularities were discovered."

Yamashita spoke up, as if helping Mori shoulder an unpleasant load. "The person of the emperor has both political and religious significance, Professor. He must be guarded from threats of many types . . ."

"I don't get it," I said.

"The emperor, as a descendent of the sun goddess, must be protected from ritual threats as well as real ones. You know something of this, I am sure," Yamashita said. I nodded. Shinto religious beliefs stress ritual cleanliness to the point of horror of spiritual contamination.

"The emperor must be protected from any source of possible pollution," Yamashita concluded.

Mori picked up the thread. "You must understand, Mr. Burke, that we Japanese place great significance on our uniqueness as a people. On our purity. We try to ensure that the emperor's guards reflect that concern."

"This recruit was an excellent candidate . . . I still believe so to this day," Yamashita said. "But when it was learned that he was the product of a mixed marriage . . ."

"His father was of Hawaiian and Japanese blood. An American who had married a Japanese national," Mori said.

He looked at me as if presenting a type of trump card. I tried to keep a blank expression on my face. I knew the

Japanese were tremendous chauvinists who believed in the "purity" of their people. To an American of my generation, it sounded absurd. But these men were deadly in earnest. Each of us in that room knew from personal experience about the Japanese feeling for outsiders. *Gaijin* are dangerous in many ways.

Yamashita continued. "Many of the other *sensei* felt it was inappropriate. Someone who was not a pure Japanese should not be Konoe-tai." He paused and looked at Mori for a minute, then at me. "I did not agree with the decision, but I was bound to support it." I nodded in reluctant understanding. The Japanese need for consensus, the devotion to group solidarity, was a powerful thing. Even Yamashita couldn't fight it.

My *sensei* swallowed and it was one of the few times I ever saw any sign of an interior emotional state, however subtle. "I was chosen to deliver the group's decision to Tomita." Yamashita set his face in a hard mask as he said it. I imagined it was the same expression he used when he came, against his will, to tell Tomita he was cast out from the group.

"It was during one of the outdoor exercises. The trainees spend so much time in the field, they say they hardly feel human. They call themselves *yaken*. Are you familiar with the word?" I shook my head no. He smiled briefly at a thought. "It means 'wild dog.' But no matter. He was a true warrior, that one. He bowed at the decision and left the field. He turned once to look at me. The expression of hatred in his eyes has remained with me for all these years."

I looked at Mori expectantly. He fidgeted under my scrutiny.

"The decision was made by all the *sensei*, Mr. Burke," he said. "Many were as deeply moved as Yamashita-san, but the will of the group . . ."

"What happened to Tomita after that?" I asked.

"We are not able to track all his movements over time," Mori said. "But we know that he continued his training with various masters."

I looked at Yamashita and he shook his head sadly. "Not I. Others. They were not the sort of teachers he needed," was all he said.

"And," Mori said grimly, "we know that, recently, he began searching for Yamashita Sensei. And the others. We do not know why. But some have already been found." The look on his face answered my silent questions about Ikagi and Kubata. But he seemed more comfortable with the story now that we were back to points that could be plotted out with clarity.

"And it's taken him this long to locate you, Sensei?" I asked Yamashita.

"I did not want to be found," Yamashita said simply.

"What has happened is regrettable, Mr. Burke," Mori interjected. "When your teacher left Japan, he maintained contact with only a select few. It is only recently that we have been in contact." Mori paused for a moment to let that sink in before he continued. "I had known for years that Tomita's humiliation was great. When I learned of the killings, I feared for Yamashita-san."

I thought of the sense of frustration Tomita must have harbored. The emotional impact of such a rejection. From hurt to hate is a small step.

"Now," Mori continued, "I believe that Tomita's search is over."

I looked at my *sensei*. "How can you be sure?"

Yamashita smiled a tight, grim smile. "Tomita hoped to deal with me the night your brother's friend was wounded. He stole Ittosai's sword to provoke me. He has tracked me through Ikagi-san . . . Kubata Sensei . . . He is here. Somewhere. He will come for me again."

They seemed so placid. "I don't believe this!" I protested.

"Please," Mori said. "There can be no doubt."

I looked at Yamashita: he merely closed his eyes in affirmation.

Mori continued. "Everything else has been prelude. The wild dog now hunts your master, Mr. Burke."

FIFTEEN

Cutting the Air

In the squad room, phones chirped and papers rustled. Detectives called to one another over their cubicle separators. There was a low-level hum of activity, the air filled with the sound of people just barely keeping the influx of information under a semblance of control. Back on the job, Micky functioned with the easy efficiency of a man in his element.

He had taken in the substance of Yamashita's statement without comment. He was silent when the D.A. let my teacher go. Now Micky was cold, dispassionate, and efficient. His words were tight and fast, as if shaped by the effort of self-control. But he didn't say a thing that revealed his anger. He was too focused on the information and its impact on the hunt for Art's attacker.

They had a name. A description. Something to narrow the odds. Motivation was less important now. Micky knew that Tomita was in the City and why he had come. He had been a cop long enough to know that you could torture yourself endlessly with trying to figure out why people did things. It was enough to know that they did them. At the very least, it kept cops employed.

There had been a conference in the Batcave, where the detective squad mapped out a strategy for finding Tomita. I had not been invited, but my brother filled me in on the nuts and bolts of a manhunt. Endless checks of hotels and their environs. A review of airline manifests. Questioning of cab drivers. The citywide distribution of a description to all precincts.

"Sounds like you've got it under control, Mick. What do you need me for?"

He squinted at me. "I've got questions." He settled back in his desk chair and rummaged around for his cigarettes. The pack crinkled. He looked at it longingly, then at the No Smoking sign Art had posted on the wall between their desks. A handwritten addition scrawled across the bottom read: "This means you!!!" Micky sighed and sat forward.

"Asa says Tomita used a sword that night in the subway."

"A *katana*," I specified.

He nodded. "OK, whatever. No weapon of this type was used in the other two homicides." I agreed.

"It tells me that Tomita probably got the weapon after Kubata was killed," he said. "I gotta assume that you don't get these things at the local cutlery store."

"There are places you can get them in New York," I answered. "If this thing is a real *katana*. And I have to believe it is, based on Asa's description and the wounds . . ." I tapered off, and thought of Art.

My brother gave me a come-on gesture. "Yeah, I know, I know. How many places like that are there around here?"

"Well, you can get cheesy imitation versions of a *samurai* sword all over town. But I don't think Tomita would use something like that. Not for something so important. There are probably two or three people who could sell you something like this . . ."

He tossed me a pad. "Names. Addresses. I'll pay 'em a visit."

"It's not that easy, Mick. Most swords like this are custom made. They have to be ordered way in advance. From Japan. You can check, but I doubt Tomita was able to get something like this on short notice."

I noticed the display catalogue from Samurai House on a

pile of papers. I never did get a chance to see the show. It seemed like something so distant as to be unreal. I picked the thing up. It was a glossy brochure that incorporated some of the stuff I had developed for Bobby Kay. "You're talking about weapons like these, Mick," I said, and waved the catalogue at him.

"OK, so where'd he get it?" Micky persisted.

I shrugged, and to stall while I thought, I leafed through the pages of Bobby's show. I was turning a page when something caught my eye. For a minute I couldn't quite figure out what was bothering me. Then it became clear.

My brother had been fidgeting in impatience but grew still as he read my body language. "What?" he asked.

"This is weird," I answered. "I had a chance to look at photos of some of the display items when I was writing that piece for Bobby. I remember this sword here." I pointed at it. "But the photo of the sword in the catalogue is different."

Micky slewed the picture around, looking at it with interest. "How so?"

I pointed the features out. "This *katana* had a *tensho-zukuri* hilt in the originals. In the catalogue, it's got a *higo-zukuri* hilt."

Micky took a calming breath. "Connor, would you please tell me something in English?"

"The handles are different shapes, Mick," I explained. "This sword is supposed to be four hundred years old. Back then, they really used them for things. A *tensho-zukuri* hilt is fluted toward the butt end. It helps you keep your grip on the sword. Modern swords tend to have a relatively straight hilt, the *higo-zukuri*." I looked up at my brother. "Somebody must have gotten the pictures mixed up. Because this sword is not the one I had written about."

"A sword like this is valuable?" Micky asked. I nodded and he smiled. "And you could still use it?"

"Sure."

"Well, buddy boy, I think maybe we've found where Tomita got his weapon."

"Huh?"

"Sure. We know he was in the gallery the night he killed Reilly. After you saw the picture of the sword. But before the catalogue was printed. He had opportunity. And a motive."

"But no *katana* was reported missing. Just the *bokken*," I protested. "You'd think Bobby Kay would want to make an insurance claim."

Micky got a crafty look on his face. "You know, all this Japanese stuff has really made this whole case hard to figure. Everything is way too exotic for my taste. But this . . . this kinda thing I get. Maybe Bobby didn't want any more adverse publicity. Maybe he didn't want to scare away backers. . . . Maybe, just maybe his insurance coverage is shady . . ."

"But he had to get all kinds of insurance for this show. He told me. Said it was costing a fortune."

Micky sat back and made some quick notes. "Precisely. And if you had to come up with a name of someone who might be likely to cut corners, who would you suggest?"

I got the point. "Bobby Kay."

My brother jumped up. "OK, I'm outta here. Got enough to work on for now."

"What about me?"

He was shrugging his coat on. "You've helped enough. Take off. Go . . . I don't know. Go do what you do."

So I did.

The tiny waterfall in Yamashita's garden flows over gray rocks. It makes a musical sound that fills the small, green space behind the *dojo*. Yamashita tends the yard with a remorseless intensity. It is (nonetheless) green and soothing in the summer and, like the man himself, the product of discipline and a fierce attention to details. We sat on the little covered porch overlooking rocks and shrubs, watching small birds bounce and flutter in the yard's stillness. Yamashita talked quietly and evenly, his voice an expression of the garden's mood. An outsider would never guess he was talking with me about the finer points of killing a man.

When I arrived, the training hall was silent. There was still tension between us, and my teacher and I had drifted down into the empty space, instinctively seeking comfort in the familiar. The afternoon sun slanted in and cast bright stripes on the deep indigo arms of Yamashita's uniform. He stood alone in the center of the room, holding a wooden sword in *gedan no kamae*, the low defensive posture. His eyes seemed focused on something far away, but as I joined him, the sword swung up to track me. The motion brought his focus back to the here and now. I had told him what the police were doing. He did not seem particularly surprised at the turn of events. But the awareness of Tomita's intentions seemed to be still sinking in.

"So . . ." he hissed and looked past me into space. "I suppose this is inevitable. The past cannot be avoided . . ."

"That would be too simple," I offered.

"Too simple?" Yamashita replied, "No. I think, rather, it is too complicated."

I looked quizzically at him.

He sighed as he gathered his thoughts. "Burke, to create a warrior of this skill level is a work of years. It requires great care. Attention must be paid, not only to technique but to the trainees. Their spirit becomes intertwined with their skills. If you take one away, the other suffers. Now we see the results."

I thought this was an interesting way to avoid dealing with his part in Tomita's past, but I said nothing.

"I sometimes doubted that the Konoe-tai had the patience to train correctly," my teacher continued. He looked up and stared at nothing. "They seek to serve the Imperial House, which is a thing of great honor. Their zeal, however, was always greater than their wisdom."

"But you were part of it," I said, and regretted it immediately.

Yamashita glided smoothly across the floor. His feet

rasped along the polished wood. He placed the *bokken* in a rack on the wall and turned to face me.

"You will learn, Burke, that the true path is not always one we can clearly see. There are times when we lose the Way." He sounded sad for a minute, and old.

"But," his voice grew stronger, "this is why we train. Because we seek the Way. And because we can never be sure that we have found it."

"Is that why you left Japan?"

Yamashita closed his eyes in affirmation. "There was difficulty there, Burke. *Budo*, the Martial Way, uses the arts of a warrior to foster peace. After a time, I was not sure that the Konoe-tai was preserving this . . . awareness . . . in what they did. After a time, I came here to see whether a different way was possible for me."

"And did you know about Tomita even then? Is that why you dropped out of sight?" I had always wondered why such a prominent master shunned the limelight so fiercely.

He looked severe for a moment. "I did not run away, Burke. I left. With Tomita . . . I was saddened by the group's decision. It was a waste of an excellent trainee. But no, I was informed of things by Mori only in the last few days. And now," he sighed, "I must decide on a course of action."

"Why now?" I asked.

"Tomita will not cease until he gets what he desires," Yamashita said. "He will continue to . . . hurt . . . those connected with me. I see that now." He looked directly at me, his night-dark eyes still and hard. "I will not have him destroy what I have built here."

"The *dojo*?"

His head swiveled on his thick neck. "No. He will strike at what I value most, Burke. Those around me. My students." Again the hard look. "You."

I felt an electric surge of panic. My face flushed. But I controlled my breathing, and gradually my heartbeat began to slow again. I thought of the destruction Tomita had left, as deep and shocking as a blade cut. And now Yamashita was certain there would be more. I needed to think of a way to stop it.

It finally came to me. Why not, I suggested after a time, lay a trap? We knew Tomita's patterns. And what he was after. How he would go about it. Why not provide him with the victim, in the way a tiger hunter stakes out a goat on a tether?

Yamashita would be the bait. He was the end point on the trail of bodies Tomita had strung across the continent. Yamashita had cast Tomita out of the Konoe-tai. He had been both father figure and *sensei* to Tomita. And the one who had rejected him. Tomita had been searching for him ever since he got to this country. Now we could dangle Yamashita in front of Tomita as bait. We knew the killer was close, biding his time. He was a predator, slowly circling in the murk, just out of sight.

Tomita needed to be attracted, I urged Yamashita, not just tracked. We would entice him to come to us. The hunt would become a seduction, made alluring by the scent of blood.

Yamashita heard out my proposition as if I were talking about a trip to the country.

"There is a logic in this, Burke," Yamashita said, nodding his head. "There is also no real trick to being the goat." He mused about this for a moment. Then those night-dark eyes bored into me. "The trick, of course, is being the goat that survives."

Which, in retrospect, is when my training really began.

My teacher had agreed to be the bait almost eagerly. There was, after all, honor involved. But he was skeptical about my assurances of safety, despite the fact that I thought that Micky would back us up. All bait, Yamashita said, can be eaten if the trap fails. So can the hunters. As a result, he treated our role in the plan as if either of us might really have to fight Tomita. "It is what he wants, after all, Burke." And so he had exacted a price from me. Yamashita thought that he would make me practice with him as he prepared

for what he thought of as the inevitable confrontation with
Tomita. "It will add some variety to your training," he commented wryly.

It had only been a few hours since that statement, and, as
we sat there on the porch, I was sore in all the ways familiar to me from decades of martial arts training. The only
difference was that now I hurt everywhere all at once. The
tiny muscles in my feet ached. My stomach muscles
spasmed involuntarily in certain positions. And I was tired.

"He hunts at night, this one," the master intoned. "He
uses the body's rhythm as a weapon. The murders occur in
the dark, when our *ki*, our vital energy, is ebbing."

I thought about the killings. All nocturnal. Most well
after midnight. The quiet time, the small hours when in-
fants awake for comfort, when sleep cycles shift. The time
when the old and the ill and the weak let life slip away and
are folded into oblivion.

"We will need to work on rhythms, Burke. You will need
to be here all through the training." It was a statement, not a
question. The link between *sensei* and student was too
strong for doubt. In some ways, it was a return to the balance of our former relationship. Yamashita sat comfortably,
a dark blue training uniform stretched over his thick torso,
squinting out into the garden as he spoke.

I moved gingerly, and he looked at me. His eyes were
flat. "Are you tired? You will be more so. We will work
more on your meditation. It will help with the fatigue."

Yamashita had a hard time getting out of the role of instructor. Even though this training was really for him, he insisted on talking like it was something he was doing for me.
I had ceased to notice it and just nodded wearily in resignation.

"Physically, there is little room for improvement. But
your skills . . ." He paused as if internally rating the catalogue of my ability. He smiled tightly, as if to himself.
Small sparrows sputtered in the waterfall's pond, scattering
droplets in a fine spray. "You are a good student, Professor.

Among my best. At each step, you have struggled, but you persevere. I like that."

I wasn't sure what he liked more about me: the fact that I had to struggle or the fact that I eventually learned much of what he taught me. It was typical of him.

With Yamashita, grading, like everything else, is a bit different from that of other arts. Martial artists talk about rank and belts and promotion. Yamashita Sensei uses a far older system. We don't wear colored belts. Some of the newer students come with their black belts wrapped around them under the *hakama* like a security blanket. Eventually, we all stop wearing them. It is not just that the belts don't make you feel secure in his *dojo*. It's that they are revealed as totally irrelevant.

In Yamashita's *dojo* there are seven different stages, ranging from *kirigami*, or initiate, to the level where the student has mastered the complete syllabus of the art, known as *menkyo kaiden*. Each level is not really a promotion, however. It's just an acknowledgment that you can do some things and are ready to try some more. It doesn't signal an end to training; there is no such thing. Only the invitation to learn more.

So when Yamashita paused and smiled, I was sure he was mentally listing my faults and reliving my past struggles, all as a preparation for judging whether I could follow him further.

"This, I think, will be hard for you." He emerged from his interior reflection and focused on me. The sounds of the world outside were muted and far away. As he spoke, they faded further, or his words swelled despite their quiet tone, so that all I could focus on was his teaching.

"It requires a total focus on the struggle. An absence of compassion. I have watched you for years. You are a good man. This type of concentration and ruthlessness are hard for you. But it would be hard for any of us. And yet, very necessary.

"The evil to be faced . . ." He inhaled suddenly as if

..ing confronted with it directly for the first time ". . . is powerful."

As he talked, he joined his hands and whispered a word. I saw the fingers knit. "*Rin*," he intoned.

I sat up a bit straighter.

"It will be as relentless as fire, Burke."

Again the pause and a new configuration of the hands. The mantra was barely audible: "*Pyo*."

His breath was cadenced. His body grew still, dense with presence, like a rock in his garden.

A new movement and the hissed word: "*Toh*."

"All techniques are needed to defeat this demon. All that the body can bear." The chant and the hand gestures continued.

Sho.

"But there is more to learn."

Kai.

"The spirit must be focused."

Jin.

"There cannot be the least gap in concentration."

Retsu.

"The luxury of mercy does not exist."

Zai.

"Or fear."

Zen.

"Or doubt."

I had seen this before. The hypnotic chant and the fluid knotting of the fingers. The breath control. *Kuji-no-in* is an ancient summoning of power. The mudra hand gestures spring from Tantric Buddhism, a ritual in which the "seals" of the gestures have been repeated over centuries to forge a link between body and spirit. The chanted mantra have echoed along dark corridors of the warrior past. They are still used in some schools of the old style as a meditation device. But with Yamashita it was something more.

He quietly began again, and I felt my fingers begin the flow in imitation of my master. This time, it was the full ritual. For each mudra, the chanted word is exhaled for eighty-one breaths. Each mantra has a name: the Single Point, the Inner Binding, the Wisdom Fist. Each is linked to a lesson: the channeling of *ki*, control, concentration.

The mind's rhythm rises and falls with the breath. The hands weave their spell. The words are murmured in the still air, small sounds that fill the space around you.

With the ritual of the ninth gesture, known as *jo-in*, completed, Yamashita lit a candle and drew paper and brush to his side. He beckoned me to approach him.

His voice seemed to come from deep inside him, from a place impossibly remote.

"Thus we intone the *kuji-in*. For strength. Compassion. Courage. This you have been taught."

I bowed formally to him. My muscles protested, but it was a curious, muffled sensation, more like a faint message from another place.

"There is yet the *ju-in*, a tenth seal, Burke. Not many know of it. Not many have the need. I will show you the character."

He brushed the dark, balanced strokes of an accomplished calligrapher on the small piece of paper. "Look at it," he ordered me, pointing at what he had written. "Do you recognize it?"

"Yes, Sensei," I whispered. He raised a hand.

"Do not say it." Then he reached out for my hand. "Trace its lines. Learn it."

I did as I was bid, tracing the lines. Yamashita ensured that my finger moved in the correct directions in the correct sequence. Our hands moved together, over and over again until I was sure.

"Now," he said, "the *kuji kiri*." The cutting with *kuji*. He raised his hands and, for each of the nine gestures, made a slash in the air in front of him, as if cutting up space. "Four vertical lines," he instructed. "Five horizontal. In the center, *to-in*."

He showed me how to make the hand shape of the tenth seal and, with my hands in that configuration, how to cut at the air, tracing the character in the center of the lines that, invisible, quivered with power and reality nonetheless.

It was the warrior's grid. A power symbol. And in the middle, *ju-in*, the tenth seal, called *to-in*. The Sword Seal.

Only then did Yamashita utter the mantra that accompanied it. He voiced it forcefully, as if pushing against the fabric of the atmosphere. I heard it and repeated.

It was an ancient word, a complex word, jumbled in the passage from Sanskrit to Chinese to Japanese, but whose meaning was clear and sharp: the destruction of evil.

"How's Art?" I asked Micky wearily. I could hear the surge of my blood in the phone receiver.

"The same," he said. "Hanging on."

"That's something, at least." I got a grunt. "Any new leads?" It wasn't a particularly animated conversation.

"We're workin' on it. I shook your pal Bobby Kay's tree a bit."

"Anything there?"

I could see the shrug, even over the phone line. "Something stinks there, but I don't have anything solid." Then he switched gears. "What are you up to? I've been trying to reach you."

"I know," I apologized. "Sorry. I got involved with something with Yamashita Sensei." I tried to sound sincere, but it was an effort holding a conversation. Yamashita had worked me ruthlessly for the rest of the day. I was sitting in one of the chairs in his living room upstairs. It was a comfortable seat. And it was good to talk. But some of the small muscles in my left hand were spasming. You could see them jump in the lamplight. My brain felt pulled in two directions.

I hadn't really told Micky about my scheme yet. I wanted to ease him into it. So I let him know that Yamashita wanted me to do some special intensive training with him. But that was all.

"It'll be a few days," I said evasively.

"Sometimes, Connor, I don't get you at all," he grumped.

"OK," he sighed, "I may need to reach you there. Give me the number."

The muscles down in my right calf near the Achilles tendon were starting to tighten up. I felt like I had tightly strung cables in my legs and was trying to ignore it and listen hard to the inflections in his voice. He knew something was up.

I gave him the number, said good-bye, and sat there with my eyes closed. Idiot, I thought. You should have told him. He's had enough of people holding out on him.

"Your conversation was upsetting." My eyes snapped open. Yamashita had slipped into the room and sat across from me. His face was impassive, but his eyes were alive.

I exhaled slowly and nodded.

"Your brother does not understand what is going on?"

"No." I shook my head guiltily, reliving the phone call.

"Burke," he said, sitting forward, "listen to me. You are wise not to involve him. A ring of danger surrounds us here. When you bring people close to you, they will be imperiled."

Not many people use the word *imperiled* anymore. When Yamashita said it, it didn't sound quaint.

"You Americans," he continued with that tight smile of his. "You want all things that are good to also be easy.

"Now I will tell you something, Professor. It is obvious you care for your brother. And you are wise not to inform him of your plans. If you can shield him, you must do so. Even if it means that he will be upset."

"I know, Sensei, but . . ."

He held up a hand, palm out. It was a small hand, but the palm was broad and the fingers were thick. Yamashita's hands looked, in fact, much like the rest of him: they were hard and capable parts of a fierce, focused human being. Even his words of comfort had a brutal tinge to them. "But nothing, Burke," he said. "Which is better, that your brother feel hurt for a time because he does not fully understand your motives, or that you gush out your secrets and he runs to your side, with all the danger it could bring? He has already suffered enough."

I nodded as he scolded me.

"If you pull him close at this moment, you will place him within the dark circle. He is, I am sure, a good policeman. But he has no place here."

Yamashita looked up and gazed out the window. Lights fought the darkness, cutting at it, beating it back in spots, but ultimately, on the edges of light, the brightness bled away, surrendering to the infinite strength of night. Yamashita's eyes were unfocused, as if he were intent on something beyond mere sight. For a moment, in the lamplight, I could see the toll of years on him. Maybe, in his own way, he was trying to explain why he had kept things from me for so long.

"Make no mistake, Burke," the old man said. "Tomita is coming. I can feel it."

In the night, I slept fitfully. Outside Yamashita's *dojo*, cars rumbled by, radios pounding. Distant horns sounded. Sirens shrieked and died away. I drifted into a drowsy half-sleep. My body jerked involuntarily as muscle tension began to dissipate. I didn't think I slept, but the *sensei* startled me when he woke me.

"Get up, Burke. It is two-thirty." I stood and focused on his stolid silhouette beside me in the dark.

"Time to train," my teacher said.

SIXTEEN

Forlorn Hopes

The heavy fire door boomed open, echoing in the empty *dojo*. Yamashita and I had rested at dawn, and Mori and his hired help had arrived shortly afterward. The two senior men conferred quietly, while the thug waited in the shadows for something to happen. The first floor practice room was empty of students, but Mori's watchdog scanned the empty air with an idiot vigilance.

Mori had a flat, reserved face that gave you the illusion of total control. But he was not as cool as he pretended to be: he looked up sharply at the sound when the door banged.

I went to see who it was. It was one of those automatic things you do for your *sensei*. Before I could even get to the foot of the stairs, however, the thug had jumped in front of me. His pistol appeared in one fluid motion, almost like that of a magician pulling a bouquet out of the air with a simple flourish.

He glided across the floor ahead of me, the gun's muzzle a black snout cutting through the space. Yamashita followed me down but said nothing, watching the action with professional dispassion.

The intruder stood with hands on his hips and regarded

the watchdog. He looked at me, then back at the man with the gun, and clearly felt the need to defuse the situation.

"Take it easy, you dickwad," he said. "I'm a cop, remember?" My brother had come visiting.

Looking at him, you could almost forget he was a policeman. Off duty, he looked like any other tired guy in rumpled clothing. He had the cop eyes, of course, but from a distance he looked just like the person I had grown up with. He had been through a hard few days, though, and as I got closer it showed in his face. But I was glad he had come. When Micky pushed open that *dojo* door, he let in street sounds, heat, and the almost palpable tug of memory. All the drills and lectures and mantra had begun to make me feel like a man in suspended animation. We may have been setting a trap, but I was the one who felt imprisoned, set off from the real world. Micky restored my sense of connection. I could guess that Yamashita thought my brother's presence was bad for the training he was trying to accomplish. I, however, grinned like an idiot.

My brother stood there dressed in sneakers patched with duct tape, a pair of old khaki pants, and a dark blue NYPD T-shirt with a little yellow badge on the breast. He looked at Mori's hired gun with that placid expression he used to calm dangerous people. Or lull the unwary. He gingerly held his empty hands out at his sides to show he had no weapon.

"Hey, c'mon," I said. "We've been through this before." Eventually, the thug relaxed, although he looked annoyed that he hadn't been able to shoot anyone. Micky glared at him silently, came upstairs, and said hello to Yamashita. It wasn't a warm greeting. I held my breath. My brother had a long memory and a short temper. From his perspective, Yamashita was partly to blame for this mess. And Micky felt there were still things he wasn't being told. He was right, of course, but now I was the one holding out on him.

Mori didn't say much when Micky showed up. The two men eyed each other warily, but Micky didn't even acknowledge him. Instead, he looked at Yamashita and said, "I came to take him off your hands for a while, Yamashita."

Yamashita looked at me like he was judging a prospective meal. He turned to my brother and nodded. "He has been behaving. Enjoy the afternoon." My teacher gestured toward the street like he was inviting us to explore Xanadu.

What we got to see instead was the brick and blacktop of Brooklyn baking in the sharp summer glare. We drove up to Fifth Avenue and headed through Sunset Park. Both sets of grandparents had lived around here, and we had spent an awful lot of childhood Sundays visiting the area, watching relatives decay and the neighborhoods change. Fifth Avenue was different now from the street of our childhood, but it certainly was lively.

People were wandering in and out of local bodegas. Racks of summer dresses and T-shirts were on display on the sidewalks. Even though we had the car windows closed and the AC on, I could hear the Latin music that the merchants piped out onto the street.

"How you doing, Mick?" I asked. His face had that tired, drawn look crash survivors have. But his eyes were clear.

He nodded. "I'm OK. You, on the other hand, look like hell."

I hadn't paid attention to a mirror in a while, but I imagined that all the training with Yamashita showed. I said nothing and let him drive. There was a point to the visit, and Micky would get to it when he was ready.

"Hey, look," Micky said. "OLPH."

The parish of Our Lady of Perpetual Help was marked by a large church complex looming over one whole block. Down Fifty-ninth Street, the school building was tucked away in the back. Micky parked in the driveway entrance to the school parking lot. Perverse creatures, schools hibernate in the summer. The entrance gate to the lot was chained shut—Property of the Diocese of Brooklyn, Violators Will Be Towed—and the building was dark and silent. Micky tossed his NYPD card on the dashboard and walked away without a second thought. It was one of the great things about being a cop: ordinary parking rules did not apply. Then again, my brother was in a line of work where Kevlar vests were considered appropriate Christmas gifts from your loved ones, so the trade-off was probably even.

The church itself was a huge, sandstone-colored building with a red tile roof. Its large arched entrance doors faced the avenue, an imposing multistory presence built of stone and old wood and leaded stained-glass windows of deep-sea blue and red as rich as blood. The old locals called it "the Basilica." The cavernous hall of the main church, up one flight of stone steps from the street, was dark and locked, but the smaller lower-level church was open. My family had baptized, married, and buried three generations in this church, and it was familiar ground for both of us. As kids, we had spent what felt like an eternity at a host of rituals there. They didn't do much for our piety, but they did create our immense capacity for tolerating boredom. We also developed the ability to sit very quietly for long periods of time. They also taught us endurance.

Micky went in, and I followed. Working with Yamashita had put me in a heightened state of suspicion and sensitivity. I didn't think it was likely Tomita would be anywhere near at this time of day, and he certainly wouldn't be interested in me. But, as my *sensei* kept drilling into my head, awareness was the key to survival. I took a hard look around.

The ceiling in the lower church was not very high, nothing like the soaring vaults one story up, and the view of the altar was blocked by the pillars that supported the floor of the church above. It broke up your line of sight, and the feeling was that almost anyone could be lurking there. Maybe even God. I scanned the room. An old man was slowly shuffling down the center aisle toward the doors. To our right, a woman knelt, obscured in a kerchief and dark blue raincoat. Her eyes were red-rimmed and moist. Her lips were dry and worked in a constant, mumbled litany. Beads made faint clicking noises. It was the sad cast of characters you find in any church in the daytime.

The room smelled of wax and the memory of incense. The pews were old and dark, polished by the friction caused by generations of human emotion and ritual choreography. Gaudy statues of saints lined the walls, and banks of candles flickered in front of them like whispered entreaties.

My brother walked slowly into the church, like someone just awakened who was trying to remember the details of a particularly vivid dream. I followed him to one of the side altars where a statue, dark with age, was located.

Most of the statues in the church were the smooth, pious type. Bland, sightless eyes were set in creamy complexions, and tidy robes with flowing lines helped obscure the awareness that any of these figures had been corporeal at one time. They were neat but not particularly powerful figures.

Micky made his way to a dark corner where a different type of statue stood, obscured in shadow. It was unpainted, a monochrome presence that glowered there, all angles and force. Someone knew what he was doing when he made it. Most of the statues in that room looked faintly ridiculous and anemic, like porcelain tamed up to distract you from their lifeless essence. But the form Micky stood before was fierce.

It was a dark cast-copper figure. The dull luster made you want to reach out and feel the hard surface. One booted foot, closest to the rank of candles, had been rubbed shiny by decades of supplicants unable to resist the impulse. The winged form was armed with a sword and a lance. The shaft pierced a writhing form, half snake, half dragon, while the stern face of the saint gazed upon the world as if trying to judge whether it was worth all this effort. He was supposed to be a holy man, but he looked more like a warrior.

Michael. The Archangel. God's champion.

My brother's namesake.

Micky stood staring at the form for a while. Then he turned and went outside without saying a word. I touched Michael's foot before I followed. The weepy lady in the back looked right through us.

*   *   *

We walked slowly around the perimeter of the church. The sidewalk was wide, and there were young trees planted in large squares of earth at regular intervals. They didn't do much to cut the sun's glare. Small, bronze plaques were set into the pavement near the trees. The metal was a dark blue-green with age.

As we walked, my brother looked down at the plaques.

"You remember Dad telling us about these trees?" he asked. "Well, not these trees, exactly. These are replacements. But the originals?"

"No. Not really," I said.

He went right on, the older brother determined to pass me this piece of family lore. We walked down the long block toward Sixth Avenue, past the rectory entrance as he spoke, still with that far-away look in his eyes. "There was some retired army guy who started a marching band in the parish. I forget his name. A big deal for the neighborhood. A working-class boy makes good. Becomes an officer.

"Well, he retires and comes back to the parish. Gets this marching band going. Uniforms and music, fifty, maybe a hundred boys. The pride of the parish. Then the First World War breaks out. The guy pulls some strings, gets back on active duty, and organizes a volunteer brigade. All those boys who grew up marching to his orders and trusting him . . ."

It was hot and the light color of the sidewalk threw up glare. It was hard to see Micky's expression very well. His voice was flat.

"So off they go to the Big War. They get a huge send-off here. Flowers and speeches. The pride of the area, all those kids, all dressed up and eager to go . . ."

We rounded Sixth Avenue at the rear of the complex. Micky had been looking at each plaque as we passed. Now he looked up and stared into the distance, down the long avenue that led south to the sea.

"Most never came back, Connor. They were used to marching band stuff moving in step, colorful uniforms, patriotic speeches. They got over there and what they got was interlocking fields of fire, machine guns, and artillery barrages. They were churned into mud."

Coming up Fifty-ninth Street, he continued. "It destroyed the parish. They never forgave the commanding officer for taking their kids off to that butcher's yard. There's a tree planted here for each boy lost."

"That's some story, Mick," I said quietly. We were at the car again and stood facing each other across the hood.

"Yeah, but do you get the point?" he asked. We got into the car and sat there in the stuffy quiet. Micky stared out the windshield for a minute, then let out a thin stream of air from pursed lips and turned to me.

"Look, Connor. You're different, all right? Even as a kid. Interested in weird things. Mom and Dad knew it. And you were stubborn . . ."

"Still am." I smiled. It didn't make a dent in Micky's seriousness.

"You always have to do things your way. On your terms. Look at graduate school. Yamashita. The way you make a living."

I said nothing, waiting to see where he was going with all this.

"But the point is"—and here he turned to look right at me—"this is different. Let me be the cop here. We're searching for Tomita right now. It's just a matter of time." I stayed silent. "I know what you're up to," he prompted. "You think you're gonna trap him."

He said it with such finality that I knew there was no dodging the accusation. "We've got a good chance," I protested, but he cut me off.

"No. You listen to me. For once in your life, listen." He was angry, but it wasn't the usual loud anger. This was quiet and white hot, with a voice focused and sharp.

"You can't deal with this on your terms. This is not some fucking game or contest. The guy is a killing machine. He kills because he can. Because he has to."

" 'Only where love and need are one,' " I quoted.

"What?" he hissed.

"A line from a Robert Frost poem," I said.

He exploded. "Will you cut that shit out!"

The air in the car was stifling. We were both sweating, but it was more than the heat.

Micky paused a minute as if trying to contain himself. "Look at the trees out there," he began again. "Every one of those kids thought he was going out to fight on his terms. Some romantic battle. Good and evil. Most never even came back in boxes. They're bits of bone that get plowed up by farmers in Belgium.

"You think all this martial arts stuff is gonna help you stop this guy? It's not."

I started to protest, to tell him that the idea was to entice Tomita into a trap where we could deal with him. Besides, I explained, even if all else failed, there was Yamashita . . .

Micky started the car and the air conditioning began to wash some cool air over us. It seemed to leach some of the tension from the atmosphere as well.

"Connor, this martial arts stuff," he said. "It's a hobby. You're good at it, but it's a hobby. A sport."

"It's more than that, Mick," I said quietly.

He waved that point away and swung the car out onto the road. We stopped at the light and watched the summer pedestrians.

"How many people have you killed, Connor?"

I said nothing.

"Tomita's killed three we know of. He tried to kill my partner." The light changed and we rolled on. Micky stared straight ahead. "I don't want him killing you."

We were quiet for a time. The familiar rhythm of driving acted like a tranquilizer: the whoosh of the air conditioner, the faint bumping of the tires as they hit road seams, the syncopated click of the turning signal. We watched the other cars and other people as if their presence were a guarantee of normality.

Finally, Micky asked, "OK, what's the plan? How do we do this?"

"We?" I said.

"We. You think I'm showing up at Mom's with the bad news that some lunatic killed you?" He smiled a little at the thought of it.

So I gave him the briefing. Most of it, he knew. The pattern of Tomita's attacks was at night or early morning in secluded places where the ritual duel could take place. I didn't dwell too much on Yamashita's past and Tomita's connection to people associated with the Kunaicho. At this stage of things, it was just so much background noise.

"With Yamashita as bait," I concluded, "we should be able to catch him."

"So you're not gonna kill him?"

"I'd like to," I admitted. Then, I said, "Nah. We just need to stop him. Get him off the streets." I wasn't sure deep down about how truthful I was being here. But I wanted to allay Micky's concerns. "You said it yourself," I added. "Killing people is not my strong suit."

He pulled the car over and turned once more to look at me directly. "OK," he acknowledged. "But there's another thing, Connor. Why do you think Mori is involved here?"

"Well, because he wanted to warn Yamashita. And to catch the Kunaicho's wild dog, Tomita. I think we have a good chance of doing it."

"Fair enough, as far as it goes," my brother said. "But now lemme remind you about guys like this. He's a company man. All that stuff about warning his friend is fine. But there's gotta be more to it."

"OK," I said, not really seeing the point.

"OK," he mimicked me. "So tell me, Mr. Smart Guy. How does this situation benefit Mori?"

"He gets to catch Tomita," I answered.

"You mean arrest him?"

"Sure," I replied, at a loss to figure out what was generating the skepticism in his voice.

"And this guy is from some Jap bodyguard outfit? And

he's gonna bust this guy, this killer? In New York? The papers would be all over it."

"What do you mean, Mick?"

"I mean the last thing Mori wants is to bust this guy. It would attract too much attention."

"So what's he after?"

"You figure it out. You got the doctorate. But first, you ought to know something else. Since Art got hurt"—his voice got husky for a moment like it hurt him to say it—"we've been trying to work the Japan angle . . ."

"It's a foregone conclusion. We know that now."

". . . yeah, but we should be getting more cooperation on this. But we're not. It's like they're stalling."

"Why?"

"Someone's doing a favor for the Japs. And they sent Mori here. But to do things quietly." He paused to let it sink in. "Mori isn't here just to catch Tomita, Connor. He's here to make sure no one finds out about him."

"And so . . ."

"And so, he wants to kill him. That's why he brought that moron with the dye job. He's a shooter, plain and simple. He's got the look. They're gonna stake Yamashita out, and when their man gets into the kill zone, they're gonna open up with everything they've got."

He pulled back out into traffic and let me digest that for a while.

"So whattaya think?" he continued.

"Makes sense. There's only one problem," I said.

"What's that?"

"Yamashita's got his own plan. And he's better than they think," I said. I turned to look at my brother, who was one of the most competent people I knew. "He's even better than you think, Micky. And so am I."

He looked into my eyes. What he saw there, I don't know. Finally, he spoke. "Let's hope so."

He said it like he didn't have much hope. We rode in silence for a few blocks and he continued. "Of course, Mori and his goon also have another big problem."

"What?" I was preoccupied thinking about the new angles Micky had presented.

"Now I'm on their case."

We pulled up in front of the *dojo*. Micky slotted the car into a No Parking zone.

"That's true, Mick. You are the biggest pain in the ass I know."

He smiled ruefully. "All part of the service, buddy boy."

But the things he said bothered me for the rest of the day. When Yamashita had finished with some late-day training, I asked him what would happen if things fell through. I didn't ask Yamashita whether he could deal with it. It would be insulting. But, as Micky had laid things out that afternoon, a sudden, troubling thought hit me: What was the worst-case scenario? The thing I feared most? What if the trap didn't work? If Micky missed? If Yamashita failed? What if I had to face Tomita?

I screwed up what little courage I had and asked my teacher what would happen then. He sat there and looked at me with those hard, dark eyes.

"You," he said, "are capable. Like most people, you are capable of more than you suspect. Whether you are ready, however, is another question. I cannot tell. Let us hope that it is something that is not asked of you."

Which was not exactly the response I was hoping for.

SEVENTEEN

Mantra

As the light began to fade, Mori's shooter started getting more focused. The untrained would have started to fidget with tension. The kid with the gun just seemed to grow more still, absolutely immobile with the effort of waiting. Yamashita looked at him and nodded with reluctant appreciation. Tomita's pattern was to strike late at night, when the energy and focus of his victims were at their lowest ebb. But Tomita was also unpredictable. He had succeeded in besting the highly skilled before; no one wanted to take chances. We sat quietly. Moved slowly and carefully. Only our eyes shifted quickly.

If the shooter was like a predator hunkered down in the tall grass, his leader seemed more like a tightly wound spring. Whatever his relationship to my *sensei* in the past, I think that it paled in comparison to his driving need to neutralize Tomita. Deep down, I imagine he looked at Yamashita and myself as a secondary concern. We were, in the final analysis, just bait. An expedient. Nothing more.

When my brother came back with me and parked himself in a chair, Mori started to protest. Micky flashed his shield and gave him a wicked smile.

My teacher looked at me. "Is this what you wish, Burke?" I nodded.

He sighed and started to say something, but after a moment, he merely swiveled his head toward Mori and said, "This man is a guest." It seemed to settle the issue. But Micky's presence clearly didn't sit well with Mori. It was one more element he didn't have complete control over.

My *sensei* spent the evening hours talking with me about the way a challenger went about confronting someone in a training hall. I had seen the aftermath of Mitch Reilly's attempt, but it wasn't very informative. Considering how he ended up, Reilly wasn't a particularly good role model.

"When I was younger, Professor," my teacher began, "challenge matches between students in different schools—*taryu jiai*—were not uncommon. They were prohibited in Japan a generation ago, but one occasionally hears of them even today."

"What were they like, Sensei?" I asked. We were seated in the garden again. Somewhere in the building, Mori and his gunslinger were staking out fields of fire and having hushed conversations. As it got darker, their conversations achieved a tone of whispered frenzy. In my master's garden, the faint hoot of car horns sounded like exotic animals far back in the undergrowth.

Yamashita cocked his head to one side. His eyes were wide open but focused inward on the gloom of things past. After a few seconds' consideration, he replied, "They were . . . informative." His hands stirred slightly in his lap with nerve memory. "One could learn a great deal from the experience."

I'll bet, I thought.

"Of course"—he looked right at me—"many people were quite seriously injured in the process. That . . . and the deaths . . . were why the government eventually outlawed them.

"In the old times, Professor, a young warrior would learn all a local *sensei* could teach and then seek out 'instruction' at another *dojo*. A truly skilled fighter could go from school to school, challenging the best students and even the masters." A sip of air as he paused. "It was known as *dojo arashi*."

Dojo storming. I could imagine what it must have been like: hard young men clomping down the packed dirt roads of Japan with battered armor and well-kept weapons slung over their backs. They churned up the miles like hungry predators, hunting down new masters to defeat and new towns to prove themselves in. The good ones earned reputations. The less skilled, in the best of situations, learned to limp away quietly. Sometimes, only their ghosts moaned in phantom processional down midnight crossroads.

"The challenge needs to be delivered according to a certain form," Yamashita continued. "The challenger recites his pedigree and must request a lesson. Depending on the situation, the *sensei* may select a student to fight for him." He looked directly at me. "I do not think this will suit Tomita's purpose in this case, Burke."

Thank God, I silently thought. But I tried not to let the relief show on my face. I had thought a great deal about the prospect of fighting. I knew someone had to do it. And I wanted Tomita stopped. And punished. Destroyed for what he had done to Art. But after all the years I have spent with Yamashita I have become detached in some ways and capable of brutal honesty. I knew, when push came to shove, that there was a chance I was not good enough to face Tomita and prevail. It hurt me to admit it, but it was true. The slightest flaw in my performance would be fatal and meant that Tomita could escape. This, I rationalized, could not be allowed to happen.

But late at night, in the brief period of rest before my master would summon me for training in the darkness, the hot spark of my anger and resolve was smothered by something dense and ominous. It was the thing all warriors struggle against every time a fight beckons. No matter who stands before you, it lurks there too. We try not to name it, for words make the intangible more potent. But the thing that lurks there, cold and dense and lifeless as mud, is fear.

My master was looking at me. I had never spoken to him of this thing, and now he said nothing. But he knew.

Then his narrative continued. "The meetings were often arranged beforehand by seconds."

"Seconds?" I asked, refocusing my attention on the lesson before me.

He smiled and nodded. "It is, after all, a duel, Professor. Usually there are witnesses at the fight itself."

"I doubt it in this case," I commented.

Yamashita nodded in agreement. "Yes. So." He closed his eyes in thought. "But one of the points in engaging in a duel is having the results known. Your prowess celebrated."

"You mean winning is not enough?"

My *sensei* opened his eyes and smiled at me. "Winning in a situation like this is everything. It means you survive. But no, it is not enough."

I looked at him quizzically.

"Tomita needs others to know of his deeds. It is why he leaves the signature at the scene. It is why he takes the risks he does."

I nodded. "I talked with my brother about this. He says that the killer wants to be caught."

Yamashita's eyes narrowed. "He does not wish to be caught, Burke. He wishes to win. To humiliate me and to take revenge. In doing so, he seeks to be acknowledged. Everything else is secondary."

Off in the house, the phone rang. Micky was inside and he picked it up. I could hear the murmur of conversation as a distant background to Yamashita's lecture.

"We need to remember this about Tomita, Burke. He has a"—the *sensei* searched for the word—"need . . . to vanquish the opponent. But the duel also feeds his spirit, his ego. He will attempt to catch his opponent off guard for the duel—it is, after all, *heiho*—but he will also need to follow the ritual forms and force the victim to acknowledge his dominance."

I noticed how Yamashita always spoke of this event like it was something that would happen to someone else, and not to him. It was an interesting way to maintain a certain objectivity.

"This need is a dangerous thing," my teacher continued. "It makes Tomita very focused. Driven. His opponent needs to be focused on the surroundings and ready for him at any moment. But"—he held up a thick forefinger to mark the point—"his need for the ritual may also permit the opponent to avert disaster." My teacher's eyes were very clear as he looked at me. "The one who fights this man must use the pause before the clash to find the center."

The Japanese spoke of the center, the *hara*, as the source of focus and balance and energy, of life. It was an early martial arts lesson that we all learned, and one that was repeated in one form or another during every day of training for the rest of your life.

I thought that his comment on centering was my teacher's final utterance, but Yamashita continued. "Remember, this man needs to defeat his opponent utterly, to humiliate as well as to vanquish. The desire will create a *tsuki*—a gap—in his concentration. It is here that the wise man may find an opportunity for victory. And survival."

I was digesting that little piece of gloom when my brother came out. He seemed eager but not particularly happy.

"I got a call. We got a lead on a lone Japanese national who entered New York a day before the killing. Traveling alone. No record of him leaving the area. He was using a different name, but the description fits. . . . We're canvassing the hotels now." He made a face. "I gotta go."

I walked to the door with him. Mori's man watched us without saying a word, tracking us across the length of the dim *dojo* like a cyborg waiting to acquire a target.

"Listen," Micky said quietly at the door, "let's give this some time to play out. Stay put. There are two plainclothes guys in a car out front, so you should be fine. I'll be back. Don't go anywhere without me." He knelt down and fiddled with his pants cuff. When he stood up, there was a gun in his hand.

"Take this," he said.

"What!" I protested.

"Take it. It's my backup piece. This guy surprises you, you get real close, and don't stop pulling the trigger until it's out of bullets."

"Come on, Mick," I protested. The snub little gun was heavy in my hand. "What am I gonna do with this?"

"With luck, nothing," he said. "Stay put. Stay down and I'll be back soon."

He was out the door and I was left there, peering up and down the street—ever alert for *ninja* assassins—and feeling the heft of the pistol tug at my tired shoulder muscles.

Yamashita slid up behind me in that fluid, silent way he has. He looked at the gun with distaste. "Your brother means well but he doesn't really understand what we do."

"No, Sensei," I had to admit, "he doesn't." We turned back inside and shut the door. The lights of the living area one floor up threw a soft glow down the stairs. The *sensei* and I followed the light, climbing up the steps like moths, moving soundlessly toward the brightness.

"I am not sure what you will do with the pistol, Burke. Generally, in times of great stress, it is wise to use weapons you are familiar with." Yamashita walked over to a side table, where a black lacquered stand held the two swords, long and short, of the *samurai*. He opened a drawer beneath them and removed a smaller weapon, cased in highly polished wood. It was a *tanto*, a small knife. The hiltless handle fit seamlessly with the matching scabbard to create a smooth oblong shape, hiding a blade of razor sharpness.

"Take this. You are better with blades."

I felt a stab of panic. "What do I need any of this for?" I protested.

I thought I caught a flash of impatience surge across Yamashita's face, like the fleeting shadow of a bird moving across a rock face. "Burke. This man does the unexpected. What if he comes now and Mori and his man are not enough? What if he comes later and your brother fails you?" He paused significantly. "What if you are surprised by Tomita and he gets close? You will be in great danger, even if I am near. So . . . you must cut." And here he began pointing out the various points where major arteries would be accessible.

"Here . . ." The smooth scabbard touched my neck. "Here . . ." He moved down my leg to mime severing the femoral artery.

"If Tomita comes in to cut down like so"—he assumed *jodan*, the high stance, which often precedes a vertical cut to the head—"do not be tempted to block the descending arms or to cut at them. The momentum of the blow will carry it through to your head."

It was a familiar lesson, but I let him continue. The rehearsal, the projection of the need to act on another person, seemed to calm my *sensei*. Who was I to upset him?

"Do not cut the arms," he repeated. "Instead, slice here"—the *tanto* moved horizontally across my abdomen—"and the attacker will collapse."

He looked at me, and I nodded. "Also," he finished, "think about the eyes." As he said this, the phone rang again and I moved toward it.

"You mean watch the eyes to see where an attack will go?" I asked. It's an old adage in the martial arts. I was half-turned to pick up the phone, but I saw his look of disgusted disappointment.

"No," Yamashita sighed. "I mean think about stabbing him in the eyes."

Which was why, I suppose, I wasn't too focused when I answered the call. The mental image of ramming the *tanto* into an eye socket and burying the blade deep into a brain was a bit intense, even after the last few days.

It was Bobby Kay. A lot had happened since we first met, and even though Bobby's name had resurfaced with Micky, I hadn't really thought much about him lately. He was all charm on the phone, however, as if we were old pals.

"Hello, Professor! How are ya?" Ever the glad-hander, Bobby's mouth was often in gear way before his brain caught up. If he had paused to think even for a minute, he

would have known the answer. I was up to my ears in a
hunt for a murderer. As it turned out, his question was en-
tirely rhetorical.

"Hey, I was wondering whether you could come by,
Burke. You and Yamashita." Here a note of tension crept
into his voice. Bobby continued the conversation, oblivious
to the silence on my end. "Something's turned up. I think
you should see it."

"Oh yeah?" I finally grunted.

"Yeah. Absolutely."

"Can't you tell me over the phone, Bobby?"

"Oh. Uh . . . It's a little complicated, ya know? Better to
come here and see what I've got." He paused, then asked,
as if the thought had just sprung up, "Hey, is your brother
still working on the case?"

I could hear a voice inside me, one that sounded a lot
like Micky's, ask what is going on? And why tell this guy
anything? But I didn't listen to it. And in retrospect, I
should have. "Yeah," I replied simply, "he's out chasing
some lead right now."

"Well, let's hope it works out." Akkadian didn't sound
very sincere, but what else was new? "So, whattaya think?
Can you two come down?"

I thought that I didn't really want to see Bobby Kay just
now. I had bigger concerns. Part of me was feeling guilty
about having kept Micky in the dark for so long. I wondered whether the visit might help him. I ran through the
pro's and con's of Bobby's request in my mind.

Bobby said he had some clues that could help me. Pro.

Bobby was also a shameless creep and it could just turn
out to be a wild goose chase or some dopey scheme for him
to make money. Con.

Tomita would come at a later hour. It was his way. I
could be pretty sure it would be OK to head to Manhattan
tonight. Yamashita's *dojo* was the locus of action and there
would be plenty of time to get back. We probably wouldn't
miss anything if we went. Pro.

Micky had told me to stay put. Con.

But this might help him out. Pro.

I stopped at that point, happy with the persuasiveness of the last idea. Looking back, I know it was as stupid as a kid rigging a game of "eenie-meenie-minee-mo" to get the desired outcome. But, as someone once said, the heart has a mind of its own. Sometimes, I also wonder whether I was secretly glad to be escaping the danger that hung around the *dojo* like a heavy, oily cloud of vapor, invisible but real for all that. To this day, I'm not sure.

I quietly told Yamashita about the call. He nodded silently in agreement. Then he stared meaningfully at the pistol still in my hand. I gave it to him, and it was replaced with the smooth feel of the *tanto*.

"Where is your car?" Softly, to keep Mori unaware.

It was around the block. Yamashita digested this, then said quietly, "You go first. I will meet you at the car."

As I moved toward the front door, Mori's shooter tried to stop me and I told him I was just heading out to pick something up at the corner store. The fact that I wasn't carrying Micky's gun seemed to reassure him. From his perspective, only a lunatic would give up a weapon like that. And, with a shrug, he let me go. Eternal vigilance is a real conversation killer.

I was glad to get out. Being away from the tense atmosphere, from Yamashita's relentless training and the barely controlled tension of Mori and his shooter, made the whole situation seem so unreal. Moving down the street toward my car that night, things almost felt like normal. I saw the plainclothes unit sitting there, but nobody stopped me. They were there to watch people coming in, not going out.

Yamashita appeared out of the shadows and joined me.

"How'd you get out?" I asked.

"I used an old *ninja* trick: I slipped out the back door while no one was looking."

The night was hot, traffic was light, and, as we approached it from a distance, Manhattan had that orange glow it gets in the summer, a pulsing aura generated by the play of pollution, trapped heat, and escaping light. The water of the East River looked hard and black as we drove over the bridge. High-rise buildings were brownish-gray in the murk, dappled in random patterns by lit windows.

Midtown at night is never really at rest. It's lit with sodium lamps along the streets and avenues, a higher-visibility twilight spiked by the brighter wash of light leaking from small stores and restaurants. But when I slowed to get a look at the building where we were heading, the Samurai House looked dark. It made me worry, and rekindled the runaway paranoia that I had developed recently. You can drown out the shouting of inner voices only for so long.

I parked up the block and Yamashita and I walked slowly down the sidewalk toward the entrance, scanning the street for anything out of the ordinary. This was Manhattan, however, and even on a good day it was hard to do that. There was the usual road traffic. Sports cars with tinted windows rocked over the uneven street surface, the pulsing bass of souped-up stereos clearly audible even at a distance. Pedestrians hustled by, anxious to get through the relatively deserted commercial block and into some air conditioning. There were buses. Taxis. The occasional piece of litter—a paper receipt or a coffee cup—was crumpled in the gutter, inert in the breathless night air.

When I looked through the glass entrance, the lobby lights of Samurai House were turned way down. No security guard was in sight. But when I tugged at them, the doors to the lobby opened.

"Hello?" I called. Yamashita ghosted in beside me and stood stock still. I checked the doors to the office complex to my right. They were locked, which was odd: I expected to find Bobby there. A brief spurt of annoyance washed through me: was Bobby Kay playing some weird game? I stood for a moment, thinking. But Yamashita had trained me well over the years. My body did the things it was supposed to do, even when the mind was not functioning well. Even as a jumble of thoughts and emotions flashed through me in a swirl, there was a part of me that was working more systematically. It was listening. Sensing. Feeling.

You usually hear all sorts of noise in places like this. The wash of the ventilation system, street sounds bleeding in from the outside, the muffled clump of people in other parts of the building. But in the lobby of Samurai House, the waterfall's whisper tended to mask most other sounds. I could feel the faint press of cool air on my skin, the slight give of the lobby carpet under my feet. My eyes adjusted to the dimness from the low lighting. I stood there passive, one more shadow in a universe of shades. Waiting.

And then I knew. It was that sudden certainty again. A jolting rush of that animal intuition, arriving with such clarity that I found it simultaneously startling and impossible to doubt. They talk a great deal about the state called *mushin* in the martial arts. It's the point where the body and the mind develop such an intimate and immediate connection that you know, you react without conscious thought. Standing there, a washed-out shadow lost among all the others cast by faint light, I felt the hair on my forearms stand up, and the electric cold spread up and across my shoulders.

I sensed him.

I can't explain how I came to this awareness, but I did. I knew it with a visceral certainty. Was it a sound? A smell? A phantom pulse in air pressure? Even now, I don't know. Yamashita would say it doesn't matter. It was enough that I knew.

A glance at my teacher confirmed my intuition. He was immobile, but you got the feeling of an almost unbearable intensity building in him. He sensed danger as well.

I slowed my breathing down and strained in the silence for a clue. I could feel my eyes widen and the muscles in my face tense up. Without thinking, I had crouched down slightly, knees bent, body ready to move. Find the center. The *hara*.

On the other side of the lobby, a faint glow from the gallery and *dojo* area registered in my peripheral vision.

Lights were on in there somewhere. We headed toward the *dojo* slowly, gliding across the lobby space in front of the waterfall. I could sense the minute increase of humidity the falling water created there, and I was hoping that it would mask the sound of my approach while I was simultaneously fearful that it was doing the same for him.

Because Tomita was here. Somewhere. Waiting.

A small, panicked version of the animal in me bleated in protest. It wasn't supposed to be like this. There was no backup from Micky. No trap for Yamashita to spring on Tomita. Despite my teacher's presence, I felt alone, and the realization came with sickening clarity that Micky had been right all along. Evil arrives on its own terms, not on yours.

I was imitating Yamashita, creeping at a glacial pace, edging through the lobby, trying to move carefully, but that's only a partial explanation. I felt like a dreamer being pulled by an irresistible force toward something horrible. It was like being caught in the grip of a magnetic field. Or an undertow. And I fought against it, even though I knew I had to go in there. Because there was a dissonant chorus sounding off inside my head, each voice clamoring for attention. There was fear. And anger. Panic. A brief urge to run.

But I didn't, because over it all, a sudden voice, quiet but implacable, silenced everything. *You are meant to meet him. It was what Yamashita had feared. What he trained you for. Tomita is in there. He's waiting for you,* the voice said. And I was afraid.

It was the last despairing peep of that animal, frantic to be acknowledged. So I did. *I am afraid,* I admitted. But I kept moving. Not toward Tomita. Toward the one lesson my teacher could not guide me through.

I know I should have been using the techniques that Yamashita had taught me. Maybe *kuji-in* would have helped me focus. But, at that moment, it was all I could do to maintain breathing discipline and not let the sweat that was popping out on my forehead unnerve me. I blinked and moved forward, wading through an invisible force that pushed me forward and pulled me back at the same time.

And the image that flickered across my mind right then was not the warrior's grid of power, the figure that Yamashita had cut into the air on a quiet afternoon, laboring to etch it into my brain.

It was, instead, a hard face, cast in bronze, staring out at the world from the shadows of an old and familiar place. And that image came with its own mantra, one Yamashita had never taught me:

> *Michael the Archangel defend us in battle,*
> *that we may not perish in the fiery judgment.*

I went in.

EIGHTEEN

Dojo Storming

The setup in the cavernous room hadn't really changed since the night I had last been there. As things had turned out, I never got to walk through the display, but the exhibits were still there, dimly shrouded in the weak security lighting, like treasures abandoned in a cave. One of the major elements in the display, a façade of wood beams and shingles simulating the entrance to a Zen temple, jutted into the display space along one wall. It was essentially a latticework of beams capped with the distinctive curved roof you find in shrines. A wooden gate stood symbolically across the opening. A workman's scaffolding was pushed up against the faux temple, in preparation for the dismantling of the exhibit. The performance space was still there. A few lights, recessed into the ceiling, cast sporadic circles of brightness on the floor. The rest was dense shadow.

I edged into the room with Yamashita, hoping my vision would adjust in time. But there was no rushing attack as we entered, no figure exploding from the black wedges of shadow. Instead, in the corner to our right, was a figure. It was perfectly still for a moment, as if frozen into place by something I could not see.

We moved toward Bobby Kay and the motion seemed to

galvanize him. He approached us and broke into that horsey grin of his.

"Hey, Burke. I'm glad you could come." He looked at Yamashita and ducked his head deferentially. "Both of you."

Yamashita seemed not to hear him. He was gazing off into the room's dark corners, his thick head slowly moving to maximize his sensitivity to sight and sound.

"What's the deal, Bobby?" I was certain there was danger here. I couldn't believe this idiot couldn't feel it.

He gestured toward the temple façade. "Something's turned up. I think you should see it."

"What?"

He made a come-along motion. "You've got to see it. I can't believe it. I mean, that it should turn up . . ." He started to head toward the temple.

I grabbed his arm. The contact made his head jerk and his eyes narrow slightly, like an animal's.

"No. Right here is good enough," I told him.

He pulled his arm out of my grip with a sullen shrug of the shoulder. Then his face broke into a sly grin and he looked first at me, then at my teacher. "It's the *bokken*, Burke. Ittosai's sword. It's been returned."

"Where?" It was the first thing Yamashita had said to him.

Again the gesture toward the temple. "I'll show ya. There's some sort of note with it, but it's in Japanese. Maybe one of you can figure it out."

Yamashita began to move along with him.

"Sensei," I hissed in warning.

He held out a hand to tell me to stay put. "I will go, Burke. *Ki o tsukete*."

It was the traditional swordsman's call to awareness. My teacher felt what I did. He was sending me an instruction. And a warning.

There was a faint light within the temple display. The gate was slightly ajar. A long, cloth-wrapped shape rested inside the temple façade, only thirty feet away. Akkadian was babbling away about the sword's mysterious reappearance, but Yamashita paid him no heed. He was focused on the object, with examining it, and returning to me.

In his haste, he got ahead of Bobby. My *sensei* pushed aside the heavy gate and entered the small space. He knelt to examine the object. Bobby lagged behind, resting a hand on the gate. Then, too late, I saw he wasn't resting. He was pushing.

The gate jarred closed and the vibration shook the scaffolding. Akkadian made a motion and I heard the metallic click as a lock snapped into place. Yamashita launched himself against the gate, but for once his timing was off. He thudded against the barrier, and the scaffolding began to shift. I shouted a warning. My teacher turned and had time to raise one arm to protect himself from the collapsing pipes and boards. Then he was borne down.

The noise—the crash and splintering of wood, the ringing of metal pipes as they hit the floor—was still reverberating when I got over to him. Bobby had scuttled out of the way across the room toward a dark corner. The gate was locked and I peered in to see my teacher. But when I reached Yamashita, he was looking across the room.

My teacher was cut on the head and banged up, but the most critical injury was the arm he had used to try to ward off the collapse. He held it with that ginger pose that tells you all you need to know.

I knelt and looked at him as well as I could through the lattice of heavy wood. "It is broken." He grimaced. I started to spin around to find Bobby Kay, but my teacher's voice restrained me.

"Burke," he hissed, "it is a trap. Beware."

"Come on," I said working the lock, "let's get you out of this."

Yamashita closed his eyes in weary resignation. "It is too late for that." He looked off into the darkness and swallowed. "You must go there." I shook the gate in token protest, but we both knew what he meant. I stood slowly and turned around, away from my teacher.

Bobby Kay stood on the other side of the room and spoke. "I told you they would come," he said.

He was talking into the darkness at the far corner. I came up to him and he backed away.

A low hissing shot from the shadows. "Fool! He was to be restrained, not injured!"

Bobby blanched at the venom in the voice from the darkness. "I told you," he said again. His voice shook a bit. "Now give me the sword."

I was half-listening to the conversation, but much of my attention was on the visual field and the silent, invisible currents of *harage*. I was alive to the threat that hung in the air, dancing in the darkness just out of reach. I had learned my lesson. Even as I looked at Bobby, I angled myself a bit so I could catch any movement out of the corner of my eye.

"You set this up, Akkadian," I said, my voice choked with the last vestige of fear and the rise of anger. Something stirred in the murk. I turned all the way around toward the fat corner of the room. Bobby had started to move in that direction. I watched him as he got nearer to the shadows.

For a moment, I wanted to ask why. I wanted to scream at him. At the situation. At whatever lurked across the room. But there wasn't time. Things began falling away, all the useless distractions of emotion and random thought. I felt it, like the sensation of a series of weights falling, one by one, from my back.

There was a smooth movement in the dark and a figure began to emerge into the light. Events were accelerating and yet, simultaneously, I had the sensation of acute perception and a slow, elastic lengthening of time. Things appeared sharper, clearer. They moved with a slow, fluid inevitability.

Bobby thought he was slick, but he was way out of his league. Whatever deal he thought he had cut, Tomita would never let him walk away. After the fight was over, if Tomita survived, he would finish off his witness. It would take about three seconds.

I couldn't let that happen. Because once Tomita was done with Bobby, he would go after Yamashita.

I swallowed with the realization that another human being in this room wanted to kill me.

After that point, events, though drawn out, also seem a bit blurred in my memory: not a sequence of actions, but a long, fluid thread that spools out in my mind.

There was a host of visual and aural images being processed. And I was experiencing a series of sensations that made some of what was taking place seem remote. Increasingly, only the force emanating from Tomita seemed sharp and real.

Bobby asked for the sword again. This time, the voice that answered was clear. The accent was Japanese, but that was no surprise. The sound was remarkable, however, for the sense of power it projected. "No," it said. "You get it when I am finished. When both men are dead."

Bobby was closer to him and must have caught a glimpse of the expression on Tomita's face, because you could see the effect: Akkadian stopped dead in his tracks and backed up. All the way to the door. I moved into the center of the room. I faced the figure, trying to remain aware of everything around me. But the background sensations were getting fainter and fainter in the face of the energy Tomita threw off.

I stood there, eyes narrowed as if they could peer through the shadow, breath rising and falling in an easy, soundless rhythm. Waiting. A rock.

He came forward. He was clad in dark street clothes but was barefoot. "I am Tomita," he said and bowed.

When you know something of an individual's past, you believe you can read it on his or her face. Tomita's was unremarkable in its Asian features: a small nose, high cheekbones, the dark eyes. He was not particularly tall, but his compact form gave the impression of a tremendous energy harnessed and compacted by years of relentless training.

There was a half-smile, grimly amused, that played across his face. But behind that, there was rage. It made him seem to swell, grow fuller and more menacing. I tingled with an awareness of how dangerous this man was. I remembered Yamashita's assessment of his skill, even at the beginning of his training with the Kunaicho, all those years ago. What would he be like now? I thought of the crime scenes I had studied. I got a fleeting image of Reilly, crumpled on this very floor. The crime scene reports for Ikagi and Kubata. And I thought of Art.

But now the time for thinking was at an end. Tomita had bowed to me, and I needed to return the courtesy. Do not let your eyes drop from him, Yamashita had said. I didn't.

I looked at him again as if truly seeing him for the first time. What I saw was no longer just the typical visual impression you get of a person; it was one element that would help me form a strategy. On the street, you merely look at people. Here, I needed to *see*.

Tomita smiled and gestured to the floor. It was a very tight smile, a social nicety and not a barometer of an internal state. His white teeth glittered briefly: a flash of bone, not of emotion. I slipped off my shoes; my feet were bare. We both sat down warily, simultaneously obeying the dictates of etiquette and watching, alert for the slightest offensive movement. We were like springs being wound into a casing, tightly coiled for action. I used *tatehiza*, a sitting posture preferred by old-time warriors on the battlefield. Beginners don't like it much, but it's easier to spring up from it than from some of the more formal postures.

He saw my strategy, of course, and nodded affably in my direction. "Yes," he said thoughtfully. "You would know that . . ."

Tomita raised his voice but never took his eyes off me. "You have taught him well, Sensei."

I could hear the faint rustle of movement as Yamashita, in evident pain, stood and addressed his old pupil.

"There is no need for this," Yamashita said.

"*Ie*, Yamashita-san," Tomita said with venom. "There is every reason. I have dreamed of this. For years, I burned with shame at what you did . . . at what the others did . . ."

You could see the rage building within him, leaking out as he spoke.

"Tomita!" Yamashita protested.

It took a visible effort for Tomita to calm himself. "When that happened, I felt as if things had come adrift. Only training served as a tether."

Tomita rose slowly and walked toward my *sensei*, gazing at him as you would at a caged animal. There was contempt there. But Tomita only moved a few steps in my teacher's direction. I sensed fear as well.

"I knew someday that I would face you, Sensei," the younger man told Yamashita. "I worked for years to perfect myself. To be able to show you"—he swallowed—"just how wrong you were."

"You know the decision was not mine alone," Yamashita rasped out. "I could do no different."

Tomita snorted in disgust. "It is a weak answer. To think, all these years, I hesitated to confront you." Tomita laughed, a hard, short noise with no joy in it. "I should have seen earlier how weak you really were."

"Let me out," Yamashita coaxed. "We will see."

Tomita's eyes glinted as he smiled. "In time. If that idiot Akkadian had not damaged you, it would have been glorious. As it is now, it will merely be the end of the ritual . . ." Tomita glided back toward the center of the room, where I stood. He continued speaking but with his back to my teacher.

"Life's surprises are endless. And I have always struggled to see the purpose in it." He sighed. "You have helped me see, Sensei. You have brought me humiliation . . . and now disappointment. But after all this time, I have come to truly see. There is a curious liberation to it all, *neh*? The sense of being untethered. Free of restraint and able to act as you wish. It took me years to forge my will to this end."

His eyes didn't really seem like they were registering my presence; they were focused on some inner reality. But now they bore into me. "You would not understand, Burke. You *gaijin* never grasp the essence of the arts."

"I think I've grasped the fact that you are nuts." My voice started out raspy but gained in strength.

Tomita smiled ruefully and shook his head. "Of course. You cannot see it." Again his voice was raised for his old teacher's benefit. "You have made many mistakes, Sensei. You should never have turned me away. . . ."

"It was not in my power to prevent," Yamashita said.

"How convenient," Tomita replied contemptuously. Then he returned to his thoughts. "You should never have come to this country. You have squandered your heritage. The gift that the gods gave us . . ."

Then Tomita spoke to me. "You think I am a madman, Burke? Because of the murders?" He nodded. "You cannot see. These acts are like . . . ceremonies for the gods. They are fiercely pure. They lay bare *kokoro*, the heart of things. When the fight is done, you cannot imagine the feeling . . . the sense of . . . fusion to the world of *kami*, of spirits." He smiled again. "And it is done on my terms."

"Tomita," Yamashita breathed, "this must end."

It was a strain to just wait there, listening to them and waiting for the ritual to unfold. Down deep, I could feel the currents swirling about the room. Despite the flow of words and the smiles, there was tension here. You could feel it building slowly, ratcheting up. Behind those dark eyes, there was rage.

I said nothing.

"So," Tomita said calmly as he kneeled again, "to the task at hand." He sat up a bit straighter and said, "I am Tomita . . ."

"Formerly of the Kunaicho," I interrupted, just to rattle him a bit.

Some of the true danger in him shot out briefly from his eyes, escaping from behind the barrier he had placed there.

"I am a student of the Morita-ha Tengu-shin *ryu*. I am *menkyo kaiden* there and a *yudansha* in Yanagi-ryu jujutsu and kendo. I have killed four men in duels. I request a lesson."

It told me nothing, other than that there were more victims than we were aware of. I had never heard of the Tengu-shin *ryu*. *Tengu* are the winged mountain goblins of Japanese legend. Master swordsmen, in the old stories they sometimes teach mortals their art. Depending on how "*shin*" was written, it could refer to some sort of divine revelation, the heart, or a deity of some sort. All I really could tell was that the man before me had had a variety of training. And he killed people.

He bowed toward me at the conclusion of his recital. It was my turn.

"I am Burke," I began. The Japanese tend not to use the given name in situations like this. "I am a student of Yamashita-ha Itto *ryu*. I am *yudansha* in Shotokan karatedo and Kodokan judo. I have killed no man in a duel."

Tomita grinned ferally at me.

"Until tonight," I concluded. His grin just got harder looking.

He stood up suddenly, and so did I. It wasn't really a conscious reaction on my part. It was as if we were connected by a string.

He was watching, and he nodded again in mock approval. He was always watching, that one. Everything, every gesture, every facial tic, told him something about his opponent. He gestured languidly to the side of the *dojo*.

"Here are weapons for you to choose from."

"Why me?" I asked. I was surprised to hear the words spoken out loud. It was the last squeak of the scared animal in all of us.

He paused and looked at me. "Ah? Why you?"

I just nodded. I didn't trust my voice anymore.

"You are his *deshi*, Mr. Burke. His disciple, yes?" I didn't answer and he didn't seem to care. Part of me was glad to have him talk; it gave me time to prepare.

"Your teacher destroyed my life. I have trained for years, and now I will destroy him. But before that, I will take away what he values most."

He paused and eyed me speculatively. "Have you been a teacher, Burke? Do you know what matters most to a *sensei*? It is not life that is precious—*bushi* are trained not to fear death." He paused and glared at me. And in that look you could feel the fury that must have lanced through him every day of his life. "Before I kill him, I want him to know that I have destroyed everything he has worked to create." I tried not react in any way. "I will take away his most prized student, Burke. I will kill you."

He gestured again. A mat had been placed on the floor. Matched pairs of *bokken* and *jo* lay there. I moved cautiously toward them, stepping sideways to keep him to my front. The choice of weapon was critical, but only if I knew what he would be using.

"And you?" I questioned, gesturing at the weapons.

He faded back into the shadows and emerged, holding a familiar weapon. It was the *katana* I had seen in Bobby Kay's photos so long ago.

"You took it," I breathed.

He drew the weapon from its scabbard. The steel hissed faintly against the case. Tomita regarded the blade admiringly as the light winked along its length. "The opportunity was . . . unexpected. But the good *bushi* must act decisively."

Then Tomita gestured with it. "As I told Mr. Akkadian, I still have some use for this weapon."

He came toward me and opened his arms wide, the sword in his right hand. I put down the *tanto* my teacher had given me and picked up a *jo*.

He smiled grimly, then paused. "The *jo*, Burke? I had hoped for more of a challenge." He sighed and slowly sheathed the blade. "Very well. Let us play a little." He set down the sword and stooped to grasp a *bokken*.

The story goes that the *samurai* who codified techniques for the *jo* once challenged Miyamoto Musashi to a duel using another weapon and was defeated. Only after he had perfected the use of the short staff was he able to beat the master swordsman, Musashi. The story was pretty well known, and part of me hoped it would act subliminally to erode Tomita's confidence.

Part of me just liked the weapon.

We stood facing each other in the ready position. The *jo* is longer than the wooden sword, but the *bokken* is heavier. Tomita watched me briefly, his eyes flat and his body relaxed. Then the attack came.

They say the thing that marks a true master is not the force behind an attack, but the speed it's launched with. When Tomita moved, it was a blur. I whipped the *jo* up to meet the strike, parrying and looking for the opportunity to counter.

Looking is not the right word. It implies some sort of visual isolation and mental identification. But Tomita was so quick, that was impossible. Things were happening so rapidly that the moves seemed to merge into a fluid sequence, a continuum of extreme danger. At such a high level of play, the weapons tended to "stick"—we maintained contact with each other for as long as possible. The *jo* met the *bokken* and directed it away from the target. Tomita slid the sword forward and in along the length of the *jo*. I pulled it back into a reverse posture, but he pressed forward. I slid to my right, hoping to bring the staff up, around, and down, but he leapt out of range.

There was a tremendous amount of movement going on. We spun and surged through the alternating areas of darkness and light in the room. The effect was strobelike: the struggle pulsed and jerked in the alternating light levels. A great deal of fighting is keyed to sight cues that are extremely subtle. I could feel my eyes straining as I tried to follow and then anticipate Tomita.

At one point, there was a minute hesitation in his back step. It happens sometimes, for no specific reason that can be anticipated—an irregularity in floor surface, a muscle group flexing or contracting a split second before it should—but I leapt at the opening it presented.

The *jo* came whistling down from high on my right to smash his collarbone. He just managed to pull back from the strike and let the tip of the weapon carry on down toward the floor. I allowed the momentum to carry me in and past him, then reversed the *jo*'s direction in a tight arc, cutting upward with a *gyaku-uchi*, a reverse strike.

Tomita sensed the threat and tried to roll out to his left side. Instead of smashing squarely into him, the tip of the *jo* only nicked his ear. But it was traveling so fast it actually ripped away part of the earlobe. I saw the bright start of blood begin there. Any wound on the head bleeds.

Yamashita had drilled me over and over again to pursue the opponent's weakness without mercy. I let go of the *jo* with my left hand, and followed my momentum in toward Tomita. I slammed the open palm of my hand into the bloody side of his head, hoping to pop the eardrum. He flinched away in an automatic response. I closed with the *jo* and struck down on his right hand. The staff landed with a crack at the base of his thumb. He hissed.

There were schools of swordsmanship in the old days that specialized in cutting off the thumbs of their opponents. Without the thumb, you can't hold the sword. It was supposed to be a humane way to defeat someone without having to kill them.

I wasn't thinking humanely. Right then, I was just trying to land a decisive blow.

Tomita moved away, and I could tell that he couldn't wield the *bokken* well anymore. It's a weapon that needs two hands, and his right thumb was probably broken.

I pressed him, advancing with the tip of the *jo* pointed at his throat. Tomita exploded in a lateral dive. Landing among the weapons on the floor, he unsheathed the *katana* before I could get to him.

The long sword can be wielded with only one hand.

Lights caught on the highly polished surface of the blade. He rose from the floor in a fluid motion. I backed up, adjusting to the new threat.

The *katana*'s cutting edge is like a finely honed razor. Mere incidental cuts can slice through a human form with ease. In a fight like this, even a minimal injury was a death sentence. But the *katana*'s sharp edge is also its weak point: it is so brittle, you can shatter a blade with a wooden weapon. If you have the nerve to get close enough. And Yamashita had warned me against that.

Tomita moved toward me. Almost subliminally, I registered the slight droop of the sword tip that comes before a strike. It was a common error, and I should have been suspicious. But momentum has a power all its own, and I was drawn to the apparent flaw. The end of my *jo* touched the side of his blade. I tried to follow the *katana* up as Tomita pulled it over his head for the strike. But suddenly, he lunged forward with his foot raised, and brought it down with a stomping kick directed at my left thigh.

It was a bone-breaking move. The idea is to distract the enemy by making him focus on the sword, then deliver a lower-level attack with another weapon. And I almost fell for it. As it was, I had to collapse the leg and fall with the direction of the kick in order to save myself.

His foot still smashed into me with an almost paralyzing force. I rolled out and away, desperate to avoid the sword blade. I stood, trying to test the leg, which felt numb and wobbly, without letting him see what damage he had caused. I attacked.

Looking back, it was a big mistake. He was fighting left-handed, and most practice in Japanese swordsmanship is based on right-hand dominance. My leg made things even more awkward. The attack faltered. Tomita shuffled back slightly. I was overcommitted and felt myself toppling in toward him, losing my balance.

He shuffled back again, trying to pull me in more. I scrambled desperately to regain my footing, but the muscle damage in my left leg made it sluggish and clumsy. I felt myself going, losing the balance that is critical in a fight. Tomita loomed before me, *katana* raised.

Instinctively, I turned away, flinching from the blow about to come. I heard the temple gate crash open and a shout from Yamashita. Then I made a last, desperate attempt to lurch out of range. My teacher shot across my line of vision and rammed into Tomita. But the younger man deflected him and continued to move in on me. Yamashita fell hard and collapsed in a heap. I heard the whistle of the sword as it arced down. It bit into me, and I could feel the tip bump across the ribs in my back.

I was down. I knew I should keep moving, but the impact of the cut was like a paralyzing jolt from a high tension line. For a brief second, I was shocked into stillness. Then Tomita was on me.

He must have dropped the sword. Maybe he lost his grip. Maybe it would have been too easy for him to finish me that way. I was slumped there, half-sitting, holding myself up with my left arm. The dying Gaul. He came up behind me and his arm circled my neck, snaking around from the left like a thick, steel cable. The other hand pushed against the right side of my head, forcing my neck against the arm.

It's a version of *hadaka jime,* a choke hold in judo. Very simple. Very deadly. When an opponent gets it in right, you have about three seconds before the pressure on your neck cuts off the flow of blood to your brain. After that, the world turns into blackness.

The only thing I had going for me was the fact that one of Tomita's hands was less than fully functional. I tried to squirm into a better position, but he was up against me from behind, and the cut in my back seemed to be limiting my ability to move.

I struggled against the pressure he was exerting. The vertebrae in my neck made little popping sounds as I tried to resist the force of the choke. I was desperate to work my chin and jawbone down below the choking arm to protect the neck. I couldn't get there. Then Tomita spoke in my ear.

"That night after the performance, I had hoped to finish this with your master, but you interfered. He escaped, and I will take his life soon. But you, Burke," he hissed, "he values you. I see this. And now I will take you from him. It will destroy him. You are beaten, Burke. Say it." He squeezed a little tighter. "Say it." His tone almost sounded like a giggle, except the voice was too raspy, too deadly serious. "Say it and I might let him live." He paused. "Then again, maybe I won't . . ."

Part of me was listening, but part of me was somewhere else as well. Yamashita had told me this gap would appear. Tomita's need for recognition. For dominance. He was playing with me, but it was important to him that I respond. I could feel the arm tighten slowly around my neck as he talked, building to a final, mighty squeeze, timed to end as his little speech did. He was expecting me to explode. It would be the reaction he needed. The acknowledgment he sought.

I didn't need to move my jaw too far. I opened my mouth as wide as I could and bit into Tomita's arm, straining against the fabric and skin, flesh and blood. I wanted my teeth to meet. I felt his muscles jumping against my tongue as I worked at him. The hand that pressed my head actually forced my mouth deeper for a split second, then the pressure was gone.

My ears were ringing from the approach of a blackout, but his howl was clear even so. He scrambled off me, reaching once again for the sword.

I jumped on him in a faltering, desperate lurch. I hoped his right thumb was broken and I was sure I had chewed my way through some of his left arm. It made Tomita a split second too slow, his movements too clumsy.

He was on his knees, reaching for the blade when I hit him from behind. He slammed forward, and with the force of my impact, his head actually whiplashed, smacking into my face. I heard the bone in my nose go.

I climbed to one side and locked up his arm. He lay there for a second, facedown, squirming, but the lock is designed to keep you away from danger and your opponent immobilized. If he struggles, you can dislocate the shoulder, the elbow, and even break the arm. But you rarely have to, because fighting the joint lock is too painful.

But then Tomita stopped squirming and started, very deliberately, to fight the lock.

It was incredible. I had him tight and there was no way

he could get away, short of dislocating the shoulder. I could feel the grating strain the lock was putting on all the joints in his right arm. He grunted and turned his head toward me. The side of his head was bloody. I could see his right eye roll back into the corner to stare at me. It was like a glimpse of some primeval world. The glare was steady and dark and malevolent.

Then he began, very slowly and systematically, to force the shoulder dislocation that would let him escape the immobilization hold. And all the while, he stared at me, a patient, savage force waiting to be unleashed again.

It was unnerving. There was only one thing to do. I barred his upper arm with my right forearm and forced the lower limb up and through the elbow joint. It made an ugly sound, and Tomita yelped once before I slammed my elbow into the point where the neck meets the head. I grunted from the effort and the tearing sensation the move made in my back. I did it again. And again.

The tension in his body eased.

Blood

I slumped back on the floor and realized that the taste in my mouth was Tomita's blood. I spit dryly for a moment, my breath raspy in a throat that felt like it had been scoured with sand. I felt sick.

I dragged myself away from the still form of Tomita. The wooden floor was a slick, bloody mess. I stood up, but hunched over again with a wave of nausea. Burke, the puking warrior. There was blood on the floor, wet and shiny. I slumped with my good side against a wall.

Yamashita approached. He was carrying the cloth bundle that held Ittosai's sword. He looked me over and said, "We must go. Quickly." But before we left, he drifted over to the body. He stared at his old pupil for a moment, then stooped and picked something up. The *katana*.

We shuffled our way out into the lobby. It felt like a long trip.

Bobby was waiting there.

"Burke . . ." He was looking at me, taking in the damage. Then he spotted the swords in my teacher's hand.

"Hey, great," he said brightly. "Thanks, I'll take those."

Yamashita stared stonily.

"No," I told him.

"Whaddaya mean, no?" When he was serious, Bobby's

face got flat, and the long, horsey shape seemed to settle back into his shoulders.

"They will be returned to their rightful owners," Yamashita said.

Bobby seemed not to hear.

"It was the insurance, wasn't it?" I asked. I had to lick my lips clear, because my nose was still bleeding.

"I need it back. It's supposed to be covered for a hundred fifty g's," he replied. "Give it to me." It was the hard, calculating tone of the real Bobby Kay, businessman.

"I think we'll hold on to it," I said.

"It's mine," Bobby protested. He moved like he was going to keep us from getting out the lobby doors. I saw he had my *tanto* in his hands. We probably didn't look like we were much of a threat. I knew I was having a hard time standing. Yamashita looked old and used up.

I took a deep breath, and you could hear it because I had to breathe through my mouth. It made a ragged sound. "Akkadian, you get the fuck out of my way. Or I will take that knife away and gut you."

At that point, I'm not really sure that I would have been physically capable of doing much more than standing there. But Yamashita says spirit is everything. I put everything I had into the way I looked at him. For a giddy moment, I had the sensation of looking out at the world through my teacher's eyes.

Bobby's spirit was like the man himself: weak. Besides, I think my appearance scared him. I must have looked like hell.

He backed down. The knife clattered to the floor, and we inched our way out. I heard a series of faint beeps made indistinct by the rushing of the waterfall. I turned to look at Bobby. He was holding a cell phone in his hand.

Better move.

But they were already there. Bobby must have had these two goons standing by at the ready outside the building. They popped out of a parked sedan and stood there on the sidewalk. They were both big, with thick upper torsos and waists that looked tiny in comparison. My eyes were still a bit blurry but one of them had a slicked-back head of silver hair. He seemed to be in charge. The lapels of his dark, open-collared shirt were neatly spread out over his summer-weight sports coat. A gold chain glittered at his throat. As my vision cleared, I saw that he was tan and had little wrinkles at the corners of his eyes. He regarded us calmly.

His younger partner seemed jumpy. His head was shaved and he had a closely trimmed goatee. He wore a sports coat as well, but the shirt underneath it was a black collarless number. A pair of shades dangled from his jacket pocket. He turned his head from one direction to the other, checking out the surroundings. Or looking for witnesses. A small earring twinkled in the streetlight. They looked like an ad for Rent-a-Thug.

"C'mon, man, let's go," the Earring urged.

His partner didn't respond and peered a bit closer at me. "Holy shit, pal, what happened to you guys?"

"Bad night," I answered.

"No shit." His eyes shifted to a spot behind me. It was probably Akkadian coming out to join the party. "Well, no need for more trouble. Why don't you give me Mr. Akkadian's swords, and we can all call it a night?" He sounded very reasonable.

"No," I said, and he looked at me with a practiced look of professional disappointment combined with anticipation.

The young one started to move toward us. As he did, he reached into his jacket and pulled out a gun. It looked a lot like the one Mori's shooter used.

"Aww, this is bullshit," he protested. "Let's do this guy and the old man, grab the stuff, and get the fuck outta here."

As he was moving toward us I could see over his shoulder. The headlights of a car were getting bigger fast. Someone was in a hurry, the car swerving a little as it sped up the street. The sound of the revving car engine made Earring turn around.

The vehicle bounced up the curb, clipping a fire hydrant, and jerked to a stop on the sidewalk. The driver's door flew open before the car stopped, rocking on its springs.

"Freeze!" It was hard to see in the dark, but you could make out the shape of a gun pointing through the space between the open door and the windshield. Earring hesitated for a moment. "I said FREEZE!" the voice shouted.

The noise seemed to jolt the younger man into movement. The gun came up.

"No, Richie," the older one called out. But it was too late.

I dove down and away. Yamashita was right behind me. I heard him grunt as he hit the pavement. The stud in the young man's ear glinted again in the night, his pistol came up into position, and he fired. From my position behind him, the muzzle flash highlighted his silhouette for a millisecond. Then three tightly spaced shots rang out from the car on the sidewalk, and you could see them punch into the young man's body, driving him back and crumpling him onto the sidewalk.

His partner stood with his hands in the air, not moving a muscle.

Micky came out from behind the car. "Connor?"

I felt dizzy and sat down on the pavement by the curb. I hoped it was cooler there. I hoped there would be more air. I held my head in my hands and closed my eyes. My blood roared intermittently in my ears as I gulped for air. I listened to the sounds washing around me.

Micky's voice got closer. I heard Richie's gun skitter across the cement as Micky kicked it away. Then the click of the handcuffs. They always cuff the suspect, no matter what.

"Thank God you're here." Bobby's voice was all oily relief.

"Shut the fuck up, Akkadian," my brother told him. Sirens howled in the distance.

I opened my eyes as a new set of lights washed the scene. They were from Mori's black Lexus. The illumination glittered across the dark pool slowly spreading from Richie and oozing into the street. I sniffed and a drop of blood spattered, fat and round, down between my feet.

Then a cop car pulled up, lights cycling around, and two uniforms jumped out. There was another faint rushing in my head, but I could hear more sirens on the way, the static chatter of the cop's radio, and voices of various types.

"Who's the dead guy?" one of the cops asked Micky.

My brother ignored him. "Connor, you OK?" he shouted at me. I didn't answer.

"Yamashita!" Micky turned to my teacher. "Is he OK?"

I felt Yamashita's hands on me, keeping me upright. He must have answered Micky. I nodded my head in affirmation as well. It hurt to do it. Then Micky went over to the silver-haired man. "Well, if it isn't Charlie G. What brings you here?"

"Just passing by, Burke. No interest."

"Who's the stiff?"

Charlie G. shrugged. It was the first time he had moved since his accomplice had been shot. "Beats me." He looked at Bobbie Kay, who nodded sagely in return.

"Sure," my brother said.

He gestured to one of the uniformed cops, who cuffed Charlie.

Mori slid smoothly out of his car, spotted me swooning at the curb with Yamashita beside me, and strode over. "Yamashita-san, where is he?" His shooter was with him, vigilant and confused at the same time.

"Hey, I'm bleeding," I said in amazement to no one in particular.

"No shit, Sherlock," Micky said as he came up to the other side of me. With Yamashita's help, he eased me down.

"I need to know where he is!" Mori insisted. He sounded like he was going to explode.

Micky ignored him and knelt down beside me. "How you doin', buddy boy?"

"How'd you know? Where I was?" My voice sounded thick.

"Yamashita called before he left."

I tried to smile, but it hurt my nose. I swiveled my head around to look at Yamashita. He smiled. Then I squinted at Mori and jerked my head. Gently. "In there," I told him. He and the shooter disappeared into the building.

By this time the EMTs were on the scene. They laid me down on my side while they cut things away and prepped me. "You a good guy or bad guy?" one asked. It didn't slow his actions down any and he didn't seem really interested: just making small talk.

"Huh?" I said.

The EMT looked at my brother. Micky pointed to the thug with the earring. "Bad guy." Then me. "Good guy." He looked at my teacher for a minute, then pointed very deliberately again. "Good guy." Yamashita bowed slightly.

The EMT nodded. "Way to go."

They loaded me up into the ambulance while another team checked out Yamashita. Before the ambulance doors closed, I saw Mori and his goon emerge from the building. They got into their car and drove off smoothly, sedately. No need to attract attention.

Micky was at the doors to the ambulance. "These guys will take care of you," he told me. "Yamashita's in another unit. I'll follow."

I gave him a little grin and tried to wink. "Hold onto those swords," I said.

The doors closed and they strapped me in. Then they put the oxygen mask on me and I tried to relax as they hit every pothole in Manhattan on the way to the hospital.

Epilogue

After jumbled darkness, a long season of light.

The summer months were almost at an end, but their heat lingered: I could still feel it through my blue blazer. The warmth felt good. The back wound had healed, but my muscles were still tight where the sword had sliced through them, and I found myself drowsing, lulled by the sensation, as the speech I was listening to went on and on.

On a day like this, with the dignitaries assembled on the steps of the university library, Dorian almost lived up to the collective delusion of its public relations image. Stately brick façades and well-manicured pathways gave the campus the impression of confident, measured purpose. In a week, students would return and the dysfunctional nature of modern college life would be suddenly revealed. For now, we held our breath and pretended. University functionaries in attendance looked bright and professional: dark suits for the men, prim business outfits for the women. The proceedings were lent a fake erudition by the sonorous buzz of Domanova's welcoming speech. Ever the pedant, he pronounced each and every syllable, rolling the words around in his mouth.

The donors were in place, the press was present, and the cameras were rolling. Micky and I sat in the second row of seated dignitaries lined up behind the podium. We were on the end, far enough away to be able to make fun of things.

My brother screwed his mouth around to the side. "Your boss is, of course, a lunatic."

I smiled at the small crowd assembled for the ceremony and nodded in agreement. "True. But this is academia. No one really notices."

Akkadian was there, strategically placed as far away from the Burke brothers as possible. A Japanese executive sat stolidly, gripping a small leather folder. And in the audience, next to the immobile countenance of Yamashita, there was Art. Thinner, moving with the convalescent's stiff caution that I sometimes saw in the mirror. But moving.

July and August had been a time for pulling things together: muscles, bones, and memory.

Tomita was dead. I learned that from the cops who came to get my statement at the hospital. Through the buzz of weariness and painkillers, I gave them my version of things. Micky later told me that Tomita had been found faceup, a *tanto* planted with almost surgical precision deep into his heart. Micky thought it was a nice gesture but confided to me that I had already broken Tomita's neck.

We both knew that I hadn't used the knife. In the press of the EMTs' arrival, no one really paid much attention when Mori and his shooter slipped into Samurai House. I thought back to the glimpse I caught of them emerging a few minutes later, hustling away into the night without a backward glance. We were all pretty sure Mori had used the knife. The police later discouraged any close inquiries about that. Diplomatic courtesy, I suppose. When Micky pressed things, his lieutenant told him to drop it. Or else.

Part of me still didn't get why Tomita targeted me before Yamashita. But my teacher later told me that he always knew that he would come. He waited until I was out of the hospital for that little discussion.

"You knew all that time that he would come for me? For me? And you didn't say anything?" I was incredulous.

When you've been injured people cut you a great deal of slack. He had been hurt too, but I had him beat because I had needed surgery. It gave me a slight advantage and I figured I could get away with that tone of voice for a while longer.

The old Yamashita gazed at me, remote, calm, totally certain. "Of course not. Think of what it would have done to your training. It was a distraction you did not need."

"But he might have killed me, Sensei!" I said in exasperation.

"What did you think when you began the Way of the Sword, Professor? That it was a game?"

Later, after watching me brood, my teacher took up this issue again. "Burke, I have watched you train for years. And, with time, I began to see that there was potential here . . ." He took a sip of air and changed tack. "The selection of a primary disciple is not an easy thing. It is often marked by blood."

He looked at me significantly. The founder of his style, Ittosai, dealt with this issue centuries ago and had left his successors through the generations a ruthless model. The master, blessed with two remarkable students of apparently equal skill, had brought them together. He had placed the scrolls of the style and the document of succession on the ground, along with a ceremonial sword. Then he had calmly informed the two disciples that the individual who left the room alive would be his successor.

Yamashita, like many of us, pushes into the future while dragging along old baggage from the past. Now I stood there with him, helping drag the load.

I was angry for a time. And confused. But it was familiar territory. As a master, Yamashita pushes you to do things you never would have dared do yourself. And at the end, you're not exactly grateful, just changed.

I heard that a reporter was writing a book about the murders that was filled with all the dark overtones and twisted logic of mental pathology: theories of abuse and the need for recognition. The urge to break free and yet to belong, to

seek out authority figures, to become like them. To destroy
them. Oedipus and sibling rivalry. The need to get close to
what we can't have but crave desperately. I could follow
the argument on an intellectual level, I suppose. But I had
little interest left in it. I wanted to face away from the dark.

My brother would never make a good writer. He could
sum it up in one sentence. And did, when the reporter inter-
viewed him: "It was revenge, you dope."

A polite rippling of applause made me sit up a bit
straighter and open my eyes. A press conference like this is
well scripted, and Dean Ceppaglia had briefed me carefully
on my role. The notoriety of the case—complete with a
string of murders, the almost fatal attack on Art and his
long, slow climb back to health as well as the violent showdown at Samurai House—was too good to pass up. Like a
shark smelling blood in the water from a great way off, Domanova and his cronies had carefully crafted the event we
were currently attending. It served as a way to link the university, the fruits of capitalism, and the triumph of good
over evil in one neat photo opportunity.

If Domanova had his way, I would have been nowhere in
sight. But the showbiz potential of the "battling professor"
getting his reward was too good for anyone to ignore. I had
spent my convalescence fending off moronic reporters asking questions like "Is the pen really mightier than the
sword?" Now this.

But I rose on cue and Mr. Takano, a prominent lawyer
representing the Japanese *sensei*, presented me with a ceremonial *katana*. The dark scabbard glowed with a somber
light. Takano was a thoroughly modern Japanese executive,
but he held the sword with respect anyway and turned it
over to me in the prescribed manner the Japanese have for
sword handling. I received it with equal gravity and
wrapped it in a brocade bag.

Domanova watched impatiently, petulant at being off
center stage and eager to move on to the central act in the
play. He sprang up from his seat when we had concluded.
With a flourish, the president announced the creation of an

institute for Asian Studies at the university. His relentless trolling for wealthy patrons in the turgid waters of the Samurai House reception had paid off. Through a convoluted and, I hoped humiliating, courtship, the Mad Leader had seduced Randall C. T. Ong, a local software magnate, into endowing the institute.

The deal had been brewing for weeks. Joseph Ceppaglia, whose new hobby was serving as my guardian angel, had gotten wind of it. The dean knew that the sudden gush of money would present opportunities. The president would briefly spew goodwill, scattering minor favors like feudal indulgences. So Ceppaglia pulled strings and whispered in ears, finessing the obscure process of memo, elliptical conversation, and countermemo that is academic decision making. The dean is not a bad guy. At the end of it, he had come away with exactly what he set out for while convincing everyone else that they had gotten what they wanted instead. I had to acknowledge that Yamashita was not the only master present that day.

Ceppaglia was sitting on the other side of me. He smiled placidly as Ong was introduced and the gift acknowledged. I shifted slightly in my seat—the hairline fracture in my thigh and the muscle damage was about healed, but I still got stiff now and then. As I moved, the letter in my breast pocket crinkled faintly. The dean had handed it to me earlier in the day with a big smile. In the round, pretentious prose that was his hallmark, Domanova had written to appoint me academic coordinator for the institute. What relation the title had to anything I would actually do was anyone's guess.

"What it means," Ceppaglia had said quietly, "is that you now have a job. A real job. Don't screw it up."

As Ong spoke, I looked around at my new colleagues. Ceppaglia chewed gum furiously and threw significant looks my way, convinced that through superior scheming he was responsible for everything going on. Domanova was scanning the crowd, mentally noting who was present and who was not, amending his black list accordingly. Members of the faculty sat there, stone-faced and outraged at Domanova's good fortune, seething ineffectually and dreaming of assassination.

When the gods wish to punish us, they answer our prayers.

The long ritual of institutional congratulation and shameless self-promotion eventually petered out in a champagne reception. We walked, squinting in the afternoon sun, and reached the awninged shade of the presidential manse. Yamashita stood to one side with the lawyer. The two men stared into the crowd and talked quietly in Japanese. They looked like zoo visitors watching gorillas, alternately fascinated by the species' similarities and secretly revolted by the thought that they were closely related.

We stood by the bar for a while. Art leaned on it. They can do amazing things with microsurgery, but I still couldn't believe that they reattached his hand. Even in the afternoon sun, I got a chill. For a moment, I could smell the damp and blood on the subway platform. I could see the stump of Art's wrist pulsing fluid.

I gestured at it. "How's the therapy going?"

He gingerly rotated his hand and wrist, watching it critically. Then he grinned up at me. "Slow. But it's better than looking like Captain Hook."

"Almost worth it to see Mick in a pair of green tights," I said.

Art sipped appreciatively at his champagne. "True. He never did grow up."

Micky didn't have a comeback for once. He just looked at us with a disgusted expression on his face.

I was identifying the key players at the reception to my brother and Art when Yamashita introduced the lawyer, Takano, to us. The man had absolutely no accent: his English was fluid and precise. He still bowed slightly when we were introduced, however. Some things are hard to change.

"Mr. Burke," he said as he unzipped his little folder, "I

am pleased to be able to present you with the reward for the return of Ittosai's sword." He wasn't really pleased, of course. No one likes to give away $25,000. But he hid it nicely behind gracious formality.

I nodded, equally gracious, and fished a piece of paper out of my pocket. "Takano-san," I replied. "It was nothing. I am honored, but I would be grateful if you would have separate checks made out in three names." This attracted at least one person's attention: Bobby Kay floated in the background, drawn by the scent of money.

Takano took the paper I gave him and frowned. Yamashita murmured something and Takano's look cleared. Then he placed his folder down on one of the cocktail tables and carefully filled out blank checks with the names. Bobby edged in closer for a peek. Takano finished writing, made some notes on a form, and asked me to sign to acknowledge receipt of the reward. I did. He zipped up his little folder, bowed to us, and then left.

Cops can't accept reward money. But a private citizen like myself can share it with anyone he wants.

Bobby Kay staggered away. As he lurched toward the bar, he bumped into Ceppaglia. Smooth veteran of decades of cocktail parties, the dean swerved around Bobby, never spilling a drop from his champagne glass. "That man looks absolutely appalled," he commented to us as he approached.

"Well," Micky said, "that's good. Because he's appalling."

"You know," I said to Micky, "I thought Bobby would make a bigger stink about claiming the reward for himself."

My brother smirked as he drank some champagne. He closed one eye the way my dad used to do when he was thinking. "Well," he said judiciously, "I explained to him that a murder is a complicated thing. You don't want to muddy the waters unnecessarily. It makes people wonder things."

"Such as?" Ceppaglia asked.

"It makes people wonder things like maybe Reilly's murder was some half-assed publicity stunt gone wrong. Or that maybe it wasn't and Bobby got into contact with Tomita later and promised to set you up in exchange for the return of the sword because he cut some corners and hadn't insured it properly. And that maybe he hired those two goons as his backup if things went wrong. Which they did.

"So I got him to agree that it wouldn't be good to pursue his claim to the reward money, especially since it might make me ask how come his fingerprints were on the knife."

"Were they?" Ceppaglia asked.

My brother waved the question away. "Who knows."

Ceppaglia looked from one of us to the other. "But I thought you said Connor broke Tomita's neck!" he protested.

"Gee," Micky said, "I think I forgot to tell Bobby that."

I looked for a minute at the checks Takano had given me. As a Burke, you don't see that many zeros associated with money that often, even after the three-way split. Then, with a grin, I handed one to Mick and one to Art. "You'll notice," I said, "that they're made out in your wives' names. Make sure they get 'em, OK?" I said.

The two men looked at me. For once, my brother seemed at a loss for words. He nodded and said, "Thanks, Connor."

"Yeah, well . . ."

Yamashita smiled at me. It is a rare event. "You are a good student, Burke."

From him, it was saying a lot. I bowed in his direction. "I'm a slow learner, Sensei." Sometimes I still dreamed about the fight with Tomita, and in the torpid unspooling of memory, the scars on my back still burned.

Yamashita's eyes squinted in that bullet head of his. "No," he said to me. "Any fool can wield a weapon." He took a final sip of champagne. "You, on the other hand, have learned honor quite well." My *sensei* set his glass down, bowed to us all, and turned to go. He flowed through the crowd and out of sight.

After a while, both the champagne and the conversation began to bubble off. I quietly wandered around the back garden, gingerly edged along the hedges, and made it out of the yard without being spotted by the president. I felt like a kid playing hooky.

It was quieter out here, and across the playing fields the campus glowed faintly in the hushed, humid air. From a distance, it seemed like an OK place to be.

My brother came up to me. "What now?"

I shrugged. "Your guess is as good as mine."

"Whaddaya think," he prompted, "time for one more drink?"

We looked at the crowd that filled Domanova's back-yard, eyed each other, and smiled, then spoke simultaneously: "Nah."

"I gotta go," Micky said. "Barbecue tomorrow?"

"Count on it."

My brother looked intently at me and patted my shoulder. He started to say something, but stopped.

We nodded at each other, a recognition of things shared that are beyond words. Micky went back for Art. I stood for a while, enjoying the sensation of just being alive. Then I wandered off, over the grass and into the warmth of a season still flush with possibility.

Please read on for an excerpt
from John Donohue's

D
E
S
H
I

Coming in Fall 2004
from St. Martin's Press

Everyone wants something: it's one of the few points of philosophy my brother, Micky, and I agree on. Desires shape the arc of life's trajectories, leading us to unimagined destinations.

The Buddhists say desire creates illusion, which is the source of all suffering. In the Catholic church I was raised in, desire was equally disparaged. There are few things in life really worth wanting, but we are cursed with an almost limitless capacity for imagination and need. The truly wise know that what we really need are those things that permit our true natures to emerge. We're born with that knowledge, then quickly forget it and spend a lifetime trying to remember it again.

The path a life takes is the product of that remembering. We wander along in search of the selves we once knew. The way isn't easy: it's stony, studded with obstacles. And we're not alone on the lurching journey: there are forms crumpled in the brambles by the wayside, markers to those who've lost their way. And when the path dips, there are other, still watchers waiting in the dim woods. Ghosts hungry to snatch us.

The way winds and dips. There are times when the path is unclear. Faint tracks lead the unwary off to their doom. But high up ahead, we can all glimpse the hint of something beautiful. It's faint and hard to see, but it pulls us nonetheless.

A good teacher tells you to keep looking at that gossamer image. I don't know whether it's kindness or cruelty. But it keeps the yearning alive; it makes you stay on the right path. And it prevents you from looking down.

Because when you do, you see that there is blood on the rocks.

The breeze was warm that day and the air felt soft and laden with moisture. It was the time of year when a few good sunny hours could make the plants seem to explode with buds and blossoms. You could feel it: after a time of tense waiting, something was about to happen.

Edward Sakura knew about waiting. He had learned to check the urge to act quickly with a calm, methodical discipline. The excitement and anticipation that were part of putting together a good deal never faded, of course. It was why he was in the business he was in. But he had mastered his impulses through years of trial and error. And it had paid off handsomely. Shodo, the Way of the Brush, had been a constant teacher in his quest for patience for over three decades. It was one of life's little ironies. As a young man, he had learned from his parents' experience in Manzinar that safety in America was based on conforming to American culture. In retrospect, people of Sakura's generation were puzzled why their folks did not grasp that one fact about America. After all, the Japanese themselves had a saying that the nail that sticks out gets banged down.

He had looked at the photos from the camps the American government had shunted his parents and other Japanese Americans off to. The rows of slapdash wooden barracks, geometrically arranged in the desolation of the high American desert, would have been enough to drive the lesson home to even the dimmest of observers. And by the end of the war, Americans of Japanese descent had learned to look forward into the future, simply because the past was too painful. And in so doing, they turned their gaze away from Japan.

Sakura had been a bright kid and he turned into an even brighter adult. After getting his MBA, he had developed a taste for the high-octane deals increasingly being cut in the entertainment industry. And over time, he succeeded quite well. But with middle age, he had come to yearn for some sense of connection to his past. A high-energy man in a fast-paced business, he chose an endeavor diametrically opposed to the normal pace of his days.

For thirty years, every day, no matter where he was, Sakura surrendered part of his life to the Discipline of the Brush. As his teachers directed, he would set aside his worries. Enter a realm of a quiet focus. Then, kneeling before the purity of white paper, he would slowly, methodically prepare. The cake of dried ink would whir faintly against the stone as he ground it into powder. He would carefully add water to the mix, gazing intently at the liquid, thick with promise, dense and black with potential.

Then he would breathe, calming his hand, centering himself before picking up the brush.

And when spirit and brush were one, the ink trail would spool across the paper, leaving something of Sakura frozen in time, made manifest in the stark contrast of black ink and white background.

He had carried his art with him when he relocated to New York. The growing presence of Japanese companies like SONY in the entertainment industry meant that there were opportunities for a deal maker like Sakura on two coasts. He worked in Manhattan and went home each night to a quiet, upscale neighborhood in the Fort Hamilton section of Brooklyn. It was a community that seemed tidy and green after the sprawling concrete of Manhattan. You could smell the sea in the breeze that blew in from the Atlantic. And best of all, amid the blush of life in a spring garden, it contained Sakura's small Shodo hut.

He had built it as far back away from the house as he could. The property lines in his neighborhood were set with high walls for privacy and thickly cushioned with trees. It made for a small island of tranquillity. He felt drawn to it now more than ever, a stone that sat, still and isolated, in the rushing current of his life.

The hut's location was why he didn't hear his killer approach.

It was easy enough to re-create the event. Explanation is a common skill, prediction an elusive art. In this part of Brooklyn, people value their privacy. The streets are relatively narrow, the houses old and well-established, their faces closed to the street. The lots that the houses sit on are irregular, with occasional backyards of surprising depth. The hum of traffic from the more congested avenues to the east is never absent. And one more Lexus tooling sedately through the late-afternoon streets would not have excited much comment.

People think of hunting as essentially a chase. But professional hunters, the really successful ones, get that way by wasting very little energy and planning ahead. They can chase if they have to, but they much prefer to stalk. And if possible, they would rather use the techniques of ambush. Know your prey. Know his patterns. Know where he will be. And wait there.

We don't really know for sure whether the killer snuck up on Sakura or whether he was already there, lurking in the undergrowth. It doesn't really matter. He knew where to find his victim. And with the pitiless certainty of all killers, he moved in.

The old masters, the real *sensei*, say that any Way leads to the same point. Whether you pick up the brush or the sword, the focus and training change you. It's imperceptible at first. But it is cumulative. I later saw some of Sakura's calligraphy, and it told me that his three decades of training had not been wasted.

The whole point of calligraphy is to lose yourself in it, not to dwell on distractions. It's probable that he picked up on the sensations swirling around him. Because mastering stillness means you can also vibrate like a tuning fork when conditions are right. I know. And I'll bet Sakura did, too.

Professionals don't leak much emotion. The Japanese warriors of old talked about the concept of remaining in *kage*, within the shadow or shade. You don't give anything of yourself to your opponent. You don't let enemies see what you think or feel or intend. The killer that day was probably as quiet and self-contained as they come. Yet we all leak some psychic energy, no matter how hard we try.

The atmosphere was charged with tension that day, and the victim sensed it. If you examine the record of his calligraphy from his last session and compare it to others, you can almost see something happen. The first warm-up exercises, the testing of ink consistency and brush conditions, reveal an artist forging a tactile link with his tools. Then Sakura began a quote from the Platform Scripture. The characters were classic Chinese, like many of the old Zen documents, and they revealed balance and poise and a fidelity to discipline. The characters flow across the page for four lines before something happens.

There's a break in the aesthetic structure. It's hard to describe. You need to look at a lot of this material to get a sense of the balance and rhythm. And you need to experience something of the focused concentration that facilitates it.

I work in a discipline with different tools, but the methods are the same. My teachers say that the mind can be distracted and "stick" to some extraneous thing. It creates a gap in your concentration. And you can see it revealed in subtle ways in your technique.

And that's what I see when I look at that sheet of calligraphy from Edward Sakura. An intrusion. A change in focus.

The killer parked his car on the next block and walked back to the side gate that led to the rear of the property. He eventually had to leave the concrete-and-stone surface to get to his target, so he left a trace. His footprints through the rich, dark spring earth suggest a big man. He walked slowly and quietly—the imprints are deeper on the toe and not much dirt was thrown backward. There was no need for haste and no need to make noise. He obviously knew where he was going and knew what he would find there.

Sakura's head probably came up as he sensed the killer's approach. He remained seated in the formal position, legs tucked under him, insteps flat on the floor. The awareness must have come on him with an overwhelming finality. Not a thrill of panic or an electric jolt, but a deep-seated settling, like something at the body's very core shifting down toward the earth, where it lodged, unmistakable and immovable.

There was no forced entry or any of the smashed doorjamb theatrics you might expect. There was no wasted motion. It was economical and efficient. You would almost call it civilized. Except for the end result.

The killer entered the hut from the door to the calligrapher's left. Sakura shifted slightly to view the intruder, but remained oriented toward the low table that held his paper and brush. Did his eyes get wide as the attacker loomed there? I would have been scrambling around like mad. But there was none of that either.

Sakura knew about deals. He understood how they worked and how you could work them. But people who knew him also said he had the knack of analyzing things and predicting the outcome way before most other people. He knew when you could still negotiate and knew when the deal was done. So between the phenomenon the Japanese call *haragei*—a type of intuition common among masters of the arts—and his years of business acumen, Sakura pretty much knew what was about to happen. There was no way out.

There may have been some conversation. Not much. The killer was not in a line of work that did much for verbal skills. Messages got delivered in more elemental ways. Sakura, turned slightly to gaze on the hulking reminder of mortality that glided into the hut, would want to know why. It's probably the most common last question there is.

But even then, despite the elevated heart rate and the sweat that sprung out like cold, oily drops on his forehead, Sakura was thinking. So his question wasn't just futile rhetoric. It was part of his last deal. Whether the killer picked up on it or not, Sakura was bargaining for the time he needed. To give us a clue.

He slid a fresh sheet of paper in front of him on the table. With a last look at the killer, Sakura rolled his brush in ink and sought the center one last time. It's a hard thing to do with the respiration going crazy and fear trying to hammer in through the barrier of discipline.

The brush rustled across the paper. The intruder's arm arced up as if it were an echo of the action.

The bullet punched in through the thin bone at the temple. The soft slug flattened out and gouged its way through Sakura's head. When it blew out the other side, his hand spasmed and his last work of calligraphy trailed off without control as the body collapsed.

The killer stepped over Sakura and poked the sheet of

paper in inquiry. He grunted with contempt as he read the strokes. This calligraphy before him could tell people nothing. In the distance, a car door slammed and his head jerked toward the sound, alive to the possible threat. He moved toward the door to check and, vaguely uneasy, left without a backward glance. What was there to see? A small refuge violated. A copy of the Platform Scripture. Rice paper with some meaningless brushstrokes. A small huddled figure in a spreading pool of fluid. And on the delicate *shoji* screens of the room, a pattern of small crimson dots blown there like raindrops driven before a strong wind.

About the Author

John Donohue holds black belts in both karatedo and kendo and has studied various Asian martial arts disciplines, such as karate, kendo, judo, aikido, iaido, and taiji, over the past twenty-five years. A nationally recognized authority on the topic, he is also an associate editor of the *Journal of Asian Martial Arts* and has written four nonfiction books on the martial arts. In addition, he has been a featured speaker at national and international conventions, as well as on television and radio. Visit his Web site at www.johndonohue.net.